Chloe

The Women of Ivy Manor

Chloe

A Novel

LYN COTE

NEW YORK BOSTON NASHVILLE

This book is the work of historical fiction. In order to give a sense of
the times, some names or real people or places have been included in
the book. However, the events depicted in this book are imaginary, and
the names of nonhistorical persons or events are the product of the
author's imagination or are used fictitiously. Any resemblance of such
nonhistorical persons or events to actual ones is purely coincidental.

Warner Faith
Time Warner Book Group
1271 Avenue of the Americas, New York, NY 10020
Visit our Web site at www.twbookmark.com

The Warner Faith name and logo are registered trademarks
of the Time Warner Book Group.

Printed in the United States of America

First Edition: June 2005

10 9 8 7 6 5 4 3 2 1

Library of Congress Cataloging-in-Publication Data

Cote, Lyn.
   Chloe / Lyn Cote.
     p. cm. — (The women of Ivy Manor ; bk. 1)
   Summary: "The first book in the Women of Ivy Manor series,
about four generations of women, begins with Chloe, the daughter
of a politician who comes of age in 1920s Washington D.C." —
Provided by the publisher.
   ISBN 0-446-69434-7
   1. Young women—Fiction. 2. Washington (D.C.)—Fiction.
3. Politicians—Family relationships—Fiction. I. Title.
PS3553.076378 C+
813'.54—dc22

2004026691

To my agent, Danielle Egan-Miller.
Thanks for all your hard work and for having confidence in me.
You've been great.

"Just as I am without one plea but that Thy blood was shed for me."

CHARLOTTE ELLIOT

Part One

CHAPTER ONE

Tidewater Maryland, April 1917

*C*hloe thought dying would be easier than what her father wanted her to do now. She'd just been lifted onto the open bed of a farm truck, where she gazed out from under the low brim of her straw hat. It framed the terrifying jumble of faces gawking up at her.

"Chloe," her father's voice rumbled a warning. Barrel-chested, wearing a custom-tailored suit, he hovered beside the truck fender while she stood above him trembling.

She parted her lips, desperate for air as all the faces ran together like wet watercolors.

"Chloe," her father repeated, chilling her.

She tried to think of the words that would please her father and also sway the people before her. But under her cream-lace bodice, she couldn't inflate her lungs. It was as if her corset had been laced too high and much too tight.

She tried to focus on the scene before her. The smell of fecund earth buffeted upward in warm waves. The dazzling, nearly blinding, spring sunshine glinted off the chrome of Model-T cars and trucks amidst a few old wagons and horses tethered here and there. She managed to draw in a teaspoon of the warm afternoon air.

"Chloe," her father prompted, his raw irritation bristling just under the surface.

"Klo-ee, Klo-ee!" Out in the crowd, a tall, towheaded boy called out her name and followed it up with a loud wolf whistle. An older man beside him cuffed the boy as a few chuckles and titters floated up to her, taunting her.

I can't do this. I can't—

You can do anythin', a clear, loud voice sliced through her mind.

Startled, her lungs found space to expand. Chloe sucked in air and hefted the megaphone to her mouth. "I've never done this before." Her voice came out unnatural and hollow sounding. She swallowed, trying to wet her cotton-dry mouth.

You can do anythin' you put your mind to and don't let nobody tell you diffr'nt. The plucky words gave her sudden confidence. Chloe lowered the megaphone. "I don't think I need this," she said in a loud voice. She forced a smile. "Can y'all hear me?" And she started to breathe.

As from faraway, approving murmurs from the watching crowd rippled up in reply. Men wearing denim overalls and straw hats slouched against blossoming trees, scant protection from the warm sunlight. Under the trees, women in starched print house dresses lounged primly on worn quilts where babies slept. Beside the schoolhouse, vacant on Saturday afternoon, barefoot children raced from the wooden swings to the slide and back again. Their yells and laughter drifted up to Chloe.

Still Chloe felt their eyes boring holes into her. Her father fidgeted. She sucked in air again.

"My daddy . . . asked me to talk to you today," she blurted out the truth. "I really don't know why . . ."

But that was near as could be to a lie. *I'm here to turn everyone up sweet for Daddy. I knew something was up the minute I clapped eyes on the new clothes he brought home from D.C.* The cream-colored cotton jaconet dress with its stylish, narrow skirt and high waist—the matching silk stockings, butter-soft kid shoes, and gloves—had made her edgy, not pleased. "You'll be comin' with me," he'd said before he'd left this morning's breakfast table. And she'd felt herself shrivel inside.

Now she strangled the megaphone with both hands as if she could choke words out of it. "But maybe it's 'cause I know him better than anyone else." Another lie. Or was it?

The crowd looked interested. They waited.

Then she realized it had been her granny's long-dead voice in her mind, urging her on, showing her how to talk to these folk. Her beloved granny—the one person who had always made Chloe feel loved and valuable in her own right. This thought gave her courage. "My Granny Raney—" Her voice gained weight. "—always told me, 'You can do anythin' you make your mind up to. Just look at your daddy.'" Truth at last.

She heard her father's chortle of approval. She sensed the men in the crowd listening to her. Her jittery heart still lodged in her throat, but somehow she spoke around it, striving to appear confident. "My daddy wasn't born in a big house like we live in now." Phrases from speeches she'd heard her father give over the years filtered through her nervous mind and out through her lips. "He didn't get to go to college. He taught himself law. He passed the bar and became a district attorney, then he ran and won a seat in the state legislature."

What next? She recalled the morning's headline and

grabbed at it. "In this dangerous time of the War to End All Wars, he wants to serve you as your first elected senator in Washington, D.C."

Then her mind went dead. Plumb dead. She stared out at the faces, her lips parted. No words came. An awful silence swelled. *Help me, Lord. Help me, Granny. I can't do this!*

"Does he want the women's vote?" a female called out, provoking, sassy.

The question stirred the gathering. Heads twisted, craning as a not-too-friendly muttering swelled. Chloe shaded her eyes and glimpsed—way back in the crowd—a hand in a navy glove waving to her. "Kitty McCaslin!" Chloe called out. At the sight of her best friend, tears of relief wet her eyes. "Honey, don't you know that amendment hasn't passed yet?"

The watchers chuckled and the tension eased. Chloe sensed their returning interest and voiced the next thing that came to mind. "Kitty, whatever are you doing here?"

"Causing trouble." Kitty's tone was teasing.

Chloe eyed Kitty. Her lifelong friend was her exact opposite—as dark as Chloe was fair-haired, petite as Chloe was tall, with brown eyes to Chloe's china blues. In a chic navy-and-white outfit probably straight from New York City, Kitty pouted her rouged lips. Kitty knew how to wrap folks around her little finger, all right.

I just have to follow Kitty's lead. Warm relief shot through Chloe. "The usual, you mean?" she countered, her hand on one hip. She gauged the crowd. They were enjoying the repartee. "What's your daddy going to say to you, interrupting my first campaign speech?"

"What my daddy don't know can't hurt him," Kitty quipped. "And *your* daddy won't care as long as he gets elected!"

The crowd laughed, indulgent with the daughter of the

local banker—even if Kitty was wild to a fault and had gone off to college in New York City. The general consensus was that Kitty's father was out of his mind letting his daughter go off to college in the big city. Didn't he know what could happen to innocent girls up there?

Chloe's heart beat in ragtime. But she knew she was winning; the crowd was with her. "I'm surprised you aren't running for senator yourself," she teased Kitty as if they were alone.

"Give me thirty years and I will!" Kitty crowed.

Good-natured catcalls swirled over Chloe. She wagged a finger at Kitty and laughed aloud before looking at her father in mute appeal. When would he let her step down?

Judging her work done, her father levered himself up beside Chloe and captured the dangling megaphone from her. With one hand he put it to his lips and with the other he gathered her close to his side. This part of the routine she was used to. With practiced charm, she kissed his cheek, smiled broadly, and tilted her face as though cameras were flashing. She'd learned the pose at the age of four.

"Ain't my little gal somethin'?" her father bellowed in his sandpaper voice.

The farmers applauded and the women nodded, studying her outfit, ready to copy it the next time they could afford yard goods.

"Thank ya, honey." He pinched her cheek.

It was then that Chloe glimpsed the elegant stranger. At the sight of him all thought of winning elections flew from her mind. He was tall, lean, dressed in a gleaming white shirt and dark trousers with a suit jacket folded over his arm. His hair was raven black, slicked back from equally dark eyebrows. He stood there, surrounded by the crowd, and his eyes met hers. The contact was almost electric.

The moment became too much for Chloe. The heat, her fear, the sudden stirring she felt looking at this stranger . . . The air rushed out of her and she was rendered breathless again. She wavered within her father's arm.

"Don't faint, honey," her father soothed, ever the solicitous father. "Here, Jackson, help her down. The sun's gotten to her."

Hands reached up for her and lowered her to the ground. Someone pushed a fan between her fingers. With a quick smile at those around her, she looked past them, but the man had vanished. Disappointment pierced her. Who in the world was this stranger? Why was she so affected by this man she'd never seen before?

Later, in her upstairs bedroom, Chloe gazed out her window at Ivy Manor's grounds. Through the limbs of budding magnolia trees, she watched the day dim into twilight. Her view of the rolling spring-green lawn and ancient maples, oaks, and tulip trees usually eased her nerves. But not today. She'd survived her first speech—just barely. Sliding down to her knees, she cradled her aching stomach with one arm and rested her cheek on the cool white windowsill. "I can't do that again."

Unbidden, a memory breathed through her. She was a little girl again. Fleeing another one of her parent's battles, she'd run weeping from the big house to the small cottage behind Ivy Manor. Granny Raney had been there in her old rocker, holding out her arms. Chloe slipped up onto her wide lap and buried her face in Granny's soft bosom, scented with camphor. Granny didn't ask any questions, just rocked and sang her favorite hymn in her low, soothing voice. And Chloe was comforted, as always.

Granny Raney had loved her, never failed her, and today,

though she'd been gone for years, she'd brought Chloe through the speech-making.

Chloe closed her eyes, willing away the clammy feeling that hadn't quite left her. *I won't do that again.*

Of its own accord, her mind brought up the image of the handsome, dark stranger at the schoolyard. Who was he? Had he come with Kitty? Her beau from New York? Her stomach quivered. What did that matter to her if he were?

Downstairs, the dinner bell floated up like a death knell. Both her parents were at home at the same time. Which meant dinner would be a nightmare. She toyed with the idea of staying in her room, begging off with a stomach ache. But that would only bring them up to her room, not stop them. Nothing ever stopped them.

With effort, she pushed herself onto her feet again and went to the blue-and-white willow-patterned pitcher and bowl on the stand across the room. Like everything else in her mother's house, the ewer had been in the family nearly a century. She washed her hands and face in the cool water and wondered what it would be like not to live in a museum, not to know the history of each piece her mother revered. Then, with a long sigh, she turned to examine herself in the freestanding mirror she knew Jason Carlyle had ordered from England for his bride in 1774 on the eve of the Revolution.

I look like I've been off to war and back again. She brushed her fair hair back from her face, tucking stray strands into the hairpins in the knot at her nape. Sunlight from the window made her hair shimmer like fire. Pinching her cheeks, she brought color into her pale face. She smoothed the wrinkles in her cotton outfit and then re-gathered her white silk stockings above her knees and freshly rolled her pink garters. Another glance in the mirror. She drew herself up into an elegant posture, her spine listing slightly backward, and proceeded to the hallway and the top of the stairs.

But there, a muffled feminine protest from below slapped Chloe like an open palm. She stiffened. Against her will she glanced down, already guessing what she'd see. Just below her, their maid, Minnie, stood looking up at her, a plea clear in her eyes. Chloe's father had his arms around Minnie. His hands curved along her bottom as he nuzzled her light-brown neck just above her white collar. Chloe recoiled, sickened.

Unbidden, an image flashed through Chloe's mind—the two of them, little girls, best of friends, running barefoot through wet grass while Minnie's brother chased them with a garter snake.

Another whimper. Staring up, Minnie mouthed, "Help. Please."

Chloe spun around, racing on tiptoe to her room. There she opened and shut her door—sharply this time. She waited, taking a deep, shuddering breath. Then she clicked her heels on the maple floor of the landing, returning to the top step. Below her, the hall had emptied.

Nauseated, she descended the stairs and entered the elegant white-and-robin's-egg-blue dining room with its chandelier glittering overhead. Her father had taken his place at the head of the long white-clothed table; her mother's place at his right was vacant. Along with Mr. Kimball, Mason Jackson, his campaign manager, rose at her entrance. A nondescript man in his late thirties, Jackson stood to her left. With his help she took her seat, and then the men settled back into their chairs.

The butler, Haines, Minnie's white-haired uncle, hovered with dignity behind Mr. Kimball, ready to serve dinner. Chloe swallowed as the fragrance of roast beef snatched away the last whisper of her appetite.

"Haines," her father said in an approximation of politeness, "will you send someone up to see if Miz Kimball is going to grace us with her presence at dinner?"

"I'm here, Mr. Kimball." Chloe's frail-looking mother, dressed in a stylish gown of deep maroon, sauntered into the room. The men rose perfunctorily.

Chloe observed her silver-and-brown-haired mother from under lowered lashes. Only a trained eye like her own would detect her mother's slight inebriation. What was it? Just a matter of how Mrs. Kimball held her head so steady, cocked to one side? Or the way she hesitated slightly before setting one foot down and raising the other? Whatever it was, Chloe had seen it enough times before to know.

Mrs. Kimball let Haines seat her across from Chloe. "I hear—" Without preamble, she launched the opening salvo. "—the three of you've had a busy day."

Mr. Kimball ignored her and bowed his head. "Thank you, Lord, for this food. Amen."

Chloe's mother sniffed and opened her white damask napkin, dragging it onto her lap. "I hear you forced our daughter onto a farm truck, of all places. Jackson's idea, no doubt."

"No, my dear Lily, it was mine," Mr. Kimball responded acidly with a twisted grin.

Once, Chloe had seen a dog and cat fighting in the farmyard behind the house. The cat had hissed and scratched and the dog had barked and charged. The farm manager had broken up the fight by swinging a broom. Chloe wished she had a broom now. With white gloves gleaming, Haines served a chilled fruit cup to her mother and then made the rounds of the table with the silver tray.

"Chloe's a natural," Jackson said, ignoring Mrs. Kimball's jibe and eating the fruit cup methodically, piece by piece. "I knew she would be. Pretty, charming. The perfect Maryland belle—shy and hesitant, but able to speak like the people. That down-home accent you put on, Miss Chloe, was very convincing."

"Why an accent?" her mother snapped. Her face, already pink, flushed brighter.

"Your daughter had the wit to talk like one of the people she was addressin'," her father barked and then took a bite of fruit and nodded approvingly at Chloe. "Spoke about my mother—a woman of the people."

Chloe spooned up a mandarin orange section. She had to appear to eat or draw fire to herself. She held the sweet wedge on her tongue, afraid to swallow and upset her stomach more.

Mrs. Kimball sniffed again. "Your mother never had the least use for politics and you know it. What I don't like is Chloe being dragged to these . . . events. I tolerated it when she was a child, but she's made her debut now. She—"

"She'll do—" Chloe's father overrode. "—what needs to be done to help her daddy get elected senator."

"Chloe should be attracting young suitors, not traveling around the county, making a spectacle of herself."

"Your daughter didn't make a spectacle of herself," Jackson interposed. "She spoke to a few citizens and made a very good impression. After all, women's suffrage is just around the corner and Chloe provides your husband with a golden opportunity to show his respect for women by letting his daughter speak for him."

"Respect for women?" Mrs. Kimball was too genteel to snort, but her tone and expression together were the equivalent. "I can't vote, Mr. Jackson. So don't try to electioneer me. Chloe is a lady and ladies have nothing to do with politics."

Chloe wished she could second this idea. But she wasn't a participant here, just the captive witness.

"Chloe's a lady," Mr. Kimball blustered. "No one can doubt that. She's your daughter after all, a Carlyle. And make no mistake, Lily Leigh, I'm going to win this election, so don't bother tryin' to persuade me not to take advantage of every ace I got."

He turned to Chloe. "You did a good job today, sugar." With a smile, he drew out a small jeweler's box from his waistcoat pocket. "This is for you."

Chloe accepted the small box and opened it. Inside the deep-blue velvet was a ring of dainty pearls and diamonds, set in platinum. The sight didn't thrill her, but she knew better than to violate her father's expectations. She looked up with a delighted smile in place. "Why, Daddy, you didn't have to."

"I know I didn't." He beamed his Santy Claus smile. "But you came through like a trooper today. At first, I thought Jackson had made a mistake. But he said you only learn to swim by being tossed into the river." He chuckled deep in his throat, the sound like pebbles rolling in a wood box. "Today my little girl swam back to shore all by herself."

Chloe pictured herself tossing Jackson into the nearby Patuxent River, swollen with spring rain and runoff. But she gave another false smile and slipped the ring onto her finger. "Thank you, Daddy." She rose and kissed his jowly cheek, another part of the ritual.

Her mother rolled her eyes. "I don't want Chloe put on display any more—"

"She'll do what I say and that's that." Mr. Kimball glared at his wife, bringing the discussion to an end.

"You never did understand how to treat a lady."

Jackson stiffened next to Chloe. Her father scowled. Chloe concentrated on swallowing her second orange section. *How much did Mother have to drink before dinner? Is that why she's stepping over the line?*

Her parents' bickering tonight had followed the usual pattern. Jackson was such a frequent visitor during Mr. Kimball's election campaigns that they no longer treated him like a guest. But why had her mother persisted tonight? According to custom, she should have subsided after Chloe received the ring from her father. Why hadn't she?

"I want Chloe to make a good match, Mr. Kimball," her mother declared, her voice beginning to slur slightly. "What gentleman wants his future wife making political speeches? That's as distasteful as Kitty McCaslin marching with the suffragettes in New York City last year."

"Kitty was there today," Chloe said, making an attempt to sidetrack her mother.

"That doesn't make it any better." Mrs. Kimball shuddered with refinement. "That McCaslin girl is never going to make a credible match—"

Mr. Kimball snorted. "Only if her daddy loses his bank." Jackson chortled behind the back of his hand.

"Oh, *someone* will marry her." Mrs. Kimball waved her hand in the air. "But no man of distinction, of breeding."

"Maybe she doesn't want a man of . . . of breeding." As if from a distance, Chloe heard the words come out of her mouth. Shocked, she fell silent. *Why did I say that? Why didn't I keep my mouth shut?*

"Chloe," her mother began in a scandalized tone.

"Miss Chloe's got a point," Jackson interrupted. "This is the twentieth century."

"Jackson's right," her father cut in. "I wouldn't want my daughter going to college, but McCaslin's no fool. If he thinks Kitty needs college, college is what she'll get."

"He knows," Jackson continued, "that men *and* women are going to be judged by their education in the future."

"You're both mistaken," Mrs. Kimball said haughtily.

"Men don't like brainy girls and never will. A man of breeding gets an education but does not want his future wife getting her head turned by all these modern ideas. Voting, indeed. Soon you'll tell me that you want Chloe to learn how to drive a car."

Chloe kept her eyes lowered. Would they go back to the usual routine? Had mother finished at last?

Her father laughed. "Now that's a flight of fancy. Why stop with an automobile? Why not fly an airplane?"

Jackson laughed, too.

"Why not?" a new voice interjected, startling the occupants of the dining room into silence. Grinning, Kitty McCaslin walked into the dining room. She winked at Chloe. "I think being a pilot would be fun."

Chloe fumbled with her water glass and rescued it just before it spilled onto the tablecloth. "Kitty, I didn't expect to see you tonight."

"My apologies for comin' in unannounced. We're all such old friends and I was sure Haines would be busy servin' dinner. I'm home just for a long weekend and wanted to see y'all." Kitty advanced on Mr. Kimball. "Mr. Kimball, how's the election going?"

"I'm going to be the first elected senator in this state," he said as he rose and accepted Kitty's polite kiss on his cheek.

"Good evening, Miss Lily." Kitty nodded to the other woman. "Mr. Jackson."

Chloe wondered if Kitty had overheard anything her mother had said about her. She hoped Kitty had just arrived.

Jackson had risen and now waited for Kitty to be seated. Kitty eyed Chloe. "Mr. Kimball, Miss Lily, I've come to steal your lovely, speechifying daughter away with me. Roarke's out in the car. We're on our way to the Palace. We've got to hurry or we'll miss the first evening showing."

"But Chloe hasn't had her dinner yet," Mrs. Kimball objected.

Rejoicing at this chance of escape, Chloe popped up. "Daddy," she began, knowing she needed his support.

"You go right ahead, sugar," he said without glancing at his wife. "Take a wrap. It's still chilly at night."

"Wait—" Mrs. Kimball held up a hand.

"You best hurry, sugar."

With a smile, Chloe's father waved her and Kitty out of the room. Behind them, an undercurrent of angry, slurred words poured from her mother.

In the hallway, Chloe tugged on her hat and gloves in front of the mirrored hall tree as Haines appeared with a light coat. And then she was running after Kitty down the front steps, between the white, ivied columns into the deepening twilight. Roarke's new Model-T was parked in front. Roarke, also a good friend, was leaning against its driver's side door, waiting with a smile. Beside him lounged the dark stranger.

Chapter Two

R oarke stepped forward, removing his hat. "Evening, Miss Chloe." He towered above her, broad-shouldered and large, unassuming and familiar. And, at the moment, totally overshadowed by the stranger. But with a conscious effort, she looked up at her friend and smiled. "Evening, Roarke." Then, of their own accord, her eyes drifted back to the stranger.

"Chloe." Kitty took her arm, tugging her forward. "This is Theran Black. Theran, this is Miss Chloe."

"Are you kidding me?" For the moment, the young man ignored Chloe and gave Kitty an amused glance. "We're barely south of the Mason and Dixon line. Do you really call young ladies 'Miss So and So'?"

Chloe was surprised that he'd ignored their introduction. Why? From under her low brim, she studied Kitty and Theran, trying to divine how they felt about each other.

"You should be addressing my sister as *Miss* Kitty," Roarke spoke up in his deep, lazy voice. "And you haven't yet acknowledged Miss Chloe."

"Well, I do declare," Theran mocked. "Evenin', Miss

Chloe. And I apologize, *Miss* Kitty, for my gross misconduct."

Kitty shoved his shoulder. "Don't talk nonsense. You call me Miss Kitty on campus and I'll black your eye. Let's get going. I don't want to be late for Mary Pickford."

"Oh, yes, we mustn't be late for America's Sweetheart." With a snort of laughter, Theran opened the car door and allowed Kitty to slide into the backseat before joining her. Roarke escorted Chloe around to the passenger side and ushered her into the front seat, then returned to the driver's seat and started the car. They were off.

In the short walk around the car, Chloe had gone numb inside. Theran and Kitty evidently must be an item. Kitty taking a seat beside him and Roarke claiming Chloe to sit up front with him made that a certainty. And Roarke had had to force the northerner to even say hello to her.

Then a slim hope flickered and flared. Maybe Kitty just didn't want to sit beside her brother? Perhaps that was it. But . . . perhaps it wasn't. She stared out at the maples and poplars spinning by, biting her lower lip and trying to rationalize things. *Why did I think a college man from New York City would even look twice at me with Kitty around? At least there's one good thing: being invisible is better than an evening at home with Mother and Daddy.*

In no time at all, Roarke was parking the car on the main street of Croftown. The First National Bank—Kitty's father's bank—stood imposingly on the street corner. Nearby, a glittering marquee blazoned "THE POOR LITTLE RICH GIRL."

Chloe let Roarke help her out of the car. With a solicitous arm under her elbow, he walked her up to the ticket window.

She smiled at him fondly. Roarke never made her feel uncomfortable or uncertain. He was a rock in her life, the closest thing to a brother she had. She glanced from him to Theran, who was chuckling over some joke with Kitty behind them. Chloe was surprised at how much she wanted him to notice her. But what could she do about it? Was she the kind of girl who'd steal a friend's beau? Unfortunately, no.

With only moments to spare, the four of them entered at the rear of the crowded auditorium. The aroma of buttered popcorn, the chatter of a hundred voices, and the hurry to get seats together compounded Chloe's uneasiness. Roarke found four seats in a row. He entered the aisle first, knowing Chloe hated sitting next to a stranger, and she smiled up at him for remembering. She expected Kitty to follow her in, putting herself next to Theran. But instead Kitty motioned Theran to precede her. Why? Why would Kitty want Chloe to sit next to her beau?

Chloe glanced surreptitiously at Theran and was startled when he winked at her. Confused, she sat down. Pins and needles raced up and down her arms at his nearness. On her other side, Roarke opened the box of candy almonds he'd purchased at the snack counter. He proffered the open box with a subtle rattle. She tried to say no, but the words wouldn't come. So she just shook her head and tried to smile naturally. Then the organist began to play urgently, loudly from behind them. The theater went inky black and flickering light flashed on the screen at the front.

She trained her eyes forward. She didn't want to embarrass herself with a wrong move, so she propped one elbow on the armrest between her and Roarke and tried to follow first the newsreel about the war in Europe and then the movie. But she couldn't focus on the flickering images. Her entire body was waging a battle to hide her interest in Theran. One thought filled her mind: if the dark stranger was interested in Kitty, then why had he winked at her?

Theran scanned the dim, barn-like interior of the roadhouse as Roarke ushered the four of them inside to a table at one end. Theran was accustomed to much smaller honky-tonks in New York. He'd never been to a place quite like this one. But here, just as in the city, society types like Kitty and Chloe mingled with painted ladies and some slick-looking customers. The addition of redneck farmers and their fresh-faced sweethearts added a new note.

Near them, a banjo player, a fiddler, and a piano player— the only black faces in the crowd—were pouring out excellent syncopated ragtime. Couples dancing the turkey trot crowded the floor. The place smelled of cigarettes, dime-store perfume, and liquor. "This sure isn't the Harlem," he said to Kitty.

Kitty gurgled. "No, but this place hops."

Theran glanced at Chloe. The pretty blonde had spent the evening looking everywhere but at him. Very classy, very cool. He wanted to get to know her. He wondered, would he be able to break through the aloof distance she maintained? He'd enjoy trying. "Would your parents disapprove of your coming to a place like this, Miss Chloe?" he teased as she and Kitty sat down at a tiny table.

She flashed a look at him. Huge blue eyes edged with dark lashes and such white, white skin. Mary Pickford had nothing on Chloe Kimball. His mouth went dry just looking at her.

"I've never been here before, Mr. Black," she replied, her chin down.

Her low, sweet voice in that southern-belle murmur did

things to him. He looked over at Roarke, who was at the bar placing their drink orders. Did the banker's son have an interest in Miss Chloe? If so, too bad.

Kitty giggled again. "Call him Theran, Chloe. Your mama isn't here."

Roarke came back with four glasses clutched in his hands. "Allow me." He handed glasses of amber liquid topped with white foam to Kitty and Theran. But the one he set in front of Chloe was darker and matched the one he kept for himself.

"What's that?" Theran pointed at the darker brew.

"Root beer," Roarke replied without hesitation, taking a sip. "I'm driving tonight."

Chloe gave the junior banker a tight, grateful smile and took a polite little sip. Her every movement caught at Theran, made his pulse spike. He chuckled to show Roarke he appreciated the joke. Who would have thought Kitty McCaslin would have a teetotaler for a big brother? But Theran didn't want Kitty. She was cute and fun, but . . . In the dimly lit room, the blonde next to him glittered like a Roman candle.

She looked at him over her glass. "Is this your first visit to Maryland, Mr. Black?"

"Theran. Call me Theran. Mr. Black's my dad."

Ever since this afternoon when he'd seen her back-talking Kitty from the bed of that truck, he'd wanted to touch Chloe Kimball, hold her close and breathe in her perfume. But how could he get her away from her arch protector, the banker's son? "Kitty thought I should see something besides New York for a change." He played for time. "This is my bold adventure south of the Mason and Dixon."

Chloe blushed and sipped again. The turkey trot ended and the couples moved back to tables or the bar.

"Hey, Kitty, Roarke." Breathless from dancing, another couple dragged over chairs and plunked down at the small table, crowding everyone closer together. Theran wished Kitty had maneuvered him next to Chloe like she had at the movies. He didn't pay much attention as Kitty introduced the new couple, giving them no more than a nod. Then he realized the new arrivals had solved his problem. Now he could ask the blonde to dance without leaving Kitty to sit here or dance with her brother.

Theran stood and motioned toward the piano player. "Hey, Mac, how about a tango?" The pianist nodded and hit the ivories. The fiddler joined in. "Let's dance." Theran claimed Chloe's gloved hand.

"I can't tango." She held back.

"You can." He pulled her to her feet and then onto the dance floor. "Easy as pie. Just step-step-step-step-close. You'll be doing it in no time." He tucked her close to him, pressing her against him in the provocative tango posture. "Just follow my lead."

As her body learned the sensual movements of the Latin dance, Chloe's senses reeled—shocked, thrilled. She clung to the dark stranger, moving with him. Within his arms, she'd been plunged into a tropical sea and the swells were carrying her away. She struggled to hear his words above the beating of her heart.

"Press your cheek to mine," he instructed. "It's a must when you tango."

Slowly, she let her face drift nearer his until . . . *What would Kitty say?* She froze, holding to decorum. But he closed the inches between them and firmed his hand over the small of her back. "Relax. This is fun."

Chloe surrendered and felt as if her skin had been slipped off. All her senses were heightened, sharpened. Intense sensations she'd never felt bombarded her. They were exhilarating, more devastating than anything she'd ever known.

The compelling two-four beat of the Latin dance pounded through her mind. She clung to Theran and moved in time with him. Through a blur, she glimpsed other couples joining them. Kitty waved as she pressed herself to the other young man from their table. Wondering what her friend was thinking, Chloe misstepped.

"Relax," Theran whispered, "you're a natural. Get ready. I'm going to dip you. Just let go and let me move you. It'll be great."

He dipped her and she reveled in the strength he exerted over her. She felt suddenly that if he wanted to he could levitate her to the ceiling or even outside into the dark sky. He was a magician and he was working his magic on her. He turned her. With a confidence she'd never known, she followed his slightest shift, molding her body to his, letting him carry them through the bold, stylized pauses. He sang to her under his breath. And she felt unlike herself—for once daring and free.

All day, she'd tried not to imagine what it would be like to have Theran's arms around her and now she was in his embrace. Surely, he couldn't hold her like this and be Kitty's beau. Surely not.

The final chords of the song vibrated in the air. *No, don't let it end.* But the next thing she knew Theran had spun her out the back door and they were alone in the chill moonlight. And the way he looked at her . . .

"No," she said, her face suddenly burning. Anyone could have seen them leave. Would this reach her parents' ears? She tried to pull away. "What will Kitty say?"

But he still held her in his arms as if about to dance. "Kitty and I are just friends."

"Does Kitty know that?" she managed to ask.

He laughed. "Yes, we dated awhile, but decided we'd make better friends than lovers."

Lovers? The concept rocked Chloe. She'd heard all the whispered gossip about Kitty going to college up north. But Kitty wouldn't take lovers, would she?

Theran leaned his mouth to her ear. "You're the most beautiful girl I've ever seen."

She was struck dumb at the look in his eyes and could manage only a shake of her head.

He took her hand and she let him draw her away from the light over the back entrance to the dubious shelter between two cars. "Hey, I mean it. Surely you know how gorgeous you are?"

She gave him her profile. She knew she had features that were pleasant to the eye—her father's use of her for political reasons was proof of that—but no one had ever talked to her this way. His flattery left her bemused. Was he teasing her?

His hands claimed her shoulders and he turned her to face him. "You're beautiful, really lovely." His voice was low, urgent, sincere. "Kitty told me about you but I didn't believe it. That's why I came home with her this weekend—to meet her friend Chloe."

In the shadows, Chloe shook her head at him. She wanted to believe him, but it all seemed so unreal—to have seen this man for the first time only this morning, and yet to have him whispering in her ear now. "You can't be serious," she finally managed, trying to add a dose of commonsense to the moment.

He bent his face over hers and held it just inches away. Chloe had time to think, *He's going to kiss me.* Then his lips brushed hers and her knees became jelly. She clung to his shoulders. She'd received chaste kisses before. But there was nothing chaste about the way Theran's kiss progressed. He assaulted her mouth, insisting, invading. She was without defense. So she answered his every demand, letting her mouth become a part of his, and his a part of hers.

Finally he ended the kiss and folded her close. She heard his breathing—ragged, hard—as she rubbed her cheek against his stiff white collar and the smooth fabric of his suit jacket. Her hat fell to the earth and she didn't care. She sniffed his collar and caught the scents of soap, starch, and him, his flesh. "No one's ever kissed me like that," she admitted, unable to stop herself.

"I believe it. You're like an angel. Sweet, innocent, lovely. A man would think twice about touching you."

"You keep that up, sir—" She tried to protect herself by lightening the tone. "—and you'll turn my head."

"But I don't want an angel," he went on as if she hadn't spoken, "I want you as a woman."

His candid words shook her. What did he mean, he wanted her as a woman? "I don't know what you're talking about." Out of her depth again, she tugged free of him.

"I'm rushing you, aren't I?" He prevented her from leaving. His gaze captured hers as he cradled her face between his strong hands.

"You . . . you . . . I'm not used to men talking this way." She recalled the way her father made up to women sometimes when he didn't know she was listening. "Is that how gentlemen talk to ladies in New York? Is this your version of sweet talk?"

"This is no sweet talk," Theran whispered close to her face, his breath warm against her skin. "Kitty dared me to meet you and not fall for you. She was right. You are my doom."

"Why your doom?" Chloe felt as if she'd caught the tail

end of a hurricane. Nothing he said was making sense. Surely he wasn't serious? "Is that bad or good?"

"I know I'm rushing you, but I don't have time. I saw this war coming and I enlisted. I didn't want to miss a war from being slow. In a week, I report to training camp. I'll be heading to France in a few months."

The news struck her as if she'd known him forever—that his leaving would render her bereft and heartbroken. She reached for him. He moved closer, enfolding her, and she rested her hands on his lapels. "No."

"Yes, I told Kitty that guys who enlisted and then fell in love were idiots. A man should have better control over himself—not leave a girl behind." He shook his head. "But Kitty dared me to meet you and not fall for you. I should have known better. Kitty's as sharp as they come."

"You don't know me." Chloe slid her forefingers up and down his notched lapels. "I don't know you." *This isn't happening,* she thought.

"How long does it take to fall in love?" He lowered his mouth and paused, leaving only a breath between their lips.

She stared at his chest, at the white shirt front against the black coat, gleaming in the low light. She shook her head.

"It only took me one minute." He claimed her mouth again.

Every part of Chloe's body was jolted once more into that peculiar heightened consciousness. She clung to his lapels as the world around her softened and blended. It felt as though she had become part of the night, of Theran and earthy spring. She pressed closer to him, letting his heat flow into her, warming her against the clammy, chill April evening.

The crunch of footsteps on gravel and a low voice inserted itself into Chloe's consciousness. "Miss Chloe," Roarke said politely.

She jerked away from Theran, allowing one startled glance at him before bringing her hand to her lips and turning away, unable to look either man in the eye. She heard Theran swear softly.

Roarke acted as if he hadn't just caught them kissing. Calmly, he bent and picked up Chloe's hat and offered it to her. "It's time we went home."

"It's early yet," Theran objected, his chin jutting toward the young banker. "We'll come back inside. I'll play by your rules."

Chloe tucked her hair under her hat, flaming and vibrating with embarrassment.

"It's time we got the ladies home." Roarke took out his pocket watch and swung it in front of Theran. "After all, to-morrow is Sunday and church."

With no further comment, Roarke turned for the car. Afraid to look at Theran, Chloe followed him. Mute, eyes downcast, she walked beside Roarke, her hands tucked into her elbows, her thoughts jumbled. What did Roarke think of her kissing a man she'd just met? And kissing like *that*—so wantonly? What if her mother ever found out? Chloe hadn't behaved herself as a Carlyle of Ivy Manor should. Silent in her humiliation, she let Roarke lead her to his Model-T.

Kitty was waiting for them beside it. "Well, Mr. Black, was I right or what?" She ignored Roarke's quick, angry look.

"You win, Kit—Miss Kitty," Theran answered lightly. "I went down in flames." At that, Chloe saw Roarke's lips tighten as he handed her into the car.

For her own part, Chloe collected this strange exchange of words and promised herself she'd think them over later. Right now, all she could handle was the explosion of feeling inside her—the awareness of Theran that refused to quiet and the appalling realization that she hadn't conducted herself as a lady should. Roarke's stolid presence beside her in the car made the riot inside her even more acute.

Unaffected, Theran and Kitty chattered in the backseat while Chloe and Roarke rode in silence. After a moment, without a word, Roarke's large comforting hand covered Chloe's on the seat. It was like an unspoken acceptance of her, of her actions.

She glanced at Roarke's profile. Then, within his grasp, she turned her hand up and linked her fingers between his. He squeezed her hand and held it. And Chloe relaxed. Roarke, her dear friend, didn't think less of her and that meant a lot. Theran could go back to New York and brag about how he'd sweet-talked and kissed a Maryland girl. But she'd be okay.

In the paneled church sanctuary the next morning, Chloe sat in the Carlyle pew, the one her family had occupied since the new church had been built in 1827. The worn maple pew cradled her between her parents as she tried not to fidget. Her father always attended church during elections. Her mother attended when she was at Ivy Manor. She liked to scan her neighbors and pick out who was letting herself go, and who was flirting with whom.

Usually Chloe listened obediently to the formal liturgy and then the homily, trying to draw near to God. After all, that's what she came to church for, wasn't it? But today all her concentration honed in on the McCaslin family pew, which was to her right and several pews forward. In navy trousers and matching blazer Theran Black had come to church with the McCaslins. She couldn't take her eyes off the back of his well-shaped head.

She wondered what thoughts were going on inside that head. She felt herself burn at the thought of the kisses they'd exchanged and at her own shameless willingness. She hadn't acted like the lady she'd been raised to be. And she'd barely slept last night, going over and over what he'd said, why she'd given way like that. *He was just sweet-talking me,* she decided. *I know that. I should just be glad for the fun of dancing the tango and having a college boy kiss me.*

But it hadn't felt like fun. He'd said things no man had ever said to her. At her debut, shy young men had danced at arm's length with her and brought her glasses of punch and told her what colleges they would be attending. A few had come calling and sat with her mother and her in the parlor and drunk tea politely. But none of them had kissed her the way Theran had. None of them had talked of love and leaving for war.

Could she believe anything he'd said last night?

Everyone around her rose to say the Nicean Creed. Chloe was caught not paying attention and got to her feet a phrase into the Creed. Her mother looked at her suspiciously. Chloe closed her eyes as if in devout meditation and recited the words, "... very God of very God begotten not made being of one substance of the Father by whom all things were made ..."

The service proceeded. The priest celebrated communion and then the organ swelled with a majestic postlude. Chloe walked between her parents up the aisle. She was very aware of the fact that Theran Black strode behind them. Was he watching her, following her? A dangerous and delicious shiver slithered up her spine.

At the door of the church, her mother greeted the priest languidly and asked after his wife. Chloe shook hands with him and her father pounded him on the shoulder. "Good sermon, preacher."

Her mother's lip curled.

As they moved away down the steps, Kitty accosted them. "Mr. Kimball, Miss Lily, I don't think you've met my classmate Theran Black."

Shaken, Chloe kept her eyes downcast as Theran bowed over her mother's gloved hand and shook her father's. "It's an honor to meet you, sir. I caught part of your speech yesterday. Good luck on your candidacy."

The older man beamed.

"But," Theran said, claiming Chloe's hand, "I was most impressed by your daughter's speech for you. You, sir, are fortunate indeed to have such a lovely supporter."

Chloe couldn't stop the blush that warmed her cheeks as she gazed up at him, tongue-tied, knowing every gossip in the county had cocked an ear her way.

"You have a discerning eye, sir," her father approved. "It's too bad you're leavin' for New York today or we'd invite you to Ivy Manor."

"As it turns out, we will be taking a later train." Theran turned to the McCaslins. "Kitty here wants to stay just a bit longer. She'll miss her early Monday classes, but it will give me a chance to get to know your lovely daughter better."

For once, her father didn't appear to have a ready reply.

"May I call on you this afternoon, Miss Chloe?" Theran asked, a grin in his eyes.

Chloe glanced at her father and then her mother. Both looked startled. She took advantage of this. "Yes, of course, Mr. Black. I—My parents and I look forward to receiving you."

CHAPTER THREE

*L*ater that afternoon, Theran sat beside Chloe on the edge of an antique settee. Rich mahogany and warm maple gleamed with a mellow polish and he was aware that the room must be filled with old family pieces. The exterior alone of Chloe's home, a white-pillared and ivied manor, should have been enough to tell him he was out of his league. But the interior bespoke a daunting history of wealth and family heritage. Now, in the formal parlor, the atmosphere wasn't chilly. It was frigid.

Mrs. Kimball's nose was in the air. Across from him, she sat like the queen, her back stiffly held away from touching the matching loveseat. She'd just poured tea from a sterling silver tea service. Having refused a cup, Mr. Kimball stood by the fireplace. He had one hand on the ornate mantel and one hand in his jacket pocket and looked as if he were about to begin a speech.

Edging forward on the settee, Theran turned sideways to face both the parents. Chloe sat frozen beside him like a store mannequin. Was she having second thoughts? Her pale loveliness had captivated him all over again. She had "beauty too rich for use, for earth too dear." He didn't have words of his own to describe her, so he was left quoting Shakespeare. But she'd barely looked at him when he'd been announced by the Negro butler. He couldn't believe Chloe had a butler. Not even Kitty's family had a butler. He'd only seen butlers in moving pictures. Meeting Haines at the door had thrown him. And a young, pretty black maid in uniform had brought in the tea tray. Had he come on a fool's errand?

He stiffened his resolve and suppressed the urge to tug at his tight white collar. "Faint heart ne'er won fair lady," or something like that. He grinned. He'd never been beaten yet.

"Excellent tea, Mrs. Kimball," he said and gave the grande dame his most charming smile—one that usually sweetened up mothers and austere aunts.

"What are you studyin' up at that college?" Chloe's father asked, giving him the beady eye.

Theran smiled to himself. The old man didn't want him taking anything for granted. "I'm a civil engineering major." Theran remembered Kitty's coaching and added, "sir."

"And what does a civil engineer do?" Mr. Kimball gave Theran his full and unflattering attention. Theran was reminded of a bulldog.

"The automobile is going to change the way America travels." Theran infused his voice with confidence. "I'll be planning bridges, routes, viaducts for the new highways automobile travel will demand."

Chloe looked sideways at him. "That sounds interesting, don't you think, Daddy—"

"Think you'll make a good living at that?" Her father cut her off and rocked back and forth on the balls of his feet.

Theran gave Chloe a reassuring smile. "I'm glad you asked that, sir. Yes, I'll make a good living and will be able to support a wife. You see, that's why I'm here. I want to ask your permission to court your lovely daughter."

Chloe's lips parted, but she said nothing.

Theran wondered why. She'd acted the shy little thing yesterday—but only until he'd kissed her. After last night, she couldn't be opposed to his suit, could she? Not after the way she'd returned his kisses. His blood warmed nicely at the remembrance.

Mrs. Kimball sat up straighter and gave Theran an affronted look. "You presume too much, young man—"

Mr. Kimball was laughing. "No, he doesn't. If he'd presumed too much, he wouldn't have asked for permission."

"Just so, sir." Theran's thin china cup and saucer rattled briefly as he set them down on the piecrust table beside him. "I realize that you don't know me, but I can give you references if you wish. If Chloe were a New York coed, this would be easier. We'd date awhile and then I'd be taken home to meet her parents. But Kitty explained to me that courtship is a little more old-fashioned out of the city."

"We certainly don't act as rashly as this," Mrs. Kimball said in a dismissive voice. "You just met Chloe last night and we know nothing of your background, your family. You can't make me believe that you—"

"He's young." Her husband cut her off, his voice a slashing counterpoint to her heated tone. Theran had never heard his quiet, dignified father use that tone of voice to Theran's mother. He looked back and forth between man and wife.

"And there's a war on." Mr. Kimball paced back and forth in front of the fireplace. "He'll be drafted soon—"

"I've enlisted, sir," Theran said. "And I'll leave for officer's training camp in a week's time." He stood and faced Chloe's father squarely. "I took my final exams early and my degree will be mailed to my parents after the commencement in May. I'll be in uniform by then, trained and ready to sail for France."

"Indeed?" Mr. Kimball lifted both eyebrows, but a cagey look lingered in his eyes.

Theran didn't have time to try to figure out what that meant. "Yes, I couldn't wait around for the draft board. I like to be in the thick of things."

"Then your suit is most certainly out of the question," Mrs. Kimball declared.

"I won't be gone long." Theran turned to her. "The Germans are hanging on by their fingernails. A few sorties by fresh American troops and they'll lay down their arms and surrender. Germany is nearly bankrupt."

"I honor you, young man." Kimball used the same voice Theran had heard him use at yesterday's speech. "Europeans will be no match for our doughboys."

"That is neither here nor there," Mrs. Kimball snapped. "I'm sure you are a patriotic and even admirable young man, but my daughter will marry a gentleman—"

"Mrs. Kimball—" Theran interrupted, but to no avail. The grande dame marched on.

"The Carlyles, my family, have lived in this house for over two hundred years. Our ancestors arrived on the *Dove*, one of the first two ships to arrive in Maryland." She lifted her voice and squared her slender shoulders. "We have connections to the peerage in England. Who are your parents, Mr. Black?"

"My father owns a grocery store in Buffalo, New York." Theran looked her directly in the eye. "He's of Scottish descent. My parents don't appear on any social register."

"A grocer?" Mrs. Kimball looked aghast.

"It's an honest way to make a living." Theran was stung by her expression. "My father has a large library and is an intelligent man but circumstances prevented him from fulfilling his dream of a college education. I'm benefiting from his ambition and so will my sister. I am not now nor will I ever be ashamed of my parentage."

Mrs. Kimball frowned and glared at the same time. "No doubt, but Chloe has been to finishing school."

"Well, I won't hold that against her." Theran grinned. He couldn't be too angry with Chloe's mother. After all, his mother wouldn't be thrilled to hear he'd fallen in love with a girl she'd never even met.

Chloe smiled then, sparkling suddenly like a diamond catching the light.

Mr. Kimball burst into dry laughter. "I always told you, Lily, you make too much out of pedigree. If you'd held yourself to the same ambition you have for Chloe to marry a gentleman"—Kimball's tone taunted his wife—"you wouldn't have married me. May I remind you that you had Ivy Manor, but I had money?"

This exchange, as before, made Theran uncomfortable. He'd never heard his dad use that tone to his mother or anyone else. *I don't like you, Kimball,* he thought suddenly.

Her face rosy, Mrs. Kimball pursed her lips. Theran felt a little sorry for her, even if she was a snob. "Mr. and Mrs. Kimball, all I want is your permission to get to know Chloe. May I correspond with her?"

"No." Chloe's mother raised her voice.

"Yes, of course." Mr. Kimball raised his louder. His wife averted her face. "There's no harm in a few letters. You'll be leavin' for France soon and a patriotic American girl should give a soldier all the encouragement she can. I think I can reply for my Chloe that she'd be honored to receive your letters and write a few of her own."

Theran moved forward to shake Kimball's hand. *Maybe he's just an old blowhard after all.* Perhaps all politicians were like this. "May I take Miss Chloe for a short walk?"

"Certainly, certainly." Mr. Kimball waved them away.

Mrs. Kimball scowled but said nothing, refusing even to look his way. He didn't really care.

Outside, Chloe walked silently beside Theran. She led him into the garden at the rear of the manse. High, blazing-yellow forsythia bushes shielded them from the windows. Red and yellow tulips edged flower beds and the sun warmed Theran's back. The pastoral setting suited Chloe. She was as achingly lovely as she had been the day before. Something inside him wanted to reach out and touch her, make certain she was real. Her continued silence disconcerted him, however. Was she having second thoughts? "Chloe, what are you thinking?"

She merely paused but didn't look up.

He recalled the way he'd kissed her and how she had kissed him in return. Her passion had been sweet, innocent, stirring. Everything about her reached out to him, called for him to claim her again. This was love, wasn't it? "Last night you led me to believe that you were not averse to my . . . suit." He kicked himself mentally for sounding like a hero in a melodrama.

"Oh, Theran." With a sigh she took his hand and drew it up to her cheek. "Sometimes I hate them so."

Her touch flared through him. But her words halted him. "Who?" What had he missed?

"My parents." She frowned pensively. "I don't know how you had the . . . courage to stand up to them like that."

"They're just parents," Theran said, kissing her hand. "I didn't expect them to be crazy about the idea of a poor soldier falling for their daughter. Your mother probably thinks I'm a fortune hunter. But they'll get used to me. They'll be forced to. I'm not changing my mind."

Chloe looked into his eyes. "Will you take me away from them? Truly?"

What was she trying to find out with that searching look? "Sure. If I could, I'd marry you right after I finish training. But I don't think that would be fair to you. In any event, the war won't last long and I'll be back. We'll marry then. You'll want a nice wedding and honeymoon."

Chloe listened in wonder to Theran's confident words as he made plans for their future. It amazed her how easily he made decisions, without any hesitation.

"I don't care a thing about all that," she blurted out. "You said, last night . . . You said . . ." Her gaze implored Theran and she wished she might be able to read his mind. Did he really care for her? It still seemed so improbable that all this was happening.

"I said I'd fallen in love with you." He squeezed her hand. "I meant it then. I mean it now. I love you, Chloe Kimball, and I'm going to make you my wife."

Chloe folded her arms around his neck and leaned her cheek against his. "Then take me away, Theran," she pleaded. "If you love me, take me away from here."

Theran pulled back. "You sound . . . unhappy. What's wrong? "

Chloe tried to think how she could make him understand what her life was like. She couldn't. He wouldn't understand. He was a straight arrow. How could she explain the games her parents played with her in order to wound the other? How insignificant they made her feel. "I'm not happy here," she whispered, knowing it wasn't enough.

Theran studied her for a moment, then nodded. "Then you won't have to stay here any longer than you must," he said, folding her into his arms. "I'll come back for you after I finish training. The recruiter said I'd get a long weekend at least between training and reporting for duty. I'll head down here and come for you. We'll marry on the way back to New York. I won't get rid of my room at the boarding house. We'll go and I'll set you up to stay there." He stopped and stroked Chloe's shoulder. "That is, if you really don't care if it's nothing fancy. My boarding house isn't up to what you're used to." He nodded his head toward Ivy Manor.

"That doesn't matter." Chloe stared up at him, still disbelieving. "I've never met anyone like you before. I expected you to make excuses."

He pulled her close and kissed her. "I'm not a talker. I'm a do-er. Trust me?" He kissed her again.

She didn't feel like herself. In Theran's arms, she was a new creature. In his arms she believed she could leave behind the sad shell of her life. "Yes, I trust you." A lightness, an airiness, bubbled up inside her.

"Will you be my bride, Chloe Kimball?"

"Yes." She let herself tousle his hair over his ears. "With all my heart, yes."

"Then leave everything to me."

Chloe closed her eyes and pressed closer to him. She knew everything was moving dangerously fast. But going ahead could only be better than letting this unlooked-for chance pass her by.

Chloe stood watching Roarke drive away on the road behind Ivy Manor. She clutched the letter he'd just hand-delivered to her this morning. Ten very long and silent days had passed since Theran had proposed to her. April had deepened, reveling in sun-splashed leaves and tiny blue violets in the green grass. But Chloe's heavy heart had clung to gray winter. Now, she looked down and read the brief note once again:

Dear Chloe, my sweet love,
    I have written to you every day since I returned to New York City. I've received no reply from you. I cannot believe that you have not tried to contact me. I'm sending this letter in a note to Kitty's brother and have asked him to hand deliver it to you away from your family. If you have changed your mind and have decided to scorn my love for you, at least give Roarke a note to that effect. I count on your love, though, my little darling. All my heart forever,
Theran.

"My sweet love." It was as if Theran had caressed her with his words. *He didn't make a fool of me.* The relief came, so powerful that momentarily she felt it suck all strength from her. But how would she be able to face her mother over luncheon without tossing this note in her face?

Chloe turned to Minnie. "Let's go." Sudden anger propelling her, Chloe stalked down the dirt road toward one of her family's sharecropper's cabin.

In her maid's uniform, Minnie trotted beside her, carrying a basket of food and a blue cotton flannel layette for the sharecropper's new baby son. Minnie touched her arm, startling her. "I think I know what's in that letter Mr. Roarke just brought you." Minnie paused, watchful.

Chloe halted and stared at Minnie. "You do?"

Obviously reassured by Chloe's response, Minnie continued, "My uncle's burnin' your letters from that man. You figured that out, right?"

Chloe could only stare at her. *I should have guessed.*

Minnie looked her straight in the eye. "Are you ser'ous about that man, Miss Chloe?"

Chloe nodded, surprised Minnie was talking so openly.

"Your fam'ly never let you marry him. If you want that man, you got to run off."

"I know." Chloe looked at Minnie, realizing that this was the open way they'd talked to each other as children—before Chloe had been sent away to boarding school at thirteen. After that, her old playmate had addressed her as "Miss Chloe" and rarely looked her in the eye.

"You need help to get away. You can't make a move they don't know 'bout."

"I'm going to marry him." Chloe let her determination flow harshly into her words.

"Then I'll help you . . . if you help me."

Their eyes met again and Chloe couldn't mistake the message in Minnie's eyes. It had been the same one she'd seen—over and over—during the past year whenever her father cornered Minnie. Chloe despised her father's coarse behavior. She didn't have to ask why Minnie wanted to get away from Ivy Manor. "How?" Chloe asked, her lungs painfully constricted.

"You got to talk that banker's son up sweet. He got a car. He can help us get away."

Chloe frowned. "Mr. Black's promised to come for me and marry me after he finishes army training."

Minnie began walking again. "That ain't good enough. If he come here, your daddy can stop him, could even have him arrested. You know he got the whole county in his pocket or on his payroll."

Chloe hurried to catch up. "I know, Minnie."

"Mr. Roarke's the only one can help us. You got to sweet-talk him—"

"But I don't want to mislead Mr. Roarke."

"I'm not talkin' about you vamping him. I'm talkin' about—" Minnie changed her voice, sweetening it. "Roarke, please I'm so in love. Help me."

Chloe was forced to smile. "I don't think that would work, but I think an appeal to his sense of right and wrong would."

"You mean it ain't right that your parents burn your letters?"

"Yes. And I know Roarke's family doesn't like my father."

"Who do?"

Minnie's cool assessment of Mr. Kimball was a revelation to Chloe. Did everyone dislike her father as much as she did?

"Okay." Minnie started walking even faster. "I'll start sneakin' some of your things out little bit by little bit to my fam'ly's place. That way you be able to leave without rousin' no 'spicion. And then I'll run away with you."

Chloe hurried along with Minnie. She only nodded, unable to say all she was thinking. "Mr. Roarke said he'd let me know tomorrow if he'd help me."

"That be all right. Miss Lily like Mr. Roarke, think you'd make a nice banker's wife and then you be settled just down the road right close to home. They be keepin' a sharp eye on you. Miss Lily tell my uncle not to let you go out alone. That's why I'm with you. Today he tole me to tell him if you see anybody else or if you just go to the cropper's house like you say."

"And will you?"

"I di'n't see nobody talk to you." Then Minnie's face split into a wide smile. "You sweet-talk Mr. Roarke and I take care of the rest."

Chloe realized she was clasping and unclasping her hands. She forced herself to take a deep breath and grin at Minnie. Hope flickered once again. But everything hinged on Roarke McCaslin.

CHAPTER FOUR

*I*n the end, Roarke found he could deny Chloe nothing. Not even a runaway marriage to the wrong man. But maybe that wouldn't take place after all. On the appointed evening in May and in a new navy suit, Roarke tapped the polished brass knocker of Ivy Manor. The ivy growing up the front of the house fluttered in the evening breeze. The door opened to reveal Haines standing in the doorway backlit by the foyer chandelier. His white hair was a halo. "Evening, Mr. McCaslin."

"Good evening, Haines." Roarke handed him his hat and Roarke noticed how lined the old man's hands were. All day, things he usually didn't notice had hit him with startling clarity. Whether for good or ill, he was bound to remember this day in his life. "I'm here for Miss Chloe."

"Yes, sir." Haines bowed and motioned Roarke to precede him down the hall to the parlor. Exactly six weeks had passed since Kitty had brought Theran Black home with her and destroyed all Roarke's hopes. As if walking to his judgment day, he entered the ornate parlor and found Chloe and her parents waiting for him.

"Roarke." Mrs. Kimball, lounging on the blue sofa in one

of her pale, gauzy dresses, beamed at him. "So you've come for our Chloe again?"

Looking frail and lovely, Chloe rose and offered Roarke her hand. It was icy cold within his palm; he squeezed it to encourage her. "I'll take care of you," he whispered to her and then raised his voice. "We need to go right away, Miss Chloe," he said as they had rehearsed, "if we're going to make it to the first showing."

"I'll just be a moment." Chloe left the room.

Roarke's eyes followed her. When would he see her again after tonight? Or would she belong to him after tonight? The odds were against it, but . . .

"I'm mighty glad," Kimball boomed, rolling an unlit cigar between his forefinger and thumb, "that New York boy finally woke you up. You nearly lost your chance with my little girl."

"Yes, sir." Roarke felt better about what he was helping Chloe do. It might not be what he'd always wanted, but he'd never been able to stomach Chloe's father or her haughty mother. He was happy to be confounding her selfish parents. He grinned. *Either way, I'm enjoying outsmarting you and later telling you about it.*

"I'm ready, Roarke." Chloe had donned a perky straw hat and white gloves. She peeped up at him from under the brim that secreted half her face. Her blue eyes were round with anxiety.

Roarke closed the distance between them and imagined pulling Chloe close and kissing her. "Let me help you with your wrap." She handed him a light pelisse that complemented the green of her sprigged muslin dress. He lifted it around her shoulders and felt an ever so slight tremor shudder through her. His back to her parents, he gave her shoulders one quick squeeze.

She glanced up at him and gave him a decided nod, though her lips quivered. Then she turned. "Good-bye, Mother, Daddy."

Mrs. Kimball laughed in a practiced, cultured way, always the aristocrat—another thing that had always irked Roarke. "Have a nice evening, dear."

"Don't keep her out too late," Kimball said, pointing the cigar at Roarke. "I'm making a speech tomorrow and Chloe's comin' 'long to bolster my confidence and to show the voters what a pretty little thing my daughter is."

Mrs. Kimball pursed her lips, grimacing at her husband.

Roarke's palms itched to box the man's ears. Using his daughter for cheap political advantage. Disgusting. With a blowhard for a father and a souse for a mother, how Chloe had turned out so sweet and honest was a mystery.

"Come along, sweetheart." Roarke relished using this endearment both because he had long wanted to use it and because it threw more dust in her parents' eyes. Outside, he led Chloe to the car. Neither of them said anything incriminating; the windows of the house were open. Sparrows chattered in the boughs over the drive and the sky was still blue.

In the car, Chloe sat stiffly beside him. His own stomach felt on edge. Without a word, he drove them to the end of the rutted lane and turned down the road toward town. Soon a slender figure stepped out from the summer green bushes on the edge of a field of young spear-leafed tobacco and Roarke stopped.

"Get in, Minnie," Chloe said, her voice sounding dry, forced. "Hurry."

Roarke got out and opened the back door for the black girl, who wore a faded blue dress and a plain straw hat. Then into the trunk of the car he stowed the two valises she'd brought with her—one expensive leather and the other cheap cardboard.

"Thank you, Mister McCaslin," Minnie murmured.

Chloe waited while Roarke got back in and started on down the lane. Then she looked back at Minnie. "Your mother didn't guess?"

Minnie shook her head, her large brown eyes shining in the shadows under the arching trees lining the road. "If she did, she di'n't say nothin'. Miss Chloe, I hid everythin' and packed it just like I tole you."

Chloe nodded and turned to face forward.

Roarke paused before turning onto the main road. "Minnie, it might be uncomfortable, but lie down on the seat until we get out of the county."

"Yes, sir," Minnie said and obeyed.

"I don't," he continued, "want anyone to know you helped Miss Chloe—in case you ever come back here. We'll just hope everyone thinks it a coincidence. I'll keep your part a secret."

"Thank you, sir," Minnie murmured.

"You think of everything, Roarke." Chloe touched his arm. "How can I ever thank you?"

"No need to thank me." Roarke knew he sounded gruff. He'd been surprised when Chloe had told him Minnie was to come with her. But he'd asked no questions, saving her from the humiliation of explaining to him why this was necessary. Practically anyone in the county could have supplied Minnie's motive for fleeing. Chloe's father had a nasty reputation with women. Especially black women. Roarke's own father had been scathing in his opinion of a man in power who took advantage of young girls. And Minnie was a very pretty girl, one with little protection since most of her family was working for or in debt to Kimball. Roarke experienced another burst of satisfaction. He was killing two Kimball birds with one stone.

"Minnie, what are your plans?" he asked. He didn't want to remove the young gal from Kimball's sweaty grasp only to have her end up walking the streets of New York.

"I'll find work as a maid, sir. Miss Chloe says she give me a good letter of ref'rence."

"I'd be glad to give you one also." Roarke took a deep breath. He'd been afraid Minnie might have longed to make a name for herself singing the blues in Harlem or something else equally inappropriate for an innocent.

"Thank you, sir."

Chloe beamed at him. "I can't believe this is happening." Her voice lifted and she glowed all of a sudden as if a cloud had obscured her. "I've dreamed of getting away for so long, ever since I returned from finishing school." She leaned over and kissed his cheek. "You're wonderful, Roarke."

Her kiss went straight through him. He forced himself to keep his hands on the wheel, not to reach up and feel the tingling place where her kiss had fallen. *This isn't the way I had planned for your escape, Chloe.* But he wouldn't speak yet. They were still too close to home. So he merely nodded and drove onto the road toward Baltimore.

Chloe sighed and settled back against the seat beside him. And Roarke enjoyed her profile. His confidence in his power to persuade her to marry him edged up another notch. After all, she'd only met Theran Black twice in her life. He was dashing; but in the end, Roarke depended on Chloe to prefer the known over the unknown. And she obviously wasn't easy in her mind. She kept fidgeting with her hat and hem.

In a little town near the county line, Roarke pulled up at a cement-block gas station with one pump. "Why don't you two freshen up while I fill up with gas?"

Chloe and Minnie got out of the car and an attendant appeared to pump the gas. "We ain't got a separate restroom for her," he announced, nodding toward Minnie. "The gal'll have to go down the end of the street to the house on the right, the black preacher's place. He lets his kind use the outhouse in back."

Minnie said nothing, but marched away with her chin lifted. Roarke motioned Chloe toward the gas station and then stood by the car watching the gas meter *click-click*. Soon he was done and the women were back and they were off down the road and across the state line. They drove for another thirty minutes and then, a few miles outside of Baltimore, Roarke slowed and pulled off on the shoulder, where a faint track led away into a grove of maples and willows. The road was deserted and twilight had deepened. Roarke heard a brook trickling faintly nearby and the full and green leaves rustled and whispered overhead in the breeze. He got out.

"Why are we stopping?" Chloe sat up alert, glancing around.

"I . . . you and I need to discuss something before we go any farther. Minnie, will you excuse us?"

The maid nodded, watchful. Roarke wondered if she knew how he felt. He opened Chloe's door and offered her his hand. The look she gave him was confused, but she allowed him to lead her away from the car farther into the leafy trees where he could talk with her alone.

"What is it, Roarke?" She touched his dark sleeve, her blue eyes large with worry. "You haven't changed your mind, have you?"

"No, when I make up my mind, I rarely change it." He stopped and leaned back against a broad, gnarled oak trunk. "Are you sure you want to marry this fellow?" he asked without preamble.

Chloe blinked in surprise. "Of course."

"Why?"

Chloe's face flushed pink. "Because I love him. Why else would I marry him?" She raised her chin as if daring him to insult her.

"Maybe to get away from your parents." Roarke held up a hand to keep her from responding. She'd flushed brighter and her eyes had sparked. "Chloe, we're all alone and I'll never repeat what's said here. I have a pretty good idea of what your parents are like. I don't have much, if any, respect for them. If I were their son, I'd have left home at eighteen and never returned. So I know what your main goal is."

"Why are you bringing all this up?" Chloe didn't seem able to stand still. She tucked her hands in the folds of her elbows and fidgeted.

"Because I want to offer you a second option." Roarke steeled himself, pressing his spine against the rough bark.

Chloe made patterns in the wild grass and clover with the pointed toe of her white shoe. "What do you mean?"

"Marry me, Chloe." He said the words and then felt as if two large hands had grabbed him and were shaking him out like a tablecloth.

"But, Roarke, I've pledged myself to Theran." She took a step back, looking shocked. "*You* brought me his letters."

He understood her point. "I know, but I still think you're marrying him less from love and more from your own motive. You want to get away and Theran presented himself and obligingly proposed. How could you resist?" A warbling oriole flitted from one branch to another overhead and a breeze rustled green leaves. Chloe worried her lower lip before she replied, "I don't think you mean to insult me, Roarke. So I'll take this as concern. Theran is a good man. You don't have to worry about me. He'll take care of me."

Roarke stared at her without blinking, imprinting the way she looked in the early dusk. Her starched muslin sleek over her slender, enticing figure and the hat so artfully begging him to come closer, lift it, so he could see her whole face, taste her unrouged lips. "This has nothing whatever to do with Black."

"How can you say that? I'm going to marry him." She swallowed. "Tonight."

"Why? In Baltimore, I can leave you and Minnie at a hotel. Nothing could be more proper. Then I'll go meet him alone. I'll tell him that you've changed your mind. You won't have to face him. I'll take care of it."

"You make me sound like a coward." She stared down, still toeing the grass. "You think I'd promise to marry a man and then ask another man—" Her voice gathered momentum and strength. "—to go and tell him I'm not going to marry him. That I'm marrying the man carrying my message. What kind of girl do you think—"

In one swift move, he abandoned the tree trunk and captured her in his arms. "I love you, Chloe. I love you, your honesty, your bravery. I love you . . . and want you." He kissed her lips, parted in shock. She tried to pull away, but he encircled her more tightly and kissed her again, nudging up the low brim of her hat. She didn't struggle further, just remained within his arms, her breathing shallow and rapid.

"Let me go," she said, not looking at him. Her voice held no softness or coyness. Her face flamed.

He released her. "I don't want to lose you."

"Roarke, you shouldn't be kissing me," she insisted, righting her hat. "I'm an engaged woman. I gave Theran my promise."

"I admire you for your loyalty." He'd expected her resistance; she wasn't a tease. "But it's mistaken loyalty. You're marrying a virtual stranger. You've only met him twice."

"I'm not a jilt."

Another car rattled by, unseen but heard. "Engagements are broken all the time and new engagements are made." The words he held back for so long rushed out. He couldn't stem the flow. "I have my grandmother's engagement ring in my pocket. I'm serious, Chloe. We can get married tonight if you wish it. I've wanted you as my wife for the past five years or more."

She took a few steps away from him over the uneven ground. The evening shadows had lengthened. "Five years? Why didn't you ever say anything to me?" Her eyes held an uncertain mix of wonder and sorrow at his declaration.

A mourning dove cooed unseen, echoing his sense of impending loss and his heart constricted. "I was waiting for you to grow up while I finished my education. I would have started calling on you this spring. But Black got the jump on me."

Chloe stared at him. "But Kitty brought him home."

"Yes, and I wanted to strangle her pretty little neck for that." Roarke drew near to Chloe again.

"She didn't know that you loved me?" Chloe gazed toward him as if studying a stranger. The low light and her hat brim veiled her eyes. What was she thinking?

"Not too perceptive about her brother," Roarke said with chagrin. "'Fools rush in where angels fear to tread.' That's my sister."

"Kitty's my friend," Chloe said with a lift of her chin.

"And she's my sister. I love her, too. I just didn't need her flashing good-looking strangers in your face. I'm not handsome or a dashing soldier. But I love you, Chloe. I'll do my best to make you happy." He claimed her delicate hand, its cotton covering soft in his palm, and waited. The silence between them swelled like a force of its own. He realized he'd stopped breathing and made himself inhale normally—as normally as his speeding heart would permit.

With a sigh, she withdrew her hand from his. "I'm sorry, Roarke. I can't turn back now. I won't be a jilt," she repeated. Her voice still held a note of uncertainty.

"Theran Black isn't part of our world." Roarke played his best card. "No one will think less of you. Heck, no one but Kitty, Minnie, and I need ever know about your engagement to Black."

"I gave him my promise." Chloe sounded as if she were working hard to convince herself. The fragments of sky between the trees glowed bronze and violet now.

"I love you, Chloe. More important," he said, laying down all his aces, "I won't let your parents use you anymore. As my wife, you won't be available to them. I won't allow you to electioneer for your daddy. I won't let your mother tell you what to wear and whom you can talk to. I can't take you away to another state or city, but I can exert my authority as your husband. I'll protect you from them, you have my word."

Chloe took another step backward and then turned away. Shadows from the fluttering leaves flickered over her back. "Please don't ask me again, Roarke. My mind is made up."

Her uncertain tone didn't convince Roarke. He came up behind her and gripped her slim shoulders with tender regard. She tensed so he didn't turn her. He began to massage the tight muscles under his fingers. She didn't pull away and, emboldened, he whispered, "Chloe, kiss me. Turn around and kiss me and then tell me I don't have a chance."

She turned under his hands and looked up into his face. "Roarke, you're one of my two best friends in the world—"

He bent and kissed her. *Love me, Chloe. I'll take good care of you always. Love me.* For a moment, she remained still within his embrace. And then her lips answered his. The kiss brought her closer to him. His hopes soared.

But she tugged free, raising her hands to her mouth and shaking her head. "No. Theran will be waiting for us." She turned and hurried away over the rutted trail.

Roarke watched her run away. In spite of losing this skirmish, he didn't allow himself to think defeat yet. It would be a long night before Chloe would come face to face with taking wedding vows with Theran Black.

"All right for now, Chloe," he said just loud enough for her to hear. "But I haven't given up. Any time this evening all you have to say is 'Roarke, I changed my mind.' And I'll take care of everything."

Just after nightfall, at the Baltimore Union Station, Chloe walked—outwardly composed—beside Roarke with Minnie just a step behind her. Her insides twirled as she wondered what lay ahead. Would Roarke challenge Theran in some way? Roarke's declaration had sent her thoughts chasing themselves 'round and 'round. Why hadn't he kept silent? Wasn't this hard enough?

As arranged, Theran was waiting for them under the high arches of the main entrance. He looked like a stranger to Chloe in his khaki doughboy uniform, and she felt suddenly uncertain. Oblivious to her doubt, he hugged her confidently to him and then wrung Roarke's hand. "I can't thank you enough, McCaslin. We couldn't have done this without you." Minnie hung back, but Theran beamed and thanked her, too.

"You're welcome, sir," the girl murmured, her eyes roving over first him and then the busy train station.

"Well, McCaslin," Theran said as he drew Chloe under one arm, "you can leave Chloe and her maid in my charge. We'll be in New York late tonight. Chloe can stay at my rooming house while I bunk with friends. Then we'll get a license as soon as City Hall opens and get married there, too."

Chloe listened to these plans with relief. All she had to do was follow along. She'd thank Roarke, bid him farewell, and Theran would take care of everything.

"I've decided to come along," Roarke said in a tone Chloe had rarely heard him use. It was a challenge.

Unable to believe her ears, Chloe looked up at him. "Come along?"

Theran's look turned ugly. "Don't you trust me? Do you think I'd—"

Roarke stopped him with a hand. "I might as well ride with you to New York. I can't very well go home right away. You don't want me to be available for questioning by your future in-laws, do you? And if they know Miss Chloe's in my care, they won't make such a public fuss right away. They'll be surprised . . . shocked that we've apparently eloped, but they won't call the state police. So I might as well come along as the friend of the bride until Miss Chloe's legally married."

Chloe stared at him, a crease between her brows. Did he expect her to go back on her word? Did he sense that her resolve was paper thin? Her traitorous eyes drifted up to his compressed lips before rising to meet his rock-hard gaze. *I'm marrying Theran, Roarke. I am.*

Behind her gloved hand, Chloe stifled an unladylike yawn. The train ride had taken longer than they'd anticipated. It was full morning before they arrived in New York City. Now the four of them waited for City Hall to open. Minnie hung back at the rear while Roarke stood just ahead on Theran's opposite side. Chloe felt conspicuous in the extreme and couldn't help fearing her father might appear at any moment. He wouldn't be pleased.

Theran put an arm around her. He already held her hand. "Don't worry, sweetheart. You'll belong to me very soon." He cast an aggressive glance at Roarke.

Chloe felt as if she were in a trance. She'd never been to New York City before. The tall, grand buildings and noisy streets—crowded with red-and-green-paneled taxis, tall green buses, and hundreds of cars—made her jumpy. Even on Saturday morning, everybody was in a hurry, honking car horns and shouting in strange accents. Foreigners called to each other in languages she'd never heard. Everything felt just too big, too strange, too complicated to settle down in her mind. *I'm getting married today. I'm marrying Theran Black.* The thought was unreal. The man beside her didn't even look familiar. The man she'd planned to marry hadn't worn a doughboy uniform and his hair had been longer. Whenever she tried to look at Theran, it was like peering through binoculars that wouldn't focus.

Beside Theran, Roarke McCaslin's profile was familiar. And Roarke had proposed to her last night. That also didn't feel real. Why hadn't Roarke ever said anything, made the least overture? If she hadn't given her word, Roarke's suit might have tempted her. But it had only made things harder for her.

"Hey!" Kitty hurried up the steps, joining them. They'd called her from the restaurant where they'd breakfasted. "Isn't this thrilling?"

Chloe didn't feel thrilled. Daunted and confused, she forced a smile. "Kitty!" She hugged her and they kissed cheeks.

"My first attempt at matchmaking—and I'm a success!" Kitty hugged her brother and greeted Theran. "You brought your maid along?" she squealed. "How very proper."

"Minnie decided to seek employment elsewhere," Chloe explained, blushing.

"I don't blame her." Kitty gave Minnie a teasing wave of her hand. "Why stay buried at Ivy Manor when you have a chance at New York City?"

Chloe turned away and caught the expression on Roarke's face. He was frowning. As she gazed at him, he mouthed, "I still want to marry you, Chloe."

She looked away. A kind of panic was brewing in her stomach. Roarke's words made it churn faster and higher. She looked at Theran, who was teasing Kitty about something. *I am marrying this stranger today.* She tried to make herself believe these words. She failed. *This can't be happening.*

The imposing double doors before them were officially unlocked with a grating and snapping of the large locks. Roarke led them inside onto the marble floors, polished and gleaming. A few people walked around them up wide steps. Chloe and the rest paused to check a large directory hung on one wall. Then Theran led them to the elevators. Everything moved quickly after that. The formalities of obtaining the license took only a few minutes at a grilled window. They moved to another office where they waited for a judge. Soon, a tall thin man with thinning gray hair stalked in wearing his black robe.

"License?" Theran handed it to him. The judge read it as if looking for any discrepancies. "Young lady, you are very young to be making this decision and I don't see your parents here. Are you sure you want to marry this soldier?"

Chloe hadn't expected this. "I'm old enough to marry."

"I didn't ask you if you were legally old enough. I wanted

to know if you wish to draw back. Marriage is for life, young woman. In times of war—" The judge looked Theran up and down. "—people sometimes marry in haste and repent at leisure."

"This is none of your business," Theran objected.

Chloe looked past the judge to Roarke, who stood beside him.

Roarke mouthed, "It's not too late."

Chloe closed her eyes. Would everything feel more real if she'd accepted Roarke's proposal? That premise didn't seem viable either. "I've made up my mind to marry Theran Black." Her voice came out unexpectedly harsh.

Theran glanced back at her, startled. "Don't sound so excited about it, honey," he said, smiling. "Judge, I'm sure you mean well, but we're in love. I leave Monday for France and we're getting married before I leave. If you don't want to do it, another judge will." Theran took her arm to lead her away.

"No, I'll marry you." The judge glared at Theran. "I always try to impress on the couple what an important, life-altering step marriage is. But I can see your mind is made up. Join your right hands, please."

Without looking at them, the judge opened a small black book and began to read the wedding ceremony in a flat, un-hurried voice. Chloe tried to keep her eyes on Theran, the man she was marrying. But they insisted on drifting to Roarke. He stood as best man on the opposite side of Theran.

"Repeat after me," the judge intoned.

Chloe breathed in deeply for strength and recited, "I, Chloe Lorraine Kimball, take you, Theran Black, as my lawfully wedded husband." All the while, her desperate eyes pleaded with Roarke's. *I'm not a jilt. He's going to war. How could I throw him over?* The ceremony raced ahead. Soon, Theran was slipping a cool, gold band on her ring finger and kissing her. The judge shook their hands. Roarke and Kitty signed the certificate as the witnesses.

Chloe's life had changed in an instant. *I'm married to Theran Black.* Tears trailed down her cheeks. She tried to hold them in, but they flowed unchecked. "Don't cry, honey." Theran, her husband, pulled her close and hugged her.

In an instant, the same breathless feeling she'd felt that night after the tango caught Chloe up in its web. Desperate to know she'd done the right thing, she pressed herself against him, drawing his assurance to her. *This is my husband.* And she turned her face and kissed his lips as she had wanted to for weeks. But even though his lips were reassuringly solid, the feeling of unreality lingered.

From behind Theran, Roarke gazed at her, but differently. Now, he looked at her the way he always had before yesterday. Had she broken his heart? She couldn't believe it. But then, she'd barely believed he'd proposed to her.

Clutching her hand in his, Theran hurried them out the door and down the wide marble staircase. "Let's go celebrate."

Chloe glanced back at Roarke. He nodded to her and she smiled at him uncertainly. *I married Theran Black and it was the right thing to do.* The judge's words came back to her: "Marry in haste and repent at leisure." She closed her eyes and drew on her inner resolve. *There will be no repenting. I married for love, not for gain like my mother. We'll be fine.* Everything would turn out all right, she knew it would. *I'm married now. Let it all work out.*

The day had passed in a whirl of sightseeing. Each moment made Chloe feel more as if she were in a trance. Every few minutes, Theran would touch her in some way. His touch compelled a response from her, that intensity she'd experienced with their first kiss. She imagined them alone together—completely alone as man and wife. The thought both enticed and frightened her. She kept reminding herself that he was her husband and he would want to be intimate with her. But she had no idea what that meant beyond kisses.

Riding in taxis and buses, they'd traveled all over Manhattan and across the Brooklyn Bridge and back. They'd all strolled through a buoyant Central Park eating hot dogs—a new food to Chloe and Minnie—and ended with a tour around the stately grounds of Columbia University, now Theran's alma mater. Proud and awed, Chloe kept glancing at Theran, the stranger who held her hand. *I'm married. This is my husband.* For all their reality, she could have been saying, "I can fly. This is my airplane." The words didn't ring true.

Now, in early evening, Chloe and everyone looked out a taxi window into what Theran had announced was Harlem. Chloe noticed that the people on the street were almost all Negro. In the backseat, Minnie perched between Kitty and her. Minnie was sitting up straight and looking around, hungry for every sight, just as Chloe was.

"Minnie, you'll like it in Harlem," Kitty said, glancing at Chloe from the girl's other side.

"I 'spect I will, Miss Kitty."

"I haven't written you your letter of recommendation yet." Chloe sat up straighter. She hadn't been thinking about Minnie leaving her. Her heart suddenly sped up.

"Minnie won't be going to any employment agency until Monday," Theran soothed from the front seat. "Right now we're taking her to a nice boarding house where she can stay the weekend. When you said you were bringing her along, I thought I better find a place for her. Yesterday I talked to a janitor on campus and he recommended this place, said the landlady was very respectable. I checked and she had a room vacant, so I reserved it for your maid."

Chloe looked at the back of Theran's head. She reached forward and caressed his neck. "That's so sweet of you, honey."

Theran glanced over his shoulder. "I am sweet, sugar."

Chloe recoiled. "Sugar" was what her father called her. "Please . . . don't call me sugar."

"Okay. How about 'honey'?"

"Fine." What a silly thing to be talking about. "Fine."

The cab pulled into the curb in front of a tall, narrow house. "Here we are, Minnie."

Chloe suddenly panicked. She caught Minnie's shoulder. "Theran, give her our address. Minnie, I'll go with you Monday to the . . . employment place. I want to make certain you get settled with a nice family."

Minnie looked into Chloe's eyes and smiled reassuringly. "Yes, miss." Roarke opened the door and Minnie climbed around Kitty and out. "Good-bye, Mr. Theran. Take care of yourself and don't let them Germans hurt you none."

Theran chuckled. "Don't worry, Minnie. I'll come home singing a song."

"Minnie," Chloe said, opening her purse, "do you have money?"

"I been savin' up, miss. I'll be fine."

Chloe still handed her a dollar. "Come over after one on Monday. Theran gave you the address. I'll be seeing him off in the morning." Nodding, Minnie waved and with her cardboard valise walked up the six steps to the door of the boarding house, painted in neat gray and white.

Chloe felt tears gathering in the back of her throat. Theran would be leaving and so would everyone else familiar. Wasn't Roarke escorting Kitty home for a visit? That meant her best friend wouldn't even be here. Suddenly Chloe was very glad Minnie had come with her to New York.

The rest of the evening fled by—a festive supper at a little Italian restaurant in Greenwich Village and then Roarke and Kitty were dropping Chloe and . . . her husband off at Theran's rooming house.

Roarke hung back beside a taxi at the curb, facing Theran and Chloe. "I'm heading home right after I drop Kitty off."

"Oh, Roarke, I can't leave till after Monday," Kitty said from the front seat. "I have to meet a professor once more."

"I can't wait. I need to get home." He looked at Chloe.

She tried to read his eyes, but the curtain had come down and would not be lifted. She'd made her decision and she could see he'd accepted it. She held out her hand. "Thank you for everything, Roarke." She wished she could say more to her old friend. "Rest on the train. You didn't sleep much last night."

He touched the brim of his hat and then lifted her gloved hand to his lips. "All the best, Miss Chloe."

She nodded, unable to speak. Kitty clambered out of the car and hugged her one more time. "I'll be leaving soon, but I'll check on you Monday. You'll love it up here. Nobody watches a person's every little move like at home."

Theran shook Roarke's hand and kissed Kitty's cheek. "Thanks, Little Miss Matchmaker." Kitty chuckled. Then Roarke and she got into the taxi and drove away. Theran swept Chloe up into his arms. "Alone at last."

CHAPTER FIVE

*C*hloe stood looking out the large, dusty window in Theran's room. The view featured the rear windows of other brick houses. For a moment, she let her mind drift to the very different view from her window at Ivy Manor—green lawn and magnolia blossoms. Then she stopped herself. *I'll probably never see it again.* This brought moisture to her eyes and an ache over her heart. She'd loved Ivy Manor. That wasn't what she'd run away from.

"It's late, Chloe," Theran said, as if commenting on the weather. "I'm going to turn out the light, give you some privacy."

She froze in place. The mystery of what intimacies a wedding night entailed loomed before her and uncertainty sluiced through her like ice water. "Theran . . ."

He came up behind her and wrapped his strong arms around her, nuzzling her neck. "Don't be afraid of me, Chloe. I'd never hurt you."

"I know that." But her voice sounded low and slid over her throat like splintered wood. Theran's banded arms moved up and rested on her dress just above her corset top. The intimate contact made her inhale sharply.

"I'm going to lie down and turn my back to you." He kissed her nape again. "I'll be waiting, dearest, but take your time."

Within moments, she heard the brass bed's springs creak and then only the street sounds from below. She lowered the shade on the window; the street lamps glowed around the frayed edges. Then in the semi-darkness, she began unfastening the row of small mother-of-pearl buttons down the front of her dress. Her every move seemed layered with new significance. *This is my husband. Being together like this is right and proper.* But her fingers fumbled with the buttons and her breath came out in shivers.

Theran began humming some slow melody, something that reminded her of dancing at the honky-tonk. The sound did things to the hairs on the back of her neck. A tingling coursed through her in cadence with her shallow breathing. A problem presented itself. Her mother still insisted Chloe wear an old-fashioned corset that laced up the back—she said it was the mark of a lady to need a maid to dress herself. But Chloe couldn't call Minnie all the way from Harlem to untie her corset. There was only Theran. She tried to loosen the ties herself without luck.

Like a naughty child, she tiptoed over to the side of the bed where he lay, facing away from her. "Theran," she whispered, "I need you to loosen my corset laces." Her face burned. She was afraid he'd say something bold and embarrassment would kill her.

He said nothing. But the bed springs creaked as he sat up behind her. Then he tugged her gently and made her sit down on the bed, facing away from him. His nearness warmed her and she realized she was chilled. She felt him untie the laces and then slowly stretch them, crisscross by crisscross, his fingers brushing her spine. As her corset stays finally released her, she sighed as she always did at the sudden relief. Before she could rise, Theran kissed the back of her neck and drew her back against him. "Don't go away, my sweet bride," he murmured. "Stay with me."

She didn't move, her breath suddenly difficult to find. Theran's scent filled her head as he kissed her neck and held her spine to his chest. She felt their skin touch and she quivered with the sensation. Slowly, he turned her and drew her up beside him—so close she could hear his heart beating. Or was it hers?

"Trust me," he whispered and she put her arms around his neck and sighed with his kisses.

In the morning, Theran in a shirt and slacks went out and brought in a bag of fragrant sweet rolls and coffee. She sat up in the brass bed, suddenly flushing to have Theran gaze at her even if she'd buttoned up her prim, high-necked nightgown.

"My blushing bride." He chuckled and bent to kiss her. Then he opened the bag and handed her a paper napkin and a sweet roll. "I'm hungry and you must be, too."

Thinking of how little sleep she'd had, she blushed again. He kissed her once more and sat down beside her on the creaky bed. With a grin, he poured steaming coffee into two chipped, mismatched cups on the nightstand, handed her one, and then settled back against the headboard. "We need to talk about practical things now. Then we can just concentrate on being together the rest of the day." He gave her a private smile.

Chloe blushed warmer.

Theran chuckled and bit into his roll. After swallowing, he pulled out a small, black leather book from the nightstand drawer. "This is my bank book. I've already put your name on the account. It isn't much, but it should help you out until most of my army pay starts arriving here."

"Will you have enough?" His matter-of-fact acceptance of his leaving for war struck her as very brave.

He shrugged. "The army has to feed me and clothe me." He looked suddenly almost boyish. "I know you're used to the very best, Chloe. I promise I'll be a good provider. This war will be over before you know it and I'll get my career on track."

Chloe wanted to remind him that the "very best" had carried a price tag she'd run away from, but she couldn't. Not with him talking about leaving, about the war. She leaned over and kissed him, hoping her lips could say what her voice couldn't: *I don't want you to go. We've just started.*

Theran rested a hand on her cheek, caressing it. Then he settled back and took another bite of his roll. "Also, I've written to my parents all about you and I've noted their address inside the back cover of the bank book. I hope you will write to them. They'll help you if you need anything."

Chloe digested this sobering thought. Surely Theran's parents couldn't be anything like her own. As if reading her mind, Theran went on, "They aren't anything like your parents. I think you'll like them."

"I'm sure I will," Chloe replied obediently, ignoring the skip in her pulse.

"Before I leave on Monday, I'll show you the bank."

"Don't talk about Monday," she whispered, suddenly losing her appetite.

"We're not going to worry about this . . . war. I'm going to come home fine and we'll have the rest of our lives together." He kissed her lips, sugary-sticky from the sweet roll. This made her laugh and she wiped away a tear with the back of her hand.

"And you'll have Kitty nearby and Minnie in town. This city has parks, museums, theaters, wonderful stores—" He chucked her chin. "—and I don't want you moping around."

"I thought I might volunteer to do some war work." Chloe took a sip of hot, creamy coffee. "I read about it in the paper."

"That's my wife. You'll do fine. I remember how strange it was when I came from Buffalo. But soon you'll love it here."

Chloe felt her spirits lift. "I know I will." *Because Daddy will never find me here.*

Theran rewarded her with a smile. "No man could ask for a sweeter, prettier wife than you, Chloe."

She looked down at the black bank book. She'd only thought of escaping her parents. But even though Theran would be heading off to Europe and the war, he had thought of how to provide for her. She leaned her forehead against his. "You're a good husband, Theran. I love you."

He took the cup and half-eaten roll from her hands and pushed her back against her white feather pillow. "You love me, huh? Show me."

On Sunday morning, for the second time in two days, Quentin Kimball brushed past Maisie, the McCaslin house-keeper, and charged into the sunlit sage-green and honey-oak McCaslin dining room. Looking at him, Roarke knew this scene would live in his memory forever—the morning sunshine blazing through the diaphanous white sheers and glinting on the sterling silver coffee urn on the oak sideboard. The smell of bacon, coffee, and melted butter. Maisie's black face peering through the half-open kitchen door.

Kimball glared around and then stopped short, squaring

off across the table from Roarke. "So you got home, Mc-Caslin. Where's my little gal?" Kimball looked upward at the ceiling. "Chloe!" he roared. "Chloe, sugar, it's your daddy!"

Roarke watched the red-faced man and caught himself just in time to prevent a smile. Roarke had lost Chloe, but he still retained the pleasure of telling Kimball the truth.

"Good morning, Mr. Kimball," Roarke's mother said as politely as if the man usually dropped in unannounced for breakfast. "Would you like us to set a place for you?" All three would be leaving for church after they'd finished their coffee.

"I don't want breakfast, woman! I want to see my daughter here with a McCaslin weddin' band on her finger. Or I'm going to know the reason why."

Swallowing hot coffee, Roarke looked into the man's blotchy face, its nose reddened by too much booze. "Chloe's in New York with her husband, Theran Black," Roarke said, "so I don't know why you'd expect her to be here, wearing *my* wedding band. I was best man at their wedding." Even as he said it, each word pounded a nail in his own coffin. Chloe couldn't have run away without his help. He was paying for that now and he feared the ache that weighed on him wouldn't go away any time soon.

He watched Kimball gabble for a few moments before becoming coherent once more. "My *daughter* left my house in your care," the man's voice quavered with pent-up fury. "And you helped her run off and marry another man! You're a fool!"

If Roarke thought her father's outrage sprung from love of Chloe, he'd have been ashamed of himself. But he knew it wasn't. It was just pique at losing one of his possessions, as if Chloe was a filly in Kimball's stable. He wondered, had the man learned of Minnie's leaving yet? Acid spurted in Roarke's stomach. He longed to say, "You're the fool."

Kimball switched his glare to Roarke's father. "Thomas, did you know this yesterday?"

"Of course Thomas didn't," Mrs. McCaslin said, looking outraged.

"Of course, I didn't." Roarke's father agreed as he steepled his fingers and coolly returned Kimball's stare. "If I had, I'd have told you when you came last night."

Kimball turned to Roarke. "When you didn't come home at a decent time, I came over to ask your daddy where you were—"

"At one in the morning," Roarke's mother slipped in, quietly disapproving.

"—and your daddy told me," Kimball continued to bawl, "that he had expected his son home sooner, but in any event my daughter was safe in his son's care. So where's my daughter?"

"I told you," Roarke repeated, fatigue rolling over him, "she's in New York with her husband." *And I'm too tired to be polite very much longer.* Losing Chloe stung him like poison nettles and his temper reflected that.

"Nonsense." Kimball dismissed this with a wave of his stubby hand. "My wife is prostrate with worry. I want to know where our Chloe's run off to."

"Kimball," Thomas spoke up in a sterner tone, "my son has told you where your daughter is. I don't approve of his aiding her in an elopement. But I also don't approve of a parent who burns letters from a girl's honest beau who happens to be leaving for war. And in any event, what's done is done."

Kimball stared at Roarke's father, his eyes narrowing. "Are you tellin' me that someone burned my daughter's letters? Who?"

"I believe you should discuss this with your good lady." Thomas took a sip of his coffee. "In any case, your daughter is a married woman now."

"It was my pleasure to help them," Roarke commented and at last he permitted himself a smile. He would have rather buried his face in his arms on the table. He had lost Chloe.

Thomas held up a hand to stop Kimball, who'd just opened his mouth again. "Once more, I didn't know when you came yesterday that my son was helping Chloe elope with another man. I had hoped my words were true—that Roarke, for whatever reason, had decided to elope with Miss Chloe himself. I apologize for misleading you, but that can't be helped now."

Roarke clutched his violet-sprigged china cup with both hands, holding on to his pride, his self-control.

Kimball reached out and gripped the top of the carved oak chair in front of him. His knuckles turned white as he stared at Roarke. "My daughter had no reason to run away. I told her the doughboy could write her."

So you could include that patriotic note in your speeches. Roarke's mouth twisted into a mirthless smile. "Perhaps you should consult with your wife about that," he repeated his father's suggestion. Then he chewed his buttered toast slowly as if what Kimball wanted was of no importance to him, as if his love hadn't pledged her faith to another man while he stood silently by.

"My wife?" Kimball let go of the chair, suddenly alert to what they'd been telling him.

Roarke's mother nodded, touching a white linen napkin to her lips. "Chloe's a sweet girl and I would have loved to have her for a daughter, but that isn't what happened, Mr. Kimball."

"Where is she? What's her address?" Kimball demanded. "I'm going to bring her home."

Roarke gritted his teeth. *Never. If it weren't for you, Chloe wouldn't have run away. She would have been mine.* He shrugged. "I don't recall the address."

Kimball's index finger shot out at Roarke. "I'll find out where she is and you'll pay for this." He shook his finger in Roarke's face. "Mark my words. You'll pay." With a last glare around the room, the man stomped out.

In the silence that remained, Roarke's mother motioned the housekeeper to pour more coffee. "What an unpleasant man to have at breakfast."

Roarke hid a faint smile behind his cup. Leave it to his mother to say just the right thing. The smile was short lived, however. He knew the empty ache inside him would last a long, long time—maybe for the rest of his life. But then, he'd be drafted soon so that might not be as long as he feared.

In the midst of these dark thoughts, a fresh worry niggled at the back of his mind. He'd better call Kitty and tell her to warn Chloe that her father would be looking for her. He hoped Theran's precautions would keep Chloe hidden. Roarke had given up Chloe to free her. And it had better work.

On Monday afternoon, Chloe—wearing the green-sprigged dress, straw hat, and white gloves she'd been married in—waited on the front steps of the red-brick rooming house. The day was warm and she had come outside to force herself to stop crying. When would Minnie show up? She leaned against the black wrought-iron railing and tried not to relive the wrenching memory of Theran marching with thousands of other doughboys onto the ship. His last jaunty wave to her would live in her mind forever.

A sob tried to swell in her throat; she forced it down. "How can I miss him this much already?" she whispered to herself. She remembered the sensation of lying in his arms, so loved, so protected. Now his ship, bound for France, was hours out to sea. *Theran, please come back to me.*

Chloe caught sight of Minnie turning the corner toward her. The young black girl in a sober new gray dress and plain straw hat was staring up at the corner street signs and house numbers. "Minnie," Chloe called and waved. "Minnie!"

The maid saw her and waved in return. "Miss Chloe!"

Chloe met her up the block and impulsively hugged her. "I'm so glad to see you. How did yesterday go?"

"I found a good colored church and I met some people," Minnie said with a perky grin.

"I . . . I didn't get to church yesterday," Chloe confessed.

Minnie giggled. "I bet you didn't." Chloe blushed. Minnie giggled some more and gave Chloe a saucy look. "You sure did marry up with a good-lookin' man."

Again, it was as if they were girls again. Somehow leaving Ivy Manor behind had permitted them to go back in time. Chloe wondered if Minnie noticed this.

"People at church tole me how to get over here to you," Minnie went on, "and give me the addresses of a couple of them employment places. Agencies, they call 'em."

"Well done." Chloe was impressed. "I'm ready to accompany you."

Minnie turned and Chloe fell into step with her. "The subway station is only two blocks 'way from your place," Minnie informed her. "That's good 'cause then you can go anywhere you want, easy as pie. I rode the subway mostly yesterday afternoon so I kin get used to it and find places by myself."

"Theran taught me this morning," Chloe said, feeling a bit queasy. Subways made her stomach jump.

"New York's a big place," Minnie commented. "But I like it."

Chloe nodded, hiding her own uncertainty. "I rode the subway back all by myself from seeing Theran off." She heard her voice catch in her throat. Theran had left her. She pulled her white ruffled handkerchief from her pocket.

Minnie patted her arm. "You gone be all right. You smart an' pretty an' you married to a soldier. Nobody gone mess with you."

Chloe felt suddenly determined to put her sorrow away and help her friend. Taking a breath, she nodded firmly. "You're right, Minnie. I'm going to be fine. And so are you. Now, let's go find you a job." And with that, they were running down the steps of the subway station and buying tickets at the booth.

At the first agency, the woman looked at them forbiddingly and asked Minnie to fill out a card. Chloe also sat down and wrote a letter of reference to be put on file. When Minnie gave her filled-out card to the woman, she surprised Chloe by saying, "Ma'am, I only wants a position with someone in the theater or music. An actress or someone like that."

The agency woman looked up at her. "We don't get too many of *that* type of client."

"Well, that's what I want," Minnie said with a decided nod.

"You won't take a position in a family unless it's connected to the theater?" The woman studied Minnie with her face drawn into a frown.

"Or music, vaudeville, movies," Minnie explained. "Anythin' like that."

"Very well." The woman's lips pinched together like the end of a lemon. "Good day."

Minnie and Chloe walked out together and got into the small, brass-trimmed elevator. Chloe waited till they reached the pavement, where cars and taxis in an unbroken line blared their horns. "Minnie, I never! What are you thinking?"

"I got plans, Miss Chloe." Minnie walked with her chin held high and her back straight as a pine.

"I see you do." Chloe hurried to keep up with Minnie's snappy pace. The discordant car horns made her wince. "What are they?"

Minnie didn't reply until they turned a corner and left the noisy cars behind. "I don't want to be a maid all my life," the girl said at last.

"You don't?" The idea of a person of color being anything but a servant or sharecropper came as a novel idea to Chloe. "What do you want to do?"

"I think . . ." Minnie walked a bit farther in silence. "I think I kin be an actress in the movies."

Chloe couldn't stop herself. She laughed out loud. Minnie might have just as well said, "I want to be elected president." She gazed at her companion with rising curiosity. "But, Minnie, there aren't any Negroes in motion pictures."

"I don't know 'bout that, and I think that gone change. They can't do black-face forever; it don't look real." Minnie looked determined, her jaw firm and her voice strong. "And anyway, they do hire black actors and actresses for the theater and sometimes a colored person can do a vaudeville act. I'll find somethin' to suit me."

"But how will being the maid of an actress help you?"

This conversation held a distinct quality of unreality. Were they really talking about Minnie being an actress?

"I figure I work for people who in show business, I can learn how to get to be an actress."

Minnie's incredible ambition exploded in Chloe's mind like shimmering fireworks, stunning her to silence. Minnie, her maid, wanted to be in moving pictures like Lillian Gish. She watched Minnie from the corner of her eye as they continued down the busy sidewalk. Then, looking around at the towering buildings and the hurrying city people and all that made this place a different world from the one she knew, Chloe realized, *Why not?* "Minnie, that's about the most exciting thing I've ever heard."

Looking suspicious, Minnie glanced at her. "You think I'm crazy."

"No, I don't." Chloe shook her head with emphasis. "This past Christmas I would never have believed that by spring, I'd be married and living free in New York City. If I can get away from Ivy Manor and marry the man I love, you can have your plans, too. And what's more, I'll do whatever I can to help you."

Minnie stopped and made eye contact with her then as if checking Chloe's true opinion one more time. Then she grinned. "We gone have new lives, Miss Chloe. You wait and see."

"I'm a believer today." Chloe laughed again. "Let's see that agency address again." Even if Minnie never got to be an actress, surely being the maid to one could only be more interesting than a humdrum family.

At the second agency, they carried out the same routine and were met with a similar response, except that this woman suggested Minnie apply at an agency near the theater district. She gave them its name and address and they set off at a brisk pace. Chloe felt more hopeful with each step. Another subway ride, and Chloe and Minnie entered another imposing brick building. Chloe paused outside the door of this agency and said a quick prayer for Minnie.

Minnie whispered her own affirmation. "Come on, Jesus. I got to have a job soon." She pushed open the door and Chloe and she entered. This agency looked a bit busier. All the chairs were filled and people milled around in front of the reception desk. While Chloe stood to the side Minnie approached the desk and asked to apply for a position.

"You—" A man's imperious voice suddenly cut across the crowded office, causing Minnie, Chloe, and several other people to turn. He gave Chloe an imperious motion. "You, the blonde, walk toward me. Please." He snapped his fingers.

Chloe nearly gave a tart reply, but then, curious, she looked the man in the face. There was something in his eyes that intrigued her. Or perhaps it was the slightly continental accent he had and his well-tailored brown suit. She walked toward him.

"Turn," he ordered, "and walk to the door again."

With a raised eyebrow, Chloe obeyed, feeling everyone in the room's attention on her. But she was used to being on display and this man sounded like he had a reason. When she turned again, the man was beaming at her. He immediately strode over and handed her a gilt-edged card.

"You're just what I'm looking for." He nodded as he took her hand, ignoring her surprised look. "A friend of mine is a couturier, just come over from Paris, and I'm helping her open a shop on Fifth Avenue. We need one blonde and one brunette model."

Chloe tried to say something but her mouth wouldn't work. The man didn't seem to notice. He turned to the secretary at the desk. "This is the girl I want. Get her information and then give her the address." He looked at Chloe again and smiled. "I'll be seeing you tomorrow, then, at nine." He bowed over her hand and walked out.

Chloe stood there, still without a word to say.

"Miss Chloe, this be so excitin'," Minnie breathed into her ear. "You're gone be a model on Fifth Avenue. That's where all the swanky shops are."

"But, Minnie! I didn't come here to get myself a job. I came to get *you* a job."

"Don' you worry 'bout me. I'll get my job, too. Now don' you pass this up, Miss Chloe."

Chloe listened to the buzz of voices as everyone, heads together, whispered about her and her new job. Everyone stared at her. *Could I really do it?*

The secretary stood up. "Please come to the desk, miss. I need you to fill out a card and I'll give you the address of the couturier."

Minnie gave Chloe a push. "Go on. We'll both fill out cards this time."

Chloe couldn't resist the I-dare-you look in Minnie's eyes. It was the same look that had gotten them spanked more than once as children, and suddenly it was wonderful to see. With a grin, she marched up to the desk.

Chapter Six

❧

*T*he noisy, boisterous chatter in the café bounced off the brick walls of the tiny basement it occupied. Kitty had met them when they returned from the final employment agency and had invited them to Greenwich Village for a very late lunch. The surrounding hubbub only intensified Chloe's agitation. It reminded her of when she was a little girl and how she'd loved to watch the wide-hipped cook at Ivy Manor fry griddle cakes. The part that had intrigued her the most was when the woman had sprinkled water on the hot grease to test it; Chloe had loved watching the droplets of water dance on the pan. That was how Chloe felt now—like the water beads hopping, sizzling.

She knew there was an unpleasant task she must do soon. When Theran had been with her, she had wanted to give him every moment. Every second with him had been so dear to her. But she had to contact her parents soon. She wouldn't go back to Ivy Manor; maybe they wouldn't even want her. But a good daughter didn't just run away and never let her family know she was all right. The problem was in how she should contact them. Would Kitty know how to do it so it would leave no trail to lead them back to her? Also, she was bursting to tell Kitty everything that had happened that day—if she could believe it herself.

But behind all that, tears hovered ready to swoop down on her. Tonight, she'd sleep alone. Theran, her husband, was already beyond her reach. In two days, she'd left home, become his wife, discovered the mysteries of being married, and then waved and cheered him off to war. With a suddenly aching heart, she pressed a white-cotton-gloved hand to her mouth, holding back her sorrow, the one thing that seemed most real to her. She hadn't realized parting from Theran would hurt so. It was a physical ache, nagging, worrying her.

She closed her eyes and drew in steady breaths until a careless waitress, reeking of some dreadful perfume, plopped cups of strong black coffee in front of the three of them and startled her. Bemused, she glanced around and realized she'd never seen such a bizarre combination of people in her life. Most looked as if they didn't know how to use an iron or couldn't afford to hire someone who did. The men wore all manner of beards. Shocking women lounged in chairs, obviously not wearing corsets, and showing off rouged lips and cheeks and bleached hair. One woman across from Chloe had cut her thick brown hair chin-length and was wearing men's clothing! Chloe tried not to stare, but her eyes roved over the colorful, radical scene. "Who *are* these people?" she asked Kitty in a low, scandalized voice.

Kitty chuckled, lolling her head back and extending her arms wide. "These, my dear Chloe, are the *avant garde.* Bohemians."

"What that mean?" Minnie asked. She wasn't the only person of color in the café. In fact, even a few Oriental people were in evidence. But Minnie still didn't look at ease. She kept jittering one of her heels, making her look like a Model-T just shuddering to a start.

"It means these are painters, sculptors, journalists, philosophers, writers, actors." Kitty waved her hands around like a magician's assistant and slouched back farther into her chair, sitting like no lady ever should. "In short, my sweets, the most interesting people you'll ever meet."

"Meet?" Chloe echoed. "Do you *know* some of these people?" The idea outright floored her. Greenwich Village seemed unreal.

"I know some of these people, yes," Kitty said with airy aplomb.

"Actors?" Minnie asked, glancing around, still jittering. "Do you know any actors, Miss Kitty?"

Kitty raised one quizzical eyebrow.

"Minnie wants to find a position as a maid for someone in show business," Chloe explained without giving away all Minnie's plans.

"You want to work for actors?" Kitty looked Minnie up and down as though she hadn't known the girl ever since they were all children together.

"Yes, Miss Kitty," Minnie said, gazing around. "I want to work for somebody in show bizness."

Kitty looked thoughtful. "Why?"

Minnie looked around the room, assumedly still trying to pick out any actors. "'Cause," she declared, stopping the jumping heel, "I want to be an actress."

"How thrilling!" Kitty crowed. "Have you ever acted?"

"Not on the stage or anythin' like that." Minnie glanced away.

Chloe studied the darker girl's profile. She suddenly realized Minnie had probably been acting out a part for many years—that of the dutiful Negro maid. No wonder she was determined to do something else.

Chloe thought of the two very different roles she herself

had been forced to play—cooperative daughter for her political father and society debutante for her mother. *I don't have to lie anymore.* It was as if a load had been lifted from her shoulders. Theran had done this for her, freed her. Theran, who was gone and who knew for how long. She felt momentarily hollow.

"Miss Chloe, you gone tell Miss Kitty 'bout your new job?" Minnie propped an elbow on the table, looking more at ease now, her shoulders relaxed, her cheek on her hand.

Kitty leaned over the table toward Chloe. "Job? *You?*"

Stung by Kitty's disbelieving tone, Chloe flushed, wishing Minnie hadn't revealed this. Kitty would tease her forever about it. "I've been offered a position as model at a couturier on Fifth Avenue. But of course I won't be accepting it."

"Fifth Avenue?" Kitty's eyes widened. "Which one?"

"I . . ." Chloe faltered and then opened her bag and took out the ivory card the man had given her. "The man who spoke to me was Marshfield Crowe," she read from the card and then handed it to Kitty. "He said he was helping a new couturier from Paris set up shop here."

"He said he needed," Minnie added, "one blonde and one brunette model. He pick Miss Chloe right out of a room full a pretty ladies." Minnie looked pleased as anything.

Chloe couldn't stop her face from warming.

"Well," Kitty handed back the card, "you're gorgeous—according to your husband. And so tall and willowy. I wish I had your inches. Oh, I'd love to see the expression on your mama's face if she knew you were *working.*"

"I'm not modeling." After all the years she'd been put on display, she hated people looking at her. "Besides I'm a married woman."

Kitty smiled, almost gleaming with impish amusement at

Chloe. "I almost forgot! Roarke called me and described the fit your daddy threw in our dining room yesterday morning."

"Your dining room?" Chloe put Mr. Crowe's card carefully away in her small purse.

"Yes, I guess your daddy came over Saturday very late and then Sunday morning to find out if you'd come back with Roarke. He thought you and Roarke had run off and eloped. 'Course my daddy didn't know what had happened, but knowing you were with Roarke, he thought that, too. Anyway, Roarke told him you'd married Theran and that he'd acted as Theran's best man."

Before Chloe could voice a word, Minnie cut in, "What did Old Puff'n'guts say to that?" Then, realizing her *faux pas,* she checked herself. "Sorry, Miss Chloe." Her voice flattened. "I forgot my place."

Chloe stared at Minnie. "Is that . . . Is that what people call Daddy?"

"Among other things." Kitty chuckled and rolled her eyes. Minnie only nodded, her eyes still downcast.

That her father was generally disliked burst over Chloe like a blinding revelation. Her mouth opened and shut. "Well—Well—" she stammered. "It does describe him." She patted Minnie's arm reassuringly. *Old Puff'n'guts? What do people say about Mother?*

For some unknown reason, this gave her a lift of confidence about communicating with her parents. Today, her life was like a book and she'd turned the page into a whole new section. Everything was different and she was, too. "What did Roarke say Daddy did then?"

"He blew like an oil well," Kitty whooped. "But he couldn't do a thing 'bout it." Her expression sobered. "Say, Roarke told me to tell you to watch yourself. Your daddy says he's going to find you and bring you home."

A shiver of dread slithered through Chloe.

"How he do that?" Minnie snapped.

"I don't know." Kitty lifted both palms. "I know Theran switched rooming houses before he left for training and didn't leave a forwarding address. And I switched places, too, and didn't leave a forwarding either. Theran and I figured your daddy might try to find you through us."

Chloe looked at her friend in wonder. "You two did all that for me?"

"No trouble 't-all." Kitty squeezed Chloe's hand. "You see, the only two ways we figured that your daddy could trace you was from our addresses and through the university records. So don't worry. You should be safe in this big city."

A woman near them slapped the face of the man she was with and stormed out. Chloe stared at her as the man ran after her, calling, "Lucie! Wait!"

"Oh, I just remembered. I'm going to a NAACP meeting tonight. Minnie, do you want to come with me?" Kitty asked, sitting forward.

"What's that?" Minnie asked.

"It's the National Association for the Advancement of Colored People."

Chloe and Minnie exchanged puzzled glances. "And what is that?" Chloe ventured.

"It was started a few years ago by W. E. B. DuBois and some others." Kitty took a sip of her coffee and glanced around at the next table, where everyone was laughing. "It holds meetings here in New York City. You two should go to one with me."

"I don't know," Minnie muttered, her eyes looking from under her thick lashes at a nearby table that had a mix of white and black customers. "I don't want no trouble."

"Spoken like an oppressed worker of the world." A tall

black man in a dark suit and white shirt had come up to them, his footsteps masked by the din of voices. "Kitty, pray introduce me to your charming companions." He swung a free chair over to their tiny table and sat down facing the chair back.

"I didn't see you come in, Frank. I don't know if I should introduce you." Kitty pouted, amusement lighting her eyes. "Your shocking reputation with the ladies . . ." She raised her brows and grinned at him.

He chuckled. "Then I'll introduce myself." He turned to Minnie and offered her his hand. "I'm Frank Lawson."

Chloe had never heard a black man speak like an educated man. This man sounded white to her. Was that how black people in New York City talked?

"I'm Minnie Carlyle." Minnie shook Frank's hand though she turned her profile to him and looked as if she were starting to blush.

Chloe didn't know the etiquette of this situation, but she didn't want to be impolite. "I'm Mrs. Theran Black," she murmured.

"Mrs. Black." Frank acknowledged her with a scant nod and turned his attention to her friend again. "So, Minnie, you've never heard of the NAACP?"

"No, sir, I ain't . . . haven't." Minnie was blushing.

Chloe watched her former maid turn a dusky rose at this man's attention.

"Now you have." Frank leaned forward, resting his folded arms on the top of the chair back. "We're trying to do something to stop lynchings in the South." His tone sharpened. "Now *those* you've heard of, haven't you?"

Minnie nodded, her eyes meeting Frank's for the first time. "Sorry to say I have."

Chloe thought she'd never heard such an odd conversation. One didn't talk about lynchings like this right out in the open and in front of ladies.

"And we're working to bring about equal rights for all Americans," Frank continued, lifting his jaw. "In the future, we'll take on Jim Crow."

Chloe felt uneasy. Should he be talking like this? Should she be listening? Daddy had always said Negroes were happy as they were because they were unable to discipline themselves. They needed white people to tell them what to do. But even as she thought this, she recalled Minnie's secret ambition and how Minnie's Uncle Haines handled the running of Ivy Manor without much, if any, help from her parents. New York City was filled with the strangest people and the most revolutionary of ideas.

Chloe sighed with relief as they exited the café into the balmy afternoon. They'd passed an entertaining few hours, but she was ready to rest back in her room. Kitty quickly said goodbye and left for another appointment. But Frank lingered, accompanying Chloe and Minnie to their subway station. He chatted to Minnie and took down Minnie's address in Harlem before he left them.

"What you think of that man?" Minnie asked as they headed down the crowded subway station steps.

Chloe shrugged. "I'm a married woman. It's you he was eyeing up and down. What do *you* think of him?"

"He sure a handsome man, all right. And the way he talk, so educated."

The comment made Chloe remember Theran. Suddenly she didn't want to go back to her room. A pain like a shaft of ice sliced through her. Theran wouldn't be there.

Subdued, she followed Minnie past the ticket window

and onto a subway. Sitting there as it sped through the tunnels, Chloe let herself think over all she had seen and heard that afternoon. Advancement of Colored People? What did that—what would that—mean? Maybe it could work in a place like New York City, but back in Maryland? Her brain felt as if an egg beater had slipped in through her ear and scrambled her thoughts, making her doubt what she'd always taken for granted. As she sat next to Minnie, she wanted to ask her . . . what? What she thought of Chloe? What she thought of Chloe's father and how he'd treated Minnie? What she thought of how, on their way north, she'd had to use the black preacher's outhouse while Chloe had used the gas station bathroom?

Minnie must have been just as preoccupied as Chloe because they rode side by side in silence. They got off and were halfway up Chloe's block before Chloe halted. "Minnie, what are we thinking? I'll walk you back to—"

"Hush, Miss Chloe," Minnie shushed her and dragged her into the cover of a flight of steps in front of another house.

"What is it?" Chloe whispered.

"You hang back in the alley." Minnie shoved her toward the alley opening, only a few feet behind them. "Somethin' don't look right 'bout your place. I go take a look and then come back to you."

Chloe obeyed, her heart thudding with fear. But of what? She'd been afraid of her father finding her, but Theran and Kitty had left no trail to her. So he couldn't have found her. Surely not yet.

Minnie strolled away, then back and returned to the alley. "Miss Chloe, you got trouble. When we were walkin', I see a man, official-looking, talkin' to your landlady out on the stoop. Then I walk by and I hear him say your name. The landlady tellin' him 'bout you bein' married to a soldier."

Chloe felt her heart jerk. "What do you think he wants?" Nothing could have happened to Theran already, could it? He was just on a ship. But ships did get torpedoed by German U-boats. That was what had brought them into the war against Germany. How far did a ship travel in a day? "You don't think something happened to Theran, do you?"

"No, I do not. I think your daddy has found out you is livin' here."

Chloe gasped. "But how could he find me so fast?"

"I don't know. But you can't go back there till that man leave."

Chloe and Minnie stood with their backs against the alley wall and waited. Finally Minnie looked down the street again and said the man was gone.

Chloe looked at Minnie, uncertain. "Do you think he just went inside and is still talking with the landlady?"

"I think we go up the alley and see if we notice anythin' from that angle."

Chloe could think of nothing else to propose, so she nodded. They walked down the alley with wary footsteps and cautious over-the-shoulder glances. When they reached the black-metal fire escape at the back of the house, Minnie sized it up. "Let's go up and see if we can hear anythin'."

Chloe nodded and the two of them tiptoed up the metal ladder to Chloe's window. She'd left it open a crack. She leaned down to see if she could hear anything. "I hear a man's voice but I can't hear what he's saying."

Minnie nodded and then she tested the window. It moved easily with only the slightest whisper of sound. She shoved it up high. Chloe caught her arm. "What are you doing?"

"I'm gone get your things and we are gettin' you out a here." Minnie slid over the window sill. She went quickly around the room silently gathering Chloe's clothing and toiletries. Then she found the leather valise and started shoving things into it.

Chloe climbed in herself and found the bank book in the nightstand and slipped it into her purse. While Minnie repacked the valise she'd packed for Chloe at Ivy Manor, Chloe pressed her ear to the door and listened to the conversation. She heard a man's faint voice ask, "You're sure the girl left this morning to see her husband off and hasn't been back today?"

Her landlady replied, "That's what I've said over and over. Why don't you believe me? And why are you looking for Mrs. Black? She seems a respectable girl and her husband's left for France."

"She ran away to marry and her parents just want to persuade her to come home." The man's voice was oily.

"Why did she have to run away? I would think anyone would be proud to have a well-educated and patriotic young man like Mr. Black as a son-in-law."

"I'm just their agent, ma'am. Here's my card. If she comes back, I'd appreciate it if you'd give me a call. Her parents just want to know that she's safe."

I'll bet. Hot rage spurted inside Chloe. How had her father done it so quickly? *You're not getting your hands on me again.*

The voices of the man and landlady became fainter as evidently they moved to the front of the house. "He's leaving," Chloe whispered. She heard the front door close and then footsteps.

"We best be goin'," Minnie said.

Chloe looked around, suddenly terrified of losing this, the place she was to call home. "But how . . . what?"

The door behind them opened. The landlady stood with her hands on her wide hips. "I thought I heard that rear window being pushed up."

Chloe couldn't form a word.

"Don't worry." The woman stepped in and shut the door behind her. "I won't give you away. I think if you were forced to run away to marry such a fine young man, you must have had a good reason."

Chloe couldn't help it. She began to weep, large tears splashing down. The large woman, in an outmoded black dress, came over and wrapped her thick, flabby arms around Chloe. "Don't cry. You'll have to leave here, but I won't tell them where you've gone. Now, here." She pulled a small cloth purse from her pocket and dished out six dollar bills. "Here's the rest of your month's rent."

"How they find out Miss Chloe here?" Minnie asked, staring at the landlady.

"From the war department. Mr. Black had given them this address for his army pay." The landlady gave Chloe the once-over. "Your pa must have some real political pull to get that information, and this fast."

Chloe nodded.

"Now you go out the back. I'm afraid they may hold up your husband's army pay. But if it still comes, give me a call and I'll forward it to you—without letting anyone else know. A soldier's wife has enough to suffer without the government making it harder on her."

Chloe hugged the landlady. "Thank you. Thank you."

Minnie moved to the window. "You come on now, Miss Chloe. We best light out a here 'fore they start watchin' this place close."

Chloe waved at the landlady and hurried through the window behind Minnie. They were safely in another subway train before Chloe asked with tingling dread, "Where do I go from here?"

"I think I take you home with me tonight. We find you a new place tomorrow."

Chloe stared out at the gray concrete tunnel flashing outside their window. "I could go to a hotel."

"No, not by yourself. That don't look right. It cost a lot a money and you gotta give a name on the register, don't you?"

Chloe nodded, sucking in the tears that still wanted to fall. Theran gone and her father hot on her heels. Everything was moving too fast. She felt miserable. The only thing that kept her going at the moment was Minnie.

Within minutes Chloe was walking at Minnie's side into the boarding house. The house smelled of good food and lemon oil polish. Minnie led Chloe off the main hall into the small dining room where a very dark-skinned landlady was presiding at the head of a long dinner table with a red-checked cloth on it. An assortment of folk crowded around it. At their entrance, every black face turned to survey Chloe. She was reminded of how she felt when she was on display for her father. Blushing, she lowered her head.

Minnie set down Chloe's valise. "Mrs. Rascombe, I done brought my friend Miss Chloe home with me. She had trouble at her rooming house. Can she bunk with me tonight?"

"What's wrong at her place?" Mrs. Rascombe asked in a commanding, slightly suspicious, tone.

"Her daddy done sent somebody to take her back home. Her daddy a nasty piece of work. Her husband just ship out for France today and her daddy pulled strings in the government to find out where Miss Chloe is livin' here in the city. He want to take her home and probably annul her marriage, and she don't deserve such treatment. She got a job, goin' to be a model on Fifth Avenue, startin' tomorrow. And then we find her 'nother place to live."

"She sure pretty 'nough to model on Fifth Avenue," one of the white-haired men at the table murmured.

Flushing hotly, Chloe couldn't raise her eyes from studying the scrubbed wooden floor. But then she thought about what her father would say if he found out he was responsible for sending her to sleep at a colored boarding house. It gave her a jolt of satisfaction. If he knew where she'd fled, he'd be chewing nails.

"You say her man gone off to France?" Mrs. Rascombe asked, tapping her index finger to her lips as if deliberating a vexing problem.

"Yes, ma'am," Minnie said. "Enlisted right off."

"Then she can stay," the landlady approved regally. "Show her up to the room and I'll let you take her up a tray of supper."

Minnie confronted the table of interested faces and noted their suspicious glances. "Miss Chloe ain't like that." She turned to Chloe. "You don't mind black and white sittin' together for a meal, do you?"

Chloe thought about the afternoon at the café, of Frank Dawson's smooth English and her father being called Old Puff'n'guts. A barrier inside her crumbled. "Please. If I'm welcome . . . I don't want to be alone right now."

"You welcome, miss." Mrs. Rascombe's voice was as rough as a dry corncob, but kind. "Jasper, you push over a bit and we slide another chair in here at the end."

Within minutes, Chloe was perched at the long table, being served fragrant beef stew. "Thank you." She drew a deep, satisfying breath. "It smells delicious." Then, as the events of the day finally caught up to her, no longer to be denied, tears once again began to flow down her face.

"There, there," Mrs. Rascombe soothed, patting Chloe's

shoulder with a slender black hand. "You eat your supper and you'll feel better."

Chloe wiped her face with her handkerchief and then took a bite of stew. All eyes were upon her and when she swallowed and smiled, everyone grinned and began eating.

Much later, in Minnie's small room upstairs, Chloe slipped out of her dress and Minnie undid the troublesome corset laces for her. "Remind me"—Chloe pulled off and shook the offending garment—"to get rid of this disgusting, old-fashioned corset tomorrow and buy the new style."

"Frankly, Miss Chloe"—Minnie considered Chloe with her arms folded—"I don't think you need one at all. You is thin as a rail anyway."

Chloe gaped at Minnie. Go without a corset? That seemed too shocking, too free. Then she recalled the women at the café who had obviously already shed theirs. Musing over this, she donned her nightgown and hung up her dress. She noted a few spots of dirt on the hem; she'd have to ask Minnie how to get them out—but tomorrow, not now. She glanced toward the double bed.

"This is my side," Minnie said, claiming the one facing the door.

Chloe folded back the covers on the window side and slid under the soft, worn muslin sheets. Another night, another strange bed. Her head felt like it was spinning. So much had happened in the span of three days. Images, sensations of Theran and the two nights they'd spent together flashed through her mind. For a moment, she felt the whisper of his lips on her nape and his arms pulling her close to him. She shivered with remembered passion. *Don't think of that now.*

For a moment she tried to bring up the image of Granny

in her rocker. Chloe longed to climb back into that comforting lap. But Granny seemed too removed from her new life here in New York City. *Besides, I'm not a little girl.*

"Everythin' be all right tomorrow, Miss Chloe," Minnie comforted her. With a final smile she turned off the lamp and settled herself.

Chloe stared at the ceiling in the darkened room, city lights flickering above her. She was Mrs. Theran Black now, not Miss Chloe. "Minnie, if we're sleeping in the same bed, I think you can drop the Miss. That's all past."

"You soundin' pretty radical, Mi—Chloe," her friend teased in the semidarkness. "You watch it or you become a Bolshevik or somethin'." She giggled.

The sound stabbed Chloe. "Oh, Minnie, I miss him so."

Minnie rolled over and pulled Chloe close. Chloe struggled for a moment and then gave in. She rested her head on Minnie's shoulder and let the tears come. "I'm sorry."

"It be okay." Minnie stroked Chloe's hair, humming. "You can't help missin' your man."

"He . . . He . . ." Chloe couldn't finish her sentence. She let herself relax more, let Minnie's soft crooning soothe her, let herself breathe in her friend's faint lavender cologne and the scent of her hair dressing. It took Chloe back to when Minnie's grandmother had rocked her to sleep many nights with the same soothing touch, the same murmured songs, the same comforting scents. "Thanks, Minnie," she whispered and pulled away slightly. "Thanks."

"You be all right. We be all right."

"Yes." Chloe closed her eyes and, overcome with love for her friend, thanked the Lord. *Help Minnie. She deserves to have her dream come true. And please, God, keep my husband safe and my daddy far away from both of us.*

*   *   *

The next morning, Minnie was easy to persuade to come along with Chloe to the Fifth Avenue couturier. It was just the kind of place Minnie declared she'd always wanted to see. Fashionable Fifth Avenue and Harlem proved to be as different as day from night. Now, Chloe looked at the gilt-edged card and checked the address of the shop before her. It was the right one. The empty display windows were concealed by white paper and the door sported a hand-lettered sign that read: "MADAME BLANCHE, COUTURIER, OPENING SOON." Her heart jumping and jerking, Chloe walked up to the door and knocked.

Chapter Seven

No one answered her knock. Chloe felt a momentary relief. She could leave now and no one would even know they'd been here. But no. Fleeing Theran's rooming house meant that—for the first time in her life—Chloe needed to earn her own way. This and Minnie's presence made her push open the strange door and step into the unknown. Muffled sunlight lit the large dusty room she entered with Minnie right behind her. "Hello?" Chloe scanned the disordered room, which held a jumble of boxes, chairs, mirrors, bolts of fabric, and dressmaker dummies.

"Who is zere?" From the rear came a woman's voice in heavily accented English.

"I'm Chloe Kim—Chloe Black." She took a step forward. "I'm the . . . blonde model." She felt like a fool.

Through a door at the rear, a tall, thin woman burst into the large, dusky room. "Ze model? My blonde model?"

Shocked into silence by the stranger's appearance, Chloe couldn't reply. The woman was like none she'd ever seen before. Very tall and pencil thin, the woman wore a purple silk turban over bobbed brown hair and a matching gown with gold frogs down the front. Her face had a full, scarlet-rouged mouth, piercing black eyes, and a long, aquiline nose.

"Turn around," the woman ordered without preamble. "Pirouette." She twirled her hand in the air.

"She wants you to turn for her," Minnie murmured.

Chloe shook off her surprise and pivoted in a full circle. When she turned her back to the woman, she felt the woman's intense gaze on her.

"*C'est bon.* Now walk. Promenade. Up! Down!" the woman ordered.

Chloe walked to the rear and back to the front door, suddenly recalling watching horses being paraded around a paddock at an auction a year ago.

"Again!"

Chloe obeyed, her eyes appealing to Minnie as she passed her. Would she please or fail?

In return, Minnie winked one eye.

"*C'est bon. C'est beau.*" The woman clapped her hands and then flung them wide. "Marshfield knows *les femmes.* You are perfection."

Standing before the French woman, Chloe smiled tentatively. What did she know about being a model? "I've never—" she began.

"I am Madame Blanche," the woman interrupted and swept forward and clasped both of Chloe's hands in hers. "Such eyes, such white skin. *Peau blanc*—like a doll of porcelain!" Madame Blanche kissed the tips of her fingers. "Perfection."

"Thank you," Chloe stammered, blushing.

"Oh, an innocent!" Madame chuckled. "Have men not told you that you are divine?"

Before Chloe could reply to this embarrassing question, Madame swung to confront Minnie. "Who are you?"

"This is my friend," Chloe hurried to explain, fearing the woman might insult Minnie. "She just came along with me."

Minnie backed away. "I goin' now, Mis—Chloe. I see you later."

"*Non!*" Madame Blanche exploded. "No! Walk . . . walk for me!"

Minnie froze. "Why you want me to walk?"

"*S'il vous plaît*—like your friend." Madame Blanche stepped back expectantly, her eyes still skimming Minnie up and down.

Giving Chloe a quizzical glance, Minnie shrugged and then straightened her shoulders and walked toward the back, turned, and walked forward.

As she did so, Chloe studied her friend more closely than she ever had. Minnie had always just been Minnie. But now Chloe realized why Frank Dawson had come to their table the day before. Minnie's smooth skin was the color of extra-creamy coffee, almost a rich toffee. Her cheekbones were high and her nose was wide but well formed. Her long, straightened hair was pulled back into a tight bun at her nape. Minnie was a few inches shorter than Chloe, and her figure was rounder, but not too full. And the way Minnie walked—oh my. She let her hips sway in a way Chloe's mother would have called unladylike.

"Like ripe fruit," Madame Blanche murmured to herself. Then she snapped her fingers. "Please stand next to Chloe."

Minnie obeyed.

"Such a contrast," Madame murmured. "Such a contrast—green fruit and ripe fruit. *Blanc* and *noir*." She beamed at them. "It will shock, it will cause talk, yes! But they will come to see *le jour et la nuit,* day and night. A coup for Madame Blanche!" She clapped her hands again.

Chloe and Minnie stared at the woman and then looked to each other. "Ma'am," Chloe began.

Portly and well-dressed, Marshfield Crowe opened the front door and strode inside. "I see the blonde model has come. What do you think, Blanche?" He beamed.

"They are wonderful. I feel the juices flowing already. Such gowns I shall robe them in." Madame sprang up onto her toes and hugged herself. "Marshfield, women will die to look like them. Men will pen poems to *ma blanc* and *ma noir*. We will make *americaine* dollars, thousands of dollars!"

"Blanche, what do you mean?" The man stared at her. "I'm going back to the agencies today until I find the right brunette."

"Non!" Blanche glared at him. "This *la femme noir* will be my brunette model."

Frowning, Marshfield took a step forward. "You don't understand. This isn't Paris. Americans won't come here if we have a . . . a Negro model. It isn't done."

"Madame Blanche will do it," the Frenchwoman snapped and gave the man a look of disdain.

"Now, Blanche," Marshfield coaxed, "what did these girls talk you into?"

"These girls tell Madame Blanche what to do?" The French woman stood ramrod straight. "You are the one who does not understand. The blonde—" The woman stretched her hand toward Chloe. "—is beautiful, but look! The two of them together." She waved Chloe and Minnie to stand close to each other. "Together—see *mettre en contraste*—the contrast! *Voilà!* They take the breath!"

Screwing up his face, Marshfield studied them.

Chloe and Minnie stood side by side. Chloe could hardly breathe because of the tense silence. Would they really hire

Minnie to be a model? Was that possible? Never in her wildest dreams . . .

That night in their darkened bedroom in Mrs. Rascombe's house, Chloe lay on her side facing the window. Tonight, Minnie was lying close to her, staring up at the flickering city lights on the ceiling. The window was open, letting in a cool breeze and the night sounds—voices, laughter, car motors and horns, doors opening and closing. Harlem didn't sleep.

Scenes from the day played in Chloe's mind. Just now she was thinking of how, at the end of the work day, she and Minnie had shared a cup of coffee in the village with Kitty and Frank Dawson. Frank had also invited them to come to the NAACP meeting, but Minnie had put him off. Chloe wondered why. Was she as confused, as fearful, of such a meeting as Chloe was? But why should she be? As a black woman she should be glad to go, right?

Chloe felt at war with herself. She wanted Minnie, her friend, to achieve her dreams. At the same time, the idea of Negroes gaining equality warred with everything she'd ever been taught about black and white. What would Mother or her friends say if they saw her working alongside Minnie as equals, sleeping beside her? All her life, between the two races, matters had been just one way. Violating this unwritten code always brought consequences. Usually horrible consequences. She recalled snippets of conversations she'd overheard about "uppity Negroes," "white trash," and lynchings. Would something bad happen to Minnie for not keeping her place? But then, Chloe herself had run away, left her place, too. Would she end up paying a price?

She pushed the harrowing conflict out of her mind and thought instead of Theran. Where was her husband tonight?

How near was he to France, to the trenches? Chloe chewed the inside of her cheek. *Theran, I wish you'd stayed. Life would be simpler.* But he couldn't hear her thoughts. She wanted to write a letter to him, but she hesitated to mail anything to the army address he'd given her. What if her father was able to get access to Theran's mail and read her new return address? She sighed. Why did life have to be so . . . tangled?

Chloe folded her hands together in the dark and tried to pray. But God seemed farther away here in New York City. And she couldn't seem to concentrate on anything. In the dark, she touched her cheek. She'd never thought much about being beautiful. But she'd known all her life that others—especially her father—considered her as such. She'd never felt comfortable with it. She didn't feel comfortable now at the thought of modeling. *I don't want to have people staring at me. That's what I always hated about Daddy shoving me forward.*

She wondered what Minnie thought of being a model. Did she feel beautiful? "Minnie, are you asleep?"

"No, I can't sleep. Too much gone on in my head."

Chloe rolled to her back. "Same here. Does it seem to you like every day in New York City brings us a new surprise, a new way?"

"You got that right."

"Does it feel funny to you," Chloe ventured, "to be a model instead of a maid?"

"Yes, it do."

"Yes, it does," Chloe corrected gently. Minnie had asked her to help her learn to speak in a more educated way. Evidently, Frank's smooth, expert use of English had impressed Minnie, too.

"Yes, it does," Minnie repeated.

"I never knew I could do anything but be a wife. And now I am one, but I'm going to be a model, too. And I never wanted to do something like that."

"When Madame Blanche say she"—Minnie corrected herself—"said she wanted me to walk, I didn't know what to think."

"Me either."

"Do she—Does she think white women will put up with me being a model?"

Chloe mulled that over. "Well, this is New York City and she is French."

"I wish I could write home and tell Mamma." Minnie sounded wistful.

"Why can't you? Your mother can't drag you back."

"Mi—Chloe, you know why. Any letter I send could put your daddy on your trail and make trouble for my people. We don't know yet if your parents think we ran away together."

Chloe went up on her elbow. "You're protecting me, too, just like Kitty." And Roarke. He'd written her a few notes and his parents had sent her a wedding gift—a silver candy dish engraved with Theran and Chloe's names. Now she touched Minnie's shoulder. "Thank you. I don't know why you're helping me, but thank you."

"I told you." Minnie's voice was suddenly stronger. "You help me and I'll help you, remember? Besides, everyone at Ivy Manor be glad—"

"Would be glad," Chloe murmured.

"Would be glad, is glad you got away. People like you. You have a gentle heart, a fair heart."

Emotions Chloe couldn't identify rushed through her. One thing she knew for sure: Minnie was her friend and Chloe would never betray her, come what may. She lay back, holding in tears. "Thank you."

"You be all right, Chloe." Minnie patted her arm. "Good night."

"Good night," Chloe replied. She closed her eyes wondering what the morrow would bring.

A little over a month later, in early July, Chloe stood in the rear of Madame Blanche's shop. She was wearing another new design, a pale-blue morning frock. Two seamstresses hovered around her, making adjustments to the fabric. She'd become accustomed to this routine. Madame always wanted to see the designs on her live models at different stages of production.

Chloe worried her lower lip, thinking about their plans for tonight. They'd been invited again to attend an NAACP meeting. Should they go or not? Nearby, Minnie was decked in a red-satin evening gown with a narrow train that pooled on the polished wood floor. She also had a seamstress fluttering around her, making little fussy noises. Minnie looked at Chloe and saw the same worry, the same question, about the meeting in her eyes.

Madame Blanche swept into the room. "Tomorrow is the day. Tomorrow we open. Now *le chapeau*, the hats!" The mousy girl who'd been hired as the milliner hurried behind Madame, her arms heaped with hats. "Come, come," the Frenchwoman summoned Chloe and Minnie over to two mirrored gilt vanities with chairs. "We try them, yes?"

Chloe and Minnie sat down gingerly because of the straight pins in their dresses. One by one, they tried on hats. Such hats! So close to the head, so sleek. Nothing like Chloe had ever seen or worn. But while Minnie slipped on her hats with ease, Chloe struggled, pushing and tugged hers into place on her head. With each hat Madame frowned more. Finally, she burst forth in rapid, irritated French and from the vanity snatched up a dressmaker's sheers.

"*Le cheveu!* The hair. It ruins the hats." She grabbed the knot of hair at Chloe's nape and aimed the sheers at it.

"No!" Chloe shrieked and leaped up, pulling away. "No, I've never cut my hair."

In tableau, Madame Blanche and Chloe stared into one another's eyes. "*Mon amie,*" Madame coaxed, lowering the sheers. "The hair is too big. You are *le modele de Madame Blanche.* You must have the look of Madame Blanche. The hair is too big for *le chapeau.* We must cut."

Minnie touched Chloe's arm. "Let her. I'll go first if you want."

"No, your hair is not so big," Madame explained. "But Chloe's hair must go."

Her hair? Chloe gazed at Madame Blanche's close-cut hair. What would it feel like to run her fingers through her hair and find it short? Her mother's voice intruded into her thoughts: *A woman's hair is her glory. A decent woman never cuts it.* Chloe swallowed. What would Theran say? He'd loved her long, blonde hair, had brushed it until it danced with electricity and then buried his face in it. The sensation of Theran's touch flickered through her. But she could always grow her hair back when Theran returned. Now she was *le modele blonde de Madame Blanche.* In a fit of determination, she closed her eyes. "Go ahead."

Madame cooed her pleasure and pushed Chloe back into her chair. The hat was whipped off and with one hissing slice Chloe's long hair dropped to the floor.

"I can shape it," one of the seamstresses offered. She took the sheers and began trimming and feathering the remaining hair. Chloe peeked at the vanity mirror and saw only the girl bending in front of her, felt her clipping above her eyebrows, making bangs. Finally, the girl stepped back and Chloe looked at her reflection—a startling one. "It's not so bad, I guess." Still, Chloe stared at her head, which suddenly looked smaller, trimmer.

"You look modern," Minnie breathed in an awestruck tone. "Madame, please, can't I have my hair cut, too?"

Madame chuckled. "*Non*, your hair is small, *bon*."

Chloe laughed and pulled on one of the hats, that fit so much better now. "Look at me. I'm modern."

Feeling tired but satisfied, Chloe and Minnie, back in their own short-sleeved walking dresses, strolled out into the warm July evening. Yet, within a few paces they sobered. Minnie looked at Chloe. "Do we got the nerve?"

"You mean do we *have* the nerve?" Chloe corrected. "Well, do we?" Fifth Avenue bustled with fashionably dressed women and men, hustling with big-city rapid rhythm. Skyscrapers loomed around them. A few feet away an elegant woman wearing an ostrich feather boa, her maid behind her, was being ushered into a silver Rolls Royce by a liveried chauffeur. This sight definitely wasn't anything like they'd ever seen around Ivy Manor.

Thoughtfully, Chloe touched the back of her head, which still felt oddly naked. She didn't feel like herself at all. "We're *les modeles de Madame Blanche*," she declared. "Modern, twentieth-century women who are working and paying our own way. We have the nerve."

By now, Chloe and Minnie had attended several NAACP meetings. Tonight's meeting was at a big church in Harlem. Chloe had become at ease in Harlem, at ease being one of the few white faces among the black. It didn't feel odd anymore. It was like being a child again with her mother and father always away and her left in the care of Minnie's grandmother and the other Negro servants. Chloe still shared a room with Minnie. Mrs. Rascombe had worried over them this evening like a mother hen. "This war's stirred things up. You two will be safer at home with me."

Mrs. Rascombe had been right. Racial incidents near army training bases and defense plants were rampant in the North and lynchings rife in the South. Tonight Chloe felt her heart beating faster than usual. The church was crowded and buzzed with angry, urgent voices. Harlem was alarmed.

She followed Minnie up the wide aisle. Minnie was scanning the crowd. Then she halted. "There he is, Chloe. I mean, Lorraine."

Today, Chloe and Minnie had taken "professional" names at Madame Blanche's request. "Chloe" had sounded all right to the Frenchwoman for one of her models, but not "Minnie." But Chloe had decided that working under another name would be a good idea, another way to evade her father. So she had taken her middle name, "Lorraine," and Minnie had chosen "Mimi" for herself. Madame Blanche said that they hadn't needed new surnames. Single names were the rage in fashion.

"Wait up, Mimi," Chloe teased, hurrying after Minnie.

Frank Dawson, by now Minnie's beau, and Kitty had saved space for Chloe and Minnie near the front of the large church sanctuary. Minnie let Frank take her hand and Chloe sat down beside Kitty. The meeting opened with a prayer by the pastor of the church and then the speaker, a professor from Columbia, took the pulpit. Chloe stared up at the man as he began speaking about the war.

"Even though segregated into separate divisions, African-

American men have an unexpected opportunity through this war to show their patriotism and their abilities."

Chloe thought about her husband. She'd written him daily, telling him everything that was taking place in her life. She'd finally mailed them to the military address he'd given her. But for a return address, she'd put general delivery at a nearby post office. And Mrs. Rascombe had agreed to pick up her mail. If the post office were watched, who would think Mrs. Rascombe was doing it for her? But Chloe still hadn't received a letter in return from him. From newspapers, she knew only that he'd been in France for several weeks and she was certain he must have written to her. But how did the military deliver mail? And would her father be able to trace her to the general delivery address?

Everyone applauded and Chloe joined in, then played with the fringe on her beaded purse. Unfortunately, after all the years of listening to her father's speeches, she couldn't seem to make her mind focus on a speaker.

Chloe hadn't written to her parents. After her father finding out Theran's stateside address and making her leave that address, she'd decided they knew she had reached New York safely and had married Theran. They didn't need to know anything else. Besides, if her father hadn't interfered by finding her in New York, she wouldn't have had to move and wouldn't be afraid now that she wouldn't be able to receive Theran's letters.

"But," the speaker was declaiming as he hit the pulpit, "the white segregationist does not want to let the black soldier think he is the equal of the white. Everywhere in the South and North, unrest is stirred by black men appearing in the US Army uniform, a new sign of equality, dignity."

Chloe had written to Theran's parents and had received an oddly restrained reply from his father. It had included no invitation to come to Buffalo to meet them or any stated intention of their visiting her. Minnie had agreed that was odd. Why wouldn't they want to meet their son's wife?

Chloe became aware of a sudden rustling in the crowd, and the sound of yelling.

"Riots! Race rioting in East St. Louis!" A black man was running forward up the center aisle, waving a newspaper extra sheet. "They're killing people over jobs!"

The next morning, Chloe and Minnie peered out through a crack at the rear door into Madame's showroom, which was elegantly decorated in bold art deco in shades of white and black. A chattering bevy of fashionable prospective clients and the press gathered in Madame's showroom. Every seat had been filled. Three men stood in the rear with pen and notebook in hand. July wasn't the usual season to be launching a fashion collection. But the war had affected many things. Madame had taken out a full-page ad in the *New York Times*, announcing her collection, and then had sent out a few gilt-edged cards to the press and some well-placed, well-heeled friends of Marshfield Crowe's.

Watching the crowd, Chloe recalled the NAACP meeting the night before. In East St. Louis, a riot over jobs at a defense plant had killed nine whites and nearly forty Negroes. The NAACP reaction had been swift. The leaders were planning a show of sympathy for those who had been murdered. Did Chloe have the nerve or not to participate? Even Minnie had looked shaken last night, and even more so today. With good reason—this was the day of their debut as models. In this racially charged atmosphere, what would be the response when Minnie, the first black model on Fifth Avenue, stepped out front?

"Ladies," Madame beckoned them away from the door. "We begin. Remember: you are so beautiful that you don't care what the people think of you. You stun them with your beauty. This modeling bores you. You are rich, you are young, you are desirable, no?"

Chloe and Minnie assumed the half-reclining posture and the world-weary expression Madame had schooled them to.

"*Bon.*" Madame clapped her hands. "I go out and make the introduction." Wearing a white linen dress, diamonds, and her scarlet lip rouge, she swept out the door.

Tingling with a mix of anxiety and excitement, Chloe looked at Minnie and Minnie looked back. "I scared, Miss Chloe." The words came out in a dry gasp, and she shook with one sharp tremor. Minnie hadn't called her Miss Chloe for weeks now. She must be very nervous. The race riot in East St. Louis couldn't have helped Minnie's confidence. But bringing up all that wouldn't help either.

"You are rich, you are beautiful, you are bored," Chloe parroted, gripping both of Minnie's wrists in her hands, feeling Minnie's speeding pulse under her fingers. "You can't show any weakness." Chloe squeezed tighter, trying to dredge up words that would make Minnie bold today. "You have to act like being a model is just everyday to you, like you were born to be here and do this. And you were, Minnie. When you walk out there, you aren't Minnie, you're Mimi, *modele de Madame Blanche.* You've got to feel it. You will be acting, just like you wanted to. This is your first part, your first play."

Minnie nodded and inhaled, but shakily. Polite applause drifted back from the showroom. One of the seamstresses pushed wide the door.

Taking a deep breath, Chloe dropped her hands to her side and turned. She walked forward down the short aisle between the rows of chairs. *I am rich, I am beautiful, I am bored,* she recited to herself. The faces before her ran together but she looked over them. Her nerves were jumping with something like St. Vita's dance. Then she recalled the day she'd first seen Theran, the speech she'd made. It bolstered her. She imagined Theran standing at the rear, smiling at her. And he would. He'd love seeing her here, looking so good. His admiration swept through her like a caress, a whisper of a kiss.

Blushing, Chloe paused, posed. Suddenly the faces staring didn't bother her. They weren't interested in her, just Madame Blanche's clothing. Her father always putting her on display had made her feel cheap, but that was different than this. She smiled and then hid it. *Remember, these people bore you.* She strutted back to the rear door. Just as she reached it, Minnie emerged from the rear.

A gasp shuddered through the room, gaining momentum, wild-firing through the gathering. Minnie didn't falter. She sauntered past Chloe—without a glance to either side—paused and posed as rehearsed, and made her turn near the front door.

Chloe had reentered the partially open door. There she sheltered behind it while the seamstresses stripped off her dress. Chloe watched Minnie pause several times, pose as taught, and then walk on. Minnie's head was held high and her eyes looked over the audience as though they were so far beneath her she was barely aware of their existence. The men at the back were scribbling frantically on their pads and the women in the audience looked shocked, stunned. Then their faces bent toward their neighbors. They whispered, shaking their heads.

The second dress had been fitted and buttoned onto Chloe. She waited—breathless, keyed up, ready to make her next appearance, ready to reenter the fray. Minnie passed her and Chloe took off without a word, her chin forward. She made a grand entrance, paused, swirled, sauntered. The buzz about Minnie blossomed fuller. Chloe ignored it.

Finally at the last possible moment before she and Minnie changed places once more, she looked down her nose at the faces, daring them to object to Minnie. Chloe held the pose until one by one the audience fell silent under her disdain. Then Chloe swirled and stalked back to the dressing room. At that moment Chloe knew what she must do on the morrow. If she had the nerve.

CHAPTER EIGHT

*C*hloe wondered if she had the courage today would demand. She and Minnie stole into Madame Blanche's shop. Today the familiar shop, done in sharply contrasting white and black, struck Chloe as stark and daunting instead of vividly sophisticated as it had before.

Only yesterday Madame's fashion debut had taken place in this shop. In carrying out their parts, Chloe and Minnie had broken many rules. It left them different, changed. All the weeks of planning leading up to the preview had not prepared Chloe for the moment she'd stepped out of the back room. Nothing in her life had prepared her for the feeling of liberation that had come to her as she advanced from the role of debutante to professional fashion model. Too, nothing had prepared her to watch Minnie step above herself, leave behind her role of obedient Negro maid. The fashion showing and the celebration afterward had been liberating. But today was the day of decision. Really a day of action.

Chloe tried to ignore the tremors sliding up and down her spine. Minnie looked haunted, her lovely, creamy-tan face drawn down into deep, tense lines. "I don't want to lose this job." The words squeezed out of her.

"I know." Chloe patted Minnie's arm, feeling her own stomach clench. She tried a smile and failed.

Minnie lowered her head. "I feel like a coward. And this is New York City, not East St. Louis."

Just then Madame Blanche burst out of the back room. "I hear your voices. Why do you not rush back? See! See the papers!" With one of her customary flourishes, Madame displayed a section of the *New York Times*. The title of the full-page article read: "MADAME BLANCHE FASHIONS CROSS THE COLOR LINE."

"It is about you two. Marshfield doubted. But Blanche knows how to turn heads, how to make the splash."

Chloe took the paper and read aloud, "'Yesterday, Madame Blanche, a refugee fresh from war-torn Paris, officially opened her shop. And the newest couturier on Fifth Avenue did so with panache. The Frenchwoman's style indeed amazed, but more shocking was her choice of models. Heart-achingly beautiful blonde Lorraine modeled the Blanche designs with an airy grace. But her companion, the devastatingly beautiful Negro model Mimi, stole the show. The *modeles de Madame* made the summer collection dazzle and amaze the eye. The French have many colonies in Africa and this reporter wonders which one—perhaps Senegal— Mimi hails from. Surely no American Negress possesses the beauty and poise displayed by the divine Mimi.'"

Chloe looked up, wide mouthed. "'The divine Mimi.'"

"What trash." Minnie dismissed it with a slash of her hand. "'No American Negress possesses the beauty.' Trash. I'm gone call that man and give him what-for."

"*Non, non,*" Madame objected, waving a ring-encrusted hand. "This is better. The mystery. You need to retain the mystery. Women, men—all will come to see, to learn the truth. We will not tell them." Madame's face lifted into a mischievous smile. "Does it matter, Mimi, if you are from Senegal or from America?"

Minnie glared at the newspaper as though the reporter were standing in front of her. "I'll do whatever you want, Madame," she agreed, one side of her mouth still twisted in anger. "You give—gave me this job and I'm thankful."

Madame put an arm around Minnie. "Men are foolish. Every woman of intelligence knows this. But we women use this against them, no?"

Minnie gave a grudging smile.

Then Chloe decided the paper had another use. She inhaled deeply and flipped back to the front page. "Madame Blanche, did you see this article?" Chloe pointed to the main story: "RACE RIOTERS FIRE EAST ST. LOUIS AND SHOOT OR HANG MANY NEGROES; DEAD ESTIMATED FROM 20 TO 75: MANY BODIES IN THE RUINS, MOBS RAGE UNCHECKED."

"I did not read that." Madame turned toward the rear, brushing it aside. "It is sad, no?"

"Yes, it is," Chloe replied, her stomach churning. "Madame, there's to be a march right here on Fifth Avenue to show sympathy for those who've died in East St. Louis."

Halting, Madame turned and then gave each of them a measuring look. "Yes?"

Chloe drew herself up. "Madame, Minnie and I want to join the march today." And then she felt a little sick.

Minnie clasped and unclasped her hands. "I can't thank you enough, Madame, for giving me this job—"

"A march on Fifth Avenue?" Madame looked from Chloe to Minnie and back again.

"Yes." Chloe's lungs were being crushed by some unseen force. Fear of losing her job, fear of Minnie losing her job, and overall the threat of a violent backlash that might greet a march by the NAACP terrified her. She inhaled deeply and forced out words, "Yesterday I heard them whispering about Minnie. Just because Minnie has dark skin—why does that make her less beautiful?" Chloe felt her panic rising, but she couldn't stop the words. "Madame, you saw Minnie as she is. A beautiful woman, not a person who can't do anything but serve white people." Chloe tried to say more but could only force out, "Please."

Minnie moved close to Chloe and slipped her arm into Chloe's. "Please, Madame."

The Frenchwoman studied them for a very long moment. Chloe heard her heart pounding in her ears. Would they be fired? If they marched, would they be pelted with stones as marchers had been in other cities?

"When does this march start?" Madame tapped one toe.

"Right now," Minnie stammered. "They're gathering a few blocks from here."

"We go." Madame tossed the paper aside. "We all go."

"What?" Chloe asked. She felt hot, then cold.

"Madame Blanche and her two models—we march together!"

Minnie's mouth dropped open.

"Are you serious?" Chloe asked, her pulse dancing.

"*Oui! Liberte! Egalite! Fraternite!*" She swung around and called to the seamstresses in the rear. "We will be back soon. Watch the shop!" Madame took Minnie and Chloe each by an arm. "Come. We march. Blanche and her *modeles— blanc* and *noir.*"

Speechless, Chloe let Madame hurry them out the door into the bright July sunshine and down Fifth Avenue. The march had already begun. Within a block, they saw the protesters advancing, thousands and thousands filling the street from side to side. Leaders of the NAACP led the marchers, carrying together in front of them a long banner reading: "In sympathy with the Negroes killed in E. St. Louis."

Brushing through the bystanders along the street like a queen, Madame steered Chloe and Minnie into the ranks of marchers. *"Liberte!"* she shouted. *"Egalite! Fraternite!"* Several of the marchers joined her. Soon the motto of the French nation echoed off the fashionable storefronts. Chloe looked around at the sea of dark faces she and Madame Blanche had penetrated. How had she come to this? What if someone she knew from home saw her? What would her parents—and Roarke—think? What would Theran think if he knew?

Then Madame broke out into song. Chloe recognized it; she'd heard it played during newsreels about the war in France. It was the French national anthem. Again, more voices joined Madame Blanche. The brave song heartened Chloe. Deeply moved by the stirring melody, she felt tears clogging her throat. She glanced past the dark faces around her to the crush of white observers lining the street.

Suddenly her eye caught those of a well-dressed white matron on the curb. The woman stared at her, horrified recognition dawning on her face. Shocked, Chloe realized she'd met the woman at a party the year before. She was an acquaintance of her mother's. Chloe's knees nearly buckled. But before she could react further the crowd dragged her on and the woman was hidden from view. The joyful Madame beside her sang on loud and strong, and with the words Chloe gained strength. Come what may she wouldn't let herself be cowed.

When the line, *"Marche on, marche on,"* came again, she joined in, not knowing the words but humming along with Madame. It didn't matter if the woman had recognized her. Her parents couldn't take her home. She was the wife of a soldier, a working woman who could support herself.

I am here. I'm doing this not for Mother or Daddy or Theran. This is for Minnie. She couldn't wait to describe the scene to Theran in her next letter. She'd never felt so alive in all her life. Not even in his arms.

It was early fall. Chloe studied her reflection in one of the mirrors in the back room at Madame Blanche's, eyeing her waistline and stomach critically. For just this moment, everyone was busy looking elsewhere and Chloe was left alone there. Any moment now two favored customers scheduled to attend a private preview of Madame's fall line would pass through the front door.

I can't do this right now. Chloe closed her eyes and steadied her nerves. Even if what she suspected were true, it wouldn't be the end of the world.

She glanced toward the front of the store as the customers swept in, wearing fox fur collars and rubies. Madame Blanche's dramatic welcome drifted into the back room. Chloe turned to her dresser and let the girl straighten the shoulders of the first dress she was to model and arrange a few artful curls around Chloe's face under the snug hat brim.

"Lorraine," Madame summoned in an imperious tone, "*s'il vous plaît.*"

Putting everything else out of her mind, Chloe straightened her shoulders and strolled out to the showing area. Two fashionable society matrons sat on molded chairs, languid and spoiled, while Chloe performed the routine she could do without even thinking anymore. Madame's voice blended into the background as Chloe took up her interrupted train of thought. Her suspicions leaped back to mind, tormenting her. *I can't do this right now.*

Then something unexpected penetrated Chloe's consciousness. What was it? Chloe listened with more attention. It was Kitty's voice in the back room. Why had she come? Something sounded wrong. Chloe refused to let herself frown and obeyed Madame's instructions for her to turn once more to let one of the ladies finger the fabric. Then Chloe was dismissed and Minnie stepped out past the mirrors. She sported a morning frock of deep royal blue. Chloe reentered the back room and let the dressers converge on her. She was right; Kitty was waiting for her. "Kitty," she began, "what brings—"

Kitty threw her arms around Chloe, sobbing.

The dressers looked disgruntled. "Please, miss," one pleaded, pulling Kitty away from her, "we have to help her into the next outfit." The dressers succeeded in detaching Kitty from Chloe and piloted her friend into a nearby chair. While they began stripping Chloe and changing her, Chloe demanded, "What's wrong, Kitty?"

"I'm so sorry, Chloe. So sorry."

Kitty's words lit a fire in Chloe's heart. She froze in place. "What's happened? Tell me."

Kitty pulled a yellow telegram from her purse. "Mrs. Rascombe didn't want to bother you here, but she went to pick up the mail at the post office and this was waiting for you. She called me to come over and get it. She wanted me to break it to you. I . . . opened it, Chloe, just to be sure." Kitty's tears flowed. "Theran was my friend, too."

Was . . . Theran was . . . Chloe ceased to breathe. The room receded; a mist of flashing pinpoints of light hit her in the face. She staggered. Leaping up, Kitty grasped her arm. "You look faint. Sit down."

The urge to succumb rolled through Chloe. She clutched at what was real—the dressers, the back room, the sound of Madame Blanche's smooth selling voice . . .

Minnie appeared and the dressers, now finished with

Chloe, turned her to go out front again. They looked uncertain. One held up a hand to halt her. But without hesitation, Chloe walked through the door, her body fulfilling its
rehearsed, required task.

Theran was . . .

Flames. Then ice. Then flames, again and again, shuddering through Chloe. Outwardly, she posed like a lifeless mannequin before the two faceless women, who both fingered the
cloth. They asked her to turn. She obeyed. They asked to view
the dress from the rear. She whirled again.

Theran was . . .

In the doorway, opened just enough to peek out, Minnie
stood with tears streaming down her dusky cheeks. Posed artfully, Chloe felt fingers tugging at her skirt and heard voices.
She paid no attention. Finally, Madame dismissed her. Chloe
reached Minnie.

Minnie whispered near her ear, "I'm so sorry, Chloe. So
sorry."

Chloe couldn't trust herself to speak. She thought she
nodded. Then Minnie was gone and Chloe faced Kitty.
"When did he die?" The words scored her throat.

"Three days ago." Kitty wiped at her tears with a damp
hankie, to no avail. Fresh tears gushed from her eyes. "Of
food poisoning. Several men died after the same meal."

The dressers paused in their progress of changing Chloe's
dress and looked up, horrified. "Dead? Your husband died?
We'll tell Madame," one murmured and started off.

"No," Chloe snapped. If she didn't go on with what was
real, what was within her power, she'd fly apart. "Make the
change. Madame has everything planned out. Minnie can't
wear my dresses. The colors aren't right."

The dressers stared at her. Kitty stared at her.

"Go on," Chloe ordered, her throat thickening. "Change me. Or we'll throw Madame off." *Theran, it isn't true.*

"But, Chloe," Kitty started.

"I can't think about that right now." Chloe turned away. "I have work to do." *Theran, you promised you'd come back to me.*

Watching her with wide eyes and blinking back sympathetic tears, the dressers nimbly finished the switch and Chloe turned to face the door.

"Chloe, you look faint," Kitty repeated. "Please sit down." Minnie entered and Chloe sauntered automatically out to the showroom, Kitty's words echoing in her mind. It was over, all over. Theran would never hold her again, not in this life. She closed her eyes, drowning in remembrance.

Two weeks later, after dark, the train arrived in Buffalo, New York. Chloe alighted and scanned the platform for Theran's parents and sister. A tall man with salt-and-pepper hair who walked like Theran came forward. "Are you Chloe?"

His resemblance to Theran caught her lungs in a vise. She managed to nod. "Mr. Black?"

He reached for her valise. "I hope your trip went smoothly." He spoke gruffly and wouldn't meet her eyes.

"Yes." What did one say to the father of her late husband, a man she'd never met? "Fine."

"I've got the car over here," he said, averting his eyes. Why wouldn't he look at her? "It's only a short ride home."

The house Theran had grown up in was a tidy two-story brick home with an enclosed front porch. In the front yard, a red maple flamed under the nearby street lamp. Her father-in-law at her heel, Chloe stepped inside the neat, oak-paneled foyer and waited. A young woman with dark hair and

Theran's gray eyes walked toward her from the rear. "Hello. I'm Theran's sister, Lorna." She offered Chloe both her hands.

Chloe took them. The hands felt cold even through Chloe's kid gloves. "It's nice to meet you." Polite words were her only shield. Chloe let Lorna keep her hands as she read the sorrow in Lorna's red-ringed eyes.

"Where's your mother?" Mr. Black asked.

"She's in bed." Lorna's voice thinned. "She says she has one of her headaches and can't bear light."

Chloe felt Lorna's grip tighten. "I'm sorry to hear that," Chloe murmured.

Mr. Black chewed the corner of his mustache. "I'll go up to her. Lorna, would you get Chloe some refreshment and show her the room we've prepared for her." He hurried up the staircase without a backward glance.

"Come to the kitchen." Lorna tugged Chloe's hands. "I've got the kettle on for tea."

"Thank you." Chloe followed her sister-in-law to the rear of the house.

As she crossed the threshold into the kitchen, Lorna turned and embraced Chloe. "I know Theran loved you. He wrote me about you. I'm so glad he . . . had a love."

"I loved him, too."

Lorna nodded against Chloe's cheek. Chloe bit her lip to hold back tears. *He was my salvation, my strength. But he's gone.*

Releasing her, Lorna motioned for Chloe to sit down and then went to the stove and lifted a steaming kettle. "We're sorry, Father and I, that we didn't come and see you in New York." She choked on tears and turned away.

Chloe said something polite. Tears dripped from her eyes.

"It's terrible to meet you under these . . . sad circumstances." She set the kettle on a black iron trivet.

Chloe agreed, but wasn't able to speak.

Lorna screwed up her face as though fighting painful thoughts. "Father doesn't want me to tell you anything. But I think I ought to."

What could be worse than Theran dying so far from home, so far away that Chloe couldn't grieve over him or kiss his lips one last time? "What?" Chloe choked out.

Lorna poured boiling water into a white china teapot. "Mother is very angry . . ." Lorna's voice faltered.

Chloe tried to guess what her mother-in-law could be angry about. "About losing Theran?" she ventured.

"Well, yes. I think that's what's really upsetting her of course. But she's . . . she didn't want you to come to the memorial service."

The words made no sense. Chloe stared at Lorna's pained face. "Why not? I'm his widow."

Lorna pressed her fingers to her forehead. "I don't really understand what's happening in her mind." She put the kettle back on the stove. "Theran was always her favorite. Theran knew that and he didn't like it, didn't think it was fair. But ever since he enlisted, she's been . . . crazy with worry. And so angry with him for enlisting when he could have waited to be drafted."

"Theran wasn't like that."

Lorna smiled then, showing a glimmer of how pretty and bright she must have looked before Theran's loss had plunged her into sorrow. "He wasn't. But my mother won't accept that. She thinks he didn't have the right to endanger his life, that he owed her and Father. They sacrificed so much for his education, you see. All their hopes were on him."

Chloe pondered this, trying to understand how Theran's

mother was feeling. "What does that have to do with me coming here?"

Lorna wiped away a tear. "She didn't think it was right that Theran married . . . eloped with you. She . . ."

Lorna's face, more than her words, shook Chloe's composure. She understood now—she wasn't wanted here, wouldn't be embraced by this family as she had dreamed. Once again she was alone. The hope of finding welcome, of finding the support Chloe had cherished, flickered and dimmed.

Theran had been buried in France. So a memorial service had to suffice. The next afternoon, this formal farewell dragged on and on. Sitting in the front row beside Lorna, Chloe held on to her composure with numb fingertips. Continuous tears slipped down her cheeks. She didn't try to stop them. People didn't speak to her, but they stared at her, looked away, and then stared more. At the end of the service, a Spanish-American War veteran presented her with a triangular-folded US flag.

Finally, the ceremony ended and everyone drove in crowded cars back to the Black home. Chloe sat in a wing chair by the cold fireplace in the formal room, where lacy antimacassars lay on the arms of the stiff horsehair chairs. The flag sat on a table with a photo of Theran in uniform. Mourners, somber and formal, milled around, still glancing toward her. A few stopped by her and murmured sympathy. Chloe nodded and thanked them. But she was the stranger—the stranger who had married Theran Black the weekend before he shipped off to France. She didn't belong here among them, not without Theran at her side. Theran's mother never looked at her. Never spoke to her. She acted as if Chloe wasn't present. Waves of animosity flowed from the other woman, icy waves buffeting Chloe. Was it this that kept everyone staring at Chloe? Did everyone sense the woman's feral resentment of her?

Eventually the guests ate their fill, said their last condolences, and left. The maid hired for the occasion cleared away the dishes and went to the kitchen to begin washing them. Chloe looked up at Mr. Black, who stood by the mantel, at Lorna and Mrs. Black, who sat side by side on the sofa across from her. She'd come here with hope. She couldn't give up without even trying to bridge the gap between Theran's mother and herself. But she wouldn't say less than the truth. "Why do you hate me, Mother Black?"

Mrs. Black didn't reply at first, but she glared at Chloe, pure venom in her eyes.

Chloe repeated her question.

"My wife doesn't hate you," Mr. Black began.

"Yes, I do," his wife snapped. "I hate you, you hussy."

Chloe tried to make sense of this insult. "I'm the widow of your son. How does that make me a hussy?"

"Look at you." The older woman's words were like a slap across Chloe's face. "Your bobbed hair, your lip rouge. You've been working as a model. A respectable wife doesn't work, and certainly not at something that's as close to an actress as being the same thing."

"I had to earn my keep—"

"And what decent girl entices a young man to elope with her? A *decent* girl would have obeyed her parents and waited till her beau returned from the war. You're a wild female and you took in my son—completely. What would he know about scheming women like you?"

Chloe's lips parted, but she couldn't think of a word to say. It was all too bizarre to be happening.

"Mother, that's enough," Mr. Black said in a quelling voice. "You're upset, but—"

"This is all your fault, you vile woman," Theran's mother plunged on, heedless.

"Mother," Lorna snapped, "stop it. You're just angry that Theran eloped with Chloe instead of coming home to spend his last weekend with us."

The woman slapped Lorna's cheek.

Mr. Black swooped down on his wife, grasped both her hands and pulled her to her feet. "This will stop now. You've said too much and I'm ashamed of you. Theran would be ashamed of you. He loved this woman or he wouldn't have married her. She is the widow of our son and I won't have you abusing her in this house."

Mrs. Black wrenched away from him. "You are just as taken in as my son was. A pretty face always counts more with a man than anything else. And that soft accent. She knows just how to get what she wants. She wanted my son; he was a catch."

Chloe opened her mouth, but no words came. The quivering that she'd felt since Kitty brought the telegram increased. Theran was gone and he'd taken away her foundation, her strength, with him.

Mrs. Black struggled against her husband, swinging around to face Chloe. "Why did you ensnare my boy? Why did you have to marry so quickly? Had you let him take liberties or did you think you were pregnant by someone else so you trapped my son to cover—"

"Mother—" Theran's father seized his wife by the shoulders and turned her toward the doorway. "—you are hysterical. Lorna, call the doctor and ask him to come over as soon as he can with a sedative." He marched his wife out of the room and up the stairs. Weeping, Lorna went to the phone in the kitchen and Chloe heard her talking to the operator.

Chloe sat without moving, barely breathing. Theran was not coming back. She'd come here hoping for a welcome, for a haven. How could Theran's mother hate her when they'd only met yesterday? Why had she voiced such terrible lies? *Theran, you're never coming back to me and your mother hates me. What am I going to do?*

Suddenly, as she sat there alone, she heard once more the voice of her Granny Raney whispering in her memory, *In this world there will be troubles.* The thought did not comfort her.

"I can't do this alone," Chloe whispered to the empty room.

CHAPTER NINE

*A*fter disembarking, Chloe walked to the triple-arched entrance of the Baltimore Union Station. Each step rang through her like the clanging of discordant bells. This wasn't from her overwhelming fatigue but because of her destination. *I can't do this.* She'd thought the worst that could happen *had* happened to her. Then she'd gone to Buffalo and her circumstances had dropped to nearly unbearable. Had she hit bottom yet or did she have more to lose? She stepped out into the chilly early November night wind. She dismissed the redcap with a generous tip and then looked around, hanging back near the dimly lit entrance.

From the shadows cast by the Greek pillars, a tall soldier approached her, but stopped a few feet from her. "Chloe?"

The familiar voice splashed through her like hot wax. "Roarke?" Neither of them moved. Eyeing his unexpected khaki uniform, Chloe couldn't take a step, could hardly breathe. Roarke, a soldier? When would it all end? When everyone had been killed? "I didn't know you'd been . . ."

"Been drafted?"

Her throat clamped shut. She could barely nod. People—civilians and more soldiers—paraded around them, between them. Many glanced inquisitively at the two of them. Chloe tried to calm herself. But seeing that Roarke now stood directly in harm's way left her more shaken than ever. *God, hold me together.*

"We haven't told Kitty yet." Roarke spoke in a composed voice as though discussing a banking policy. "She had exams and we didn't want her to know until after she'd finished them." His mouth became a line. "Theran's death upset her. We thought . . ."

Chloe would never forget Kitty's face, her voice on that awful day at Madame Blanche's when Kitty had brought the telegram about Theran.

Now, Roarke looked as if he'd like to say more, but he only said, "Let me take those for you." He picked up the two valises at her feet. "My car is over here." He nudged her arm and led her to the familiar Model-T.

She was grateful for his effort to keep everything commonplace. But being near Roarke awoke memories— especially of the last time they'd been together on her wedding day, when he'd let her know he wanted her for himself. Careful not to brush against Roarke's crisp wool uniform, Chloe slipped onto the seat. She closed her eyes as the memory of Theran in his uniform waving and smiling aboard ship taunted her. The subtle tremor deep inside that never left her intensified. First Theran, now Roarke.

Roarke laid a knit afghan over her lap. "It's pretty chilly tonight." The gentle words and comforting gesture threatened to undo her completely. She looked away. Some thought, some realization, was trying to surface. But she pushed it down. She tightened her mouth, trying to stop the unremitting uncertainty of what might come rolling, tumbling out if she let her self-control ebb.

Without any conversation, he drove them out of the city

onto the darkened highway. And all Chloe could think of were the memories of the night back in May—surely a century ago—when Roarke had been driving her away from Ivy Manor. Tonight he was driving her toward it. She shivered once, sharply. *No.*

"When did you get drafted?" she asked at last, trying to sound normal.

"Over two months ago. I did my officer's training and I'm home for a week before I ship out."

"So soon." It wasn't a question, just a statement. *No. Please, no.*

"I'm glad I was here when you needed me. But if I'd been gone, my father would have come for you."

Tears slipped down her cheeks, but she made no effort to wipe them away. Maybe he wouldn't see them in the dark.

"I won't distress you by talking about Theran." Roarke passed a slower car. "But we—my parents and I—were saddened to hear about your loss . . . about the loss of your husband. He was a brave man."

She thought if she said one word that she'd shatter like one of her mother's translucent English china cups. She tried to nod, but instead stared straight ahead, quivering inside and fighting it.

"Kitty will be home from law school in a few weeks for Thanksgiving," he continued, "I think that will make it—my shipping overseas—easier for my parents."

Chloe nodded. Roarke overseas. Black-and-white images from war newsreels flashed in her mind. She closed her eyes. Warm tears still flowed.

"When I talked to Kitty earlier tonight—before leaving home to come get you," Roarke went on, "she was surprised that you were leaving New York."

Roarke said the words without any overt inflection, just

a plain sentence. Still, Chloe recognized it as a question. "I didn't tell anyone but Minnie." *I couldn't bear to tell Kitty. Kitty is sunshine and apples, not sad good-byes and black crepe.*

"I see." He let her sit in blessed silence for the next few miles. The Model-T's headlamps cast a ghostly light on stark, leafless trees.

She struggled to quell the shuddering, the insecurity, the feeling of falling apart.

Then he cleared his throat. "Chloe, I thought . . . you were . . . Why have you come home?"

She mangled her pale, embroidered handkerchief. She'd been forced to tell Minnie and Madame Blanche why she was leaving. But didn't Roarke deserve the truth, too? "I'm pregnant." The admission was like pulling a plug.

"I see." Again his tone was colorless. She knew this wasn't because he didn't care that she was pregnant and didn't care that Theran was dead but because of his exquisite politeness. Roarke had always been that way with her—thoughtful, gentle, easing her way. In a stroke, her anguish broke through the last thin tissue of her composure. She began to cry, loudly enough for him to hear. She fought it. *I can do this. I have to.* But her calm acceptance, only a veneer, shriveled up and blew away.

Roarke made no sign that he heard her weeping. Again, it was his politeness, his natural courtesy. How did he know that she teetered on the edge of hysteria? Finally, she wiped her face with her fingertips. "I'm all right," she lied.

"Of course you are. You aren't weak, Chloe. Always remember that. No matter what happens, you are a capable woman and you will face whatever comes." He claimed one of her hands and held it gently, resting on the seat, just as he had the night she'd met Theran as they drove home from the roadhouse.

Whatever comes. She let his hand cover hers, the familiar gesture helping to calm her nerves. How could she tell him, tell anyone that Theran's death had left her feeling stripped of her skin, defenseless and raw?

Whatever comes. Ominous words from a man facing a war. *I'm not the only one suffering this war. I have to be strong, face whatever comes. But how?*

"Roarke, I came home to have the . . . my baby. Madame Blanche wanted me to stay in New York and come back to work after the baby was born. But I don't think I could do that. I wouldn't want to leave my child with a nanny. I want this baby very much." The thought of the baby—a sweet little boy with Theran's thatch of black hair and his gray eyes that she could love—had been her only consolation, even if it had forced her to leave New York.

"Sometimes a person needs to be back home."

Where is home for me? I want to go back to Mrs. Rascombe's table and sit down with Minnie. But she couldn't burden them with this. For this, she needed family. Chloe drew in a ragged breath. "So you leave for France in a week?"

"Yes. Father says I'll have a rough crossing. The Atlantic isn't very friendly in winter."

"That's right." Her mind dredged up memories of the world before war. "Your parents always loved to visit London and Paris." The conversation found the mundane then. She'd known Roarke all her life. They talked of nothing and everything for the next few miles. Then, exhausted, Chloe closed her eyes and fell asleep on the front seat.

*　　*　　*

As he drove over the deserted roads and through the sleeping towns, Roarke watched her sleep. Once, twice, he touched her soft white cheek and a golden lock of her bobbed hair. She didn't stir. Then he faced forward. He had no right to speak of love now. Would he desert Chloe forever as her husband had or would he come home safely? If he did, would Chloe ever look at him the way she'd looked at Theran Black?

It was daybreak when he finally drove up the lane to Ivy Manor. The trees were leafless and the sky was pewter. The sun lent its glow to the gloom. Even the ivy around the windows looked dejected. He parked by the front door and came around for Chloe.

She didn't move, just sat staring at the house.

He wanted to turn around and drive toward his home and put Chloe into the care of his mother. But he had no right to. "Your parents aren't home," he reminded her.

She looked up at him, uncertainty pinching her lovely face. "I really appreciate you coming to get me, Roarke." Her soft voice curled through him. "You'll come for a visit before you leave, won't you?"

He tightened his control. She didn't need him showing weakness. "I'm tying up things at the bank. I hate to leave my dad right now." He paused. *I can't trust myself alone with you again, Chloe. You don't need me talking to you of love and then going off to war worrying you sick.* "If I can't come here," he went on as if this were just any day, "my mother will have you over for dinner before I leave. She wants to see you very much. She told me to tell you that. She'll be glad to do whatever she can for you." *While I'm gone.*

"Your mother has always been kind to me."

He hated the beaten-down tone of Chloe's voice, as though she had no friends, nowhere to turn. "Chloe, you can come to my mother if you need . . . anything." He meant "need someone." He tried but couldn't keep the urgency from his tone. His sweet Chloe needed him and he couldn't help her. An unusual feeling barreled through him like boiling water. He wanted to pound something into dust. *Chloe needs me and I can do nothing. This blasted war.*

"I know your mother is very kind." She let him help her out of the car.

"Will you call her if you need her?" he insisted.

Interrupting them, the door of Ivy Manor opened and Haines and Minnie's mother, Jerusha, hurried out and down the pillared steps. "Miss Chloe! Welcome." Grinning, Haines approached with a lift to his step. "We are sure glad to hear you comin' home." Haines picked up one of Chloe's valises and waved her to precede him. Jerusha—reminding Chloe strongly of Minnie—lifted the other suitcase and waited. Chloe held back. The servants waited.

"I'll call you later," Roarke said, wishing she'd given him her promise to turn to his mother if need be. "Rest."

Chloe turned and waved good-bye like a lost little girl. "Thank you again, Roarke."

He wanted to hold her, kiss her, whisper that she mustn't worry, that he'd take care of everything. But instead, he watched the beautiful, gentle-hearted woman he still loved disappear inside. Would the day ever come when he could let her know that he still adored her? Or would he end up like Theran and never return?

Two days later, Roarke admired Chloe as she sat at the Mc-Caslin dining room table. The chandelier glittered above them, highlighting Chloe's blonde hair until it looked like a fairy crown. Wind-tossed vines tapped at the French windows. Roarke tried to eat enough to show his appreciation of the delicious farewell meal Hattie, their cook, had poured her heart and soul into for his sake. But he might as well be eating army food already. *Tomorrow morning I leave for war.* But the words were gibberish.

"Chloe, honey, you certainly don't look as if you're expecting at all," his mother commented not for the first time. "I would have loved to see you modeling in that Fifth Avenue shop. I surely would."

Chloe smiled, though still looking faintly ill at ease. She didn't look very pregnant to him, either. He surreptitiously studied Chloe's figure and could detect no change. No, that was a lie. There was a subtle difference, a distinct rounding where there had only been a slender waist. The thought brought back unwelcome images of Theran kissing Chloe at the courthouse in New York. He imagined Theran holding Chloe . . . He closed his mind. *She chose him, not you. Why torture yourself?*

"Do you think you'll go back to New York after the baby's born?" his mother asked.

Not if I can help it. Roarke bit his lip, holding back objections he had no right to make.

"My dear," his father interrupted, "*Miss Chloe* will be a mother then."

"Well, *she* was raised by Jerusha's mother and her grandmother, a Carlyle tradition."

Roarke glowered at his mother.

His mother raised her eyebrows at him and adroitly changed topics. "If I'd only been born a generation later, I'd have dearly *loved* to be a model on Fifth Avenue."

"I know you would have," his father commented with an indulgent smile.

Roarke made himself take another bite of buttery corn bread. He savored the give and take between his parents, true opposites. His father so staid and serious, his mother so enthusiastic and playful. He'd always known he took after his steady father while Kitty was the image of their mother. He'd miss the byplay between his parents.

"Really, dear?" his mother teased. "I was pretty enough to be a model?"

Father nodded, looking proud, and smiled. "You are still pretty enough, my dear. And no doubt you'd like to have gone off to college like your daughter, too."

Mother chuckled. "Only if you'd been attending the same college, my sweet." She brushed his wrist in a blatantly provocative way and chuckled again.

The easy banter between Miss Estelle and Mr. Thomas, Roarke's parents, had always intrigued and surprised Chloe. What would it have been like to be raised by parents who loved each other? Chloe rested her hand low on her abdomen, under the cover of the tablecloth. *I loved your daddy, little one, and I'll make sure you know that.* But these brave words only left Chloe feeling unqualified, green. Once someone had told her that her father's name, Kimball, meant "hollow vessel." That described how she felt now.

The meal ended finally and Roarke stood up. "Chloe, I'll drive you home now."

Chloe jumped as if someone had pinched her hard. She'd dreaded this moment. She remembered all too clearly the night Roarke had proposed to her. Would he propose to her again? Surely not. Roarke was too kind, too understanding, to wound her so. But the worry nibbled at the corners of her mind.

By rote, she made her farewells to his parents. Mrs. Mc-Caslin clasped her hands around Chloe's and implored her to call if she needed "anything at all." Mr. McCaslin seconded his wife, looking at Chloe with a compassion that almost brought her to tears. More than anything she wanted to give in to their offer, to tell them that though she didn't want to be alone at Ivy Manor, she felt unequal to facing her parents when they returned. But she merely nodded and offered a smiling thank-you.

Roarke slipped Chloe's black wool coat around her without touching her. He then led her to the door. "I'll go around and get my car and pick you up in a moment."

"No, I'll walk with you." She adjusted her hat. She must get away while her shaky control held. The early winter twilight was spent and full night had come. The cold wind ruffled Chloe's bangs. Once again, she felt as though she were walking a final mile. Would this be the last time she would ever see Roarke alive? Would they say good-bye and be parted till death or the Lord came? These questions were dull knives slicing through her.

"Wait here." At the bend where the garage loomed up, Roarke stopped her with a hand on her shoulder.

Suddenly something unexpected happened inside her. She froze in mid-step. "Roarke." The unusual sensation, one she'd had only a hint of before—stronger now, and so startling, held her immobile. Slipping her hands inside her jacket, she pressed them over her abdomen. "I think I just felt the baby kick."

Roarke stood stock still, staring at her in the dim light cast from the house and garage light. "Does it hurt?"

She chuckled, feeling herself shake under her hands. A joyous release flowed through her. "Here." Impulsively, she reached over, gripped his hand, and pressed it to her. The baby kicked again.

"It feels . . . It feels like bird wings," Roarke said. "Like a baby bird flapping its wings."

"How poetic." Chloe couldn't help herself; she laughed out loud. But as the baby flutter-kicked again, she felt a completely different emotion overwhelming her. In a split second, she was weeping. "Oh, Roarke, Theran will never see his baby."

Roarke's arms came around her, his lips pressed to her forehead. "We'll all tell his child about him, about his bravery and his joy and exuberance. He was Kitty's friend, too. She'll never let Theran be forgotten."

Chloe let the scents of wool and Roarke's clean soap fill her head. She lifted her face, gazing up at him in the dim light. "Don't let them kill you, Roarke. Please come home to us. You've been my best friend, even better than Kitty. You understand me more than she does."

The words came from deep inside Chloe. She had never consciously thought this. But now she realized they were the honest truth. Roarke had always accepted her. He watched in easy silence and then did what he could to make life more pleasant for her. Kitty, on the other hand, always came in and turned things around to suit herself, usually upside down.

Chloe meant every word she'd said, but she worried at their effect on Roarke. *Don't ask me to wait for you. I don't feel that way about you. I'm sorry. I loved Theran. It's not the same, although I can't bear to lose you either.*

But Roarke said nothing, just held her in his arms. He didn't cross the invisible line from comfort to passion. Reassured, she let his warmth surround her. The baby kicked once more before apparently falling asleep in his cozy nest. Still, Roarke and Chloe clung to each other. Finally, Roarke slowly released her. "I'll be careful, Chloe. I'll do what I must, but I don't think I'm a dashing hero like Theran."

"You're a good man in a world of liars," she murmured, thinking of her father and how different he was from the man standing in front of her. Roarke was steady and trustworthy. Who could trust Quentin Kimball? Not she. Certainly she didn't know how she would be able to protect her child from him and from his squabbling with her mother. But she wouldn't voice her concerns. That wasn't Roarke's battle. He'd have enough facing the Germans.

Roarke drove her home and walked her to the door. They gazed at each other. Chloe was memorizing the way he looked tonight. Was he doing the same, memorizing her?

He lifted her hand and kissed it softly. "I'll write."

"Please."

The fragile moment was broken as the door behind her was flung open. "Chloe!" her father boomed. "My poor little gal came home."

Shocked, Chloe cringed. She hadn't expected her father to be there, and at seeing him after all this time the urge to turn tail raced through her like flame on dry grass. She took a step back.

Beside her, Roarke held her hand, tightened his grip as if saying, "Stand your ground." "Evening, Mr. Kimball," he said, giving Chloe a moment to compose herself.

"I hear you got drafted." Chloe's father rocked on the balls of his feet.

Roarke nodded. "I leave in the morning."

Her father stretched out his hand. "Good luck, soldier."

"Thank you, sir." Roarke shook his hand, patted Chloe's shoulder, and left her there, facing her father. By then she was ready for him. Roarke's confidence in her gave her the strength she needed.

"Come in, gal." Daddy stepped out of the doorway.

Too weary to even question his presence there, she entered, careful not to touch him as she passed. "I'm very tired, Daddy." She didn't know how he'd found out so quickly she was back, and she didn't care.

"I hear from Haines you're in an interestin' condition."

Chloe wouldn't look at him.

"Didn't know that college boy had it in him."

"Don't be vulgar, Daddy."

He chuckled. "So I'm going to be a granddaddy. Well, that's good. That's what we need around here—some fresh blood, new life."

Chloe couldn't come up with a single angle for this comment. He'd lost the election and wouldn't be the new state senator. Was her father already expecting to use his first grandchild to his advantage?

He patted her shoulder paternally. She resented it, but submitted. "I'm very fatigued, Daddy. I'm going off to bed."

"Does your mother know you're expectin'?"

"No, I only told the McCaslins." She wouldn't mention Minnie. "Roarke came and picked me up in Baltimore when I came down from New York."

"Well, you did right, honey. At a time like this—you losing your husband in the war and expectin' his child, you came to the right place. Your mother and I won't hold it against you, you runnin' away like that."

Chloe held her tongue but it wasn't easy.

"It was mostly her fault anyway," he continued, "havin' Haines burn the man's letters when I told him he could write to you. Your runnin' away was all your mama's doin' and don't think I didn't tell her so."

Chloe barely listened to him working himself up to a tirade. At least at the door in front of Roarke he'd behaved better than she'd hoped. "I'm plumb tired out, Daddy. I've got to get upstairs to bed."

Jerusha hurried down the hall as if on cue. "Come with me, Miss Chloe. You need to lie down and get off your feet." Her father stepped out of the way. Even though she didn't need to, Chloe leaned on Jerusha's arm. She wanted to get away and keep her father out of her room. Daddy avoided sick women.

It worked. Soon Jerusha had helped Chloe undress and she'd slipped into bed. The maid started a fire in the grate at the foot of the bed. "We need to take the chill off this room. You'll rest better."

Chloe thanked her and closed her eyes. Her last thought was *God, keep Roarke safe and bring him home. And please take Daddy far from here tomorrow.*

Her mother arrived two days later. Her father had called her at the resort in Florida to gloat about being the first to know they were expecting a grandchild. She had caught the first train home. Now she hurried into the house. "Chloe! Chloe!" she called up the stairs. "Everything will be all right now! Your mother's here."

Standing alone in her bedroom, Chloe opened her eyes and stared out her window. She wished she'd never left New York. "Don't worry, little one," she whispered to her unborn child and patted her growing abdomen. "I'll protect you. I won't let them make your life miserable. I won't." She tried to push away the fear that had been growing since her father had come home. How could she stand against them? She didn't know how she'd find the strength. But then she remembered the moment of the first fashion showing at Madame's. *I didn't think I had the nerve for that either.*

Her mother hurried into Chloe's room and embraced her dramatically. "Mother's here, my dear. I'll take care of everything."

"I'm doing fine, Mother. I'm eating and resting in the afternoons. Doctor Benning says the baby's growing just fine."

"You had the doctor here. So soon? No doubt that was your father's—"

"I called him when I returned home. I wanted to make sure everything was going as it should."

"Chloe, you don't need a doctor. You need your mother."

Her father filled the doorway. "We been doin' just fine without a mother."

Chloe's mother sniffed. "You always were an unfeeling barbarian."

He laughed out loud. "Our daughter doesn't take after you. She takes after me. Built tough. She'll do fine. Give me a strong grandson."

"Oh, you know this will be a boy then?" her mother sneered.

"Please," Chloe interrupted, "it's time for me to take my daily walk."

"Not in this sharp wind," her mother objected.

"The doc said she should walk every day unless it was icy," her father weighed in.

Chloe ignored them both and walked from the room. *I'll protect you, little one. I won't let them fight over you.*

CHAPTER TEN

France, March 1918

Cold penetrated his paralyzing fog. Roarke stirred. A moan. Was it his own? He tried to focus on his jaws. Were they open? Another groan forced its way through his slack lips. He was flat on his back and he couldn't move, not even lift a finger. Pain gnawed him with jagged, razor teeth. His eyes jerked open.

Coming through the strange, clinging mist in front of his eyes, a hand gripped his wrist. "More morphine," a man's voice ordered. A careless hand hauled up Roarke's head, and pain began peeling off his skin. He groaned long, low. Dry lips stuck together as indifferent fingers opened his mouth; a liquid trickled down his throat. To stop from gagging, he swallowed. Bitter, burning. Another moan dragged itself from his lungs.

Other sounds, moaning, whimpering, then a terrifying whistling. His heart pounded. "Shells!" he yelled, but didn't hear his voice. Were they being bombarded again? "No!" he shouted. Or was it only a whisper? His head sank back the fraction he'd managed to raise it, gasping, fighting for breath.

The agony was a vise twisting him apart. "God, help me. Help me . . . die."

"You need to make a decision, Lieutenant McCaslin," the doctor said in his clipped English accent. He stood above Roarke by his bed. The mingled odors of disinfectant, sweat, and blood were strong. The bare, white-washed walls were lined with narrow cots. Wounded men lay like cord wood, quiet or writhing and moaning. White-garbed doctors and nurses paraded purposefully up and down the center aisle as if set apart from the pointless suffering.

Roarke looked up at the doctor. The man with thinning hair was maybe ten years his senior, but looked haggard and drawn. Well, didn't they all? Roarke had been moved from the field hospital to a ward in an army hospital near Paris. A Red Cross nurse had told him that last night—or was it the night before? The passage of time had become irrelevant to him.

"Your elbow is badly shattered," the physician said, his eyes on the clipboard. "I've removed some bone fragments and have studied your X-ray. You must decide if you want your arm set straight or crooked."

"What?" Roarke asked. The question made no sense.

"You are not going to regain normal mobility of your right arm." The voice was cool and perfunctory. "I can set it so that your arm will remain extended like this." The doctor held his arm stretched taut at his side. "Or bent like this." The doctor bent his arm at the elbow as if it were in a sling.

"Bent or straight," Roarke repeated, still not sure of what was going on. "What happened to my face?" He finally made himself speak the words that had been on his mind.

"You were hit by shrapnel, I'm afraid. It's healing but you'll have permanent scarring."

"How bad is it?"

"Not bad. Just your cheek. You didn't lose an eye or an ear. Your nose is intact, too. Not bad at all."

Roarke wondered if the doctor would say it was "not bad at all" if it were his own face. Over the dressing on his face, Roarke gingerly traced the furrows carved into his right cheek. He didn't look forward to encountering a mirror.

"Well, which do you want—bent or straight?" the doctor prompted with a trace of impatience. "You're next in line. We need to know." The man looked down at his clipboard and waited.

Roarke tried to think, but his head was like a cotton ball. Someone across the aisle began moaning for "Rosie." The sound made it hard for Roarke to focus. "What do you think?"

"Me?" The doctor looked into Roarke's eyes at last. "I think I'd prefer bent. Sometimes it's awkward not to be able to bend your arm, don't you think?"

I think I'd like to go home with everything back to normal. But that wasn't what the doctor was asking. Roarke finally got it. The Englishman was telling him, "You will never be normal again."

"Bent is fine," Roarke muttered, not really caring either way. *I'll never again be able to hold Chloe the way I want to.*

"Very good." The doctor turned away. "Nurse, prepare this man. We'll set his arm in plaster now."

Roarke closed his eyes. Then, as it had done innumerable times since he'd first awakened, the awful truth of what he'd done once again blazed through him. Lying every night on his back in the dark berth, he had seen it happening again like a newsreel in his mind. Now, he held himself still so that no sob betrayed his weakness. A bent arm and a scarred face were no less than he deserved for what he had done. He deserved to die. And how could he ever face Chloe again?

Maryland, March 1918

A contraction gripped Chloe again, tightening her lower back. She watched the clock on her mahogany dresser tick second by second. She breathed in and tangled her hands in the sheets. Grinding her teeth, she resisted the urge to scream.

"That's okay, honey." Jerusha wiped her forehead with a damp cloth. "You can yell. Nobody blame you. Let it out." The woman's dark features expressed loving willingness to suffer through labor along with Chloe. The pain let go, but the tension hung on. Panting as if she'd been running, Chloe sank back onto the sheet, damp with her own perspiration. Jerusha's kind hands bathed Chloe's face with more cool water and smoothed back her bangs. The gentle touch soothed the ache in Chloe's heart. "I wish Minnie were here," she muttered.

"Me, too, honey. Me, too." Jerusha patted her face dry with a crisp linen cloth.

"Did I tell you how beautiful Minnie looked in that red-satin evening gown?" Chloe whispered.

Nodding, Jerusha lifted a cup to Chloe's lips. "Take a sip of water, honey."

Another pain seized Chloe, raking her, twisting her. Jerusha stood by with cup in hand, watching and waiting. Her thin, aging face filled with concern. Chloe was glad Minnie's mother was here to help her. For a second, she wished her mother was by her side as well. But only for a moment. Mother would only tell her that ladies didn't labor to have babies, that their maids did that for them, or something else in that vein. Chloe closed her eyes and tugged, mangling the sheet on each side of her. *I'm having your baby, Theran. Our little boy will be born soon.* The pressure wrenched harder, more potent.

Jerusha dabbed her forehead with the linen. "Let it out, honey. Go ahead."

Chloe gasped and then a groan was dragged out of her. She panted. "How long?"

"You still got a way to go, honey." Jerusha helped her sip water. "Babies don't come out till they're ready."

Gray-haired, soft-voiced Doctor Benning walked over. "I'll check her now."

Chloe closed her eyes, trying to block out the doctor's hands probing her, the pain.

Chloe lay exhausted, weak, flattened. She stared at the ceiling, feeling warm blood between her legs.

"A difficult presentation," the doctor murmured. He stood with her mother near Chloe's bed. She heard a baby wailing, wailing. "I thought I might lose her," the doctor continued.

Chloe closed her eyes. The pain had been more than she'd ever experienced before and had lasted a day and a night, but she'd done it. She'd brought Theran's baby safely into this world. *Oh, Theran, I wish you were here.*

"Chloe's always been delicate," her mother fretted, "but she'll be all right now, won't she?"

"She'll need careful nursing, very careful nursing." Doctor Benning's voice was subdued. "She'll be in bed for two weeks at least."

Did they know she was awake?

"I'd send you a trained lying-in nurse but I think Jerusha here is as good as any I could get from outside. She's done an excellent job with many of my patients who needed extra nursing after a delivery."

"I'd rather have a trained nurse—" her mother began.

"I want Jerusha," Chloe interrupted, trying to lift herself onto one elbow and failing. "I want . . . Jerusha." Minnie seemed closer with her mother nearby.

"You're awake then?" The doctor came over and gently clasped her wrist. "So you prefer someone you know?"

Chloe nodded, rubbing her head against her pillow. "Yes."

"And I think Francy Clayborn is nursing now." Doctor Benning looked at his watch. "You can get her to wet nurse your little girl."

My little . . . girl? That's right. I didn't have my little boy. Chloe knew it had been foolish to have imagined a little boy with Theran's black hair and gray eyes. But she could love a little girl as well, couldn't she? "I want to nurse my baby. My daughter." Chloe turned on her side to face Doctor Benning.

Her mother chuckled her sophisticated lady laugh. "Chloe, ladies don't nurse their babies. You'll ruin your figure."

"I don't care about my figure." Chloe wished her mother would leave. She had disappeared when labor began and hadn't returned until the baby had finally come and had been bathed. "I want to nurse my baby."

"You've been through a terrible, long labor," her mother said in a patronizing voice. "You don't need to be doing something low like nursing your child. That's for servants."

Chloe clenched her hands around the top of the soft wool blanket spread over her. "I want my baby—" She infused her voice with as much starch as she could. "And I want to nurse her."

Her mother made an exasperated sound. "Chloe, really. What will Doctor Benning think?"

"Many ladies nurse their own children," the doctor said in an easy tone. "Why don't we let Chloe try?"

Her mother clicked her tongue and tossed her head in an impatient gesture.

Jerusha helped prop Chloe up in bed with pillows. She'd never felt so exhausted, so bone weary in her whole life. But anticipation warmed her as she watched Jerusha carry the little bundle that was her baby toward her. Then the child began crying again. And Chloe wished again that she'd even held a newborn baby before. But she hadn't.

"She sound hungry." Jerusha grinned down at the baby and Chloe. "You tellin' your mama that you hungry, little one?"

Cautiously Chloe accepted the soft, cotton-wrapped bundle and looked down at the wrinkled red face. The little mouth was wide open and squalling. The doctor drew her mother away toward the door of the room.

Jerusha opened Chloe's nightgown and folded it back. Chloe looked down at her own white flesh and recalled Theran's dark head resting there. Now his little girl would rest her cheek there. "Hello, sweetheart. Hello, Elizabeth Leigh—my little Elizabeth," Chloe cooed, her heart beating fast. "Your daddy would have loved you. I love you."

The baby wailed, balling her hands into tiny fists. Jerusha showed Chloe how to hold and lead the child to nurse. The baby keened on, stretching her neck and twisting up her little face. Maybe she sensed her mother didn't know what she was doing. Chloe tensed. "Am I doing it wrong?"

"No," Jerusha began.

"You're just not strong enough to do this," her mother snapped, approaching the bed. "You need your rest."

Chloe bit back angry words and blinked away hot tears of frustration. "I am tired, but I want to hold my baby."

"Well, no one said you couldn't hold your baby, did they?" Her mother gave her a false smile. "You're making a fuss when you should be sleeping."

Jerusha said nothing, but she adjusted the baby in Chloe's arm and with a dark finger lifted the baby's pale chin to nurse. She began sucking.

Chloe hadn't anticipated the brand-new sensation of the child's suckling and jerked. The baby fussed, balling her little fists again.

"This one has a temper," Jerusha said with an indulgent smile. "She'll get it all right. You wait and see."

Chloe's mother sniffed.

Jerusha helped little Elizabeth start nursing again. In spite of the unexpected discomfort from her child's sucking, Chloe forced herself to remain still. She closed her eyes and tried not to notice the lingering pain and exhaustion that wanted to swallow her whole.

"You just need to be patient," Jerusha whispered. "It's harder at first for pale ladies like you. I don't know why, but it is."

Chloe hoped she was right. Theran came to mind again and a wave of fresh sorrow washed over her. She wanted to cry and never stop. But Theran expected better from the woman he'd married. She expected better.

* * *

Little Elizabeth was over a month old. It was after midnight in the dark and otherwise silent house. Chloe stood near the window and thought she might go crazy. She pressed the back of her hand to her mouth, buffeted by wave after wave of frustration. "What's wrong with her?" *Why doesn't she like me?*

Jerusha held the wailing baby in her arms and walked up and down the nursery floor. "Your little Bette got the colic. That's all, Miss Chloe. She can't help it. Her little tummy hurt her." Jerusha made soothing noises and rocked the baby in her arms as she paced.

Chloe had been so weak and in so much pain after childbirth that her mother had taken over Bette's care while Jerusha nursed Chloe back to health. Now, for some reason, Chloe couldn't make up for lost time with her baby. "I should be able to comfort my baby." *A good mother would be able to.*

"She know her mommy is here. She just feel so bad she gotta let us know."

"Every time I nurse her she cries." Chloe covered her face with her hands and winced, thinking of how painful nursing Elizabeth was. *I'm a bad mother. A good mother wouldn't mind the discomfort.*

"This is your first time and you gotta baby with a sore stomach. It make you nervous. That's all."

"But she screams every time I touch her." Chloe felt like sinking to the floor and never rising again. *What am I doing wrong? I must be doing something really bad. I lost Theran and now my baby hates me.* She leaned her head against the chilly window. Tears poured from her eyes and she was too weak to wipe them away.

*   *   *

It was nearly July. Chloe walked into the nursery and found her mother rocking three-month-old Bette by the cold fireplace. "I finally got her to take a bottle," her mother whispered.

Chloe drew near and looked down on her child. Was it her imagination or did her daughter glare up at her the same way Theran's mother had? The look accused her as though Chloe were the one responsible for all the pain Bette had endured, still suffered at times. *No matter how much I try my baby doesn't like me. I'm not a good mother.*

Chloe's milk had dried up over the past week. And Chloe was secretly relieved to be done with the painful, messy process. But as a consequence, her daughter would have even less to do with her. Francy, the wet nurse, still came three times a day and Bette nursed hungrily. In between, the baby liked the sweet, diluted evaporated milk Jerusha mixed up. But Bette would take this only from her grandmother.

It was almost as if Chloe had cursed her baby by giving the child both her grandmothers' names. *Elizabeth* was Theran's mother's name and *Leigh* was her mother's middle name. She'd given her daughter the name *Leigh* to placate her mother's ego. She really would have liked to name her daughter *Lorraine* after Granny Raney, who had loved her so. But she had chosen *Elizabeth* with the faint hope Theran's mother would soften toward Theran's only child. It had so far been in vain. Lorna, though, continued to write. Even Mr. Black had written her a note congratulating her on Bette's birth, but Mrs. Black had not even signed the note.

Chloe walked to the window and stared out at the black night. Her days were long and empty when she'd anticipated being busy with her baby. *But my daughter doesn't want me or need me.* Chloe walked out of the room, unable to bear listening to her mother cooing over her grandchild. She paused on the landing. Haines was looking up the staircase. "Miss Chloe, I was just comin' to get you. Telephone for you."

Chloe hurried down the steps and picked up the black receiver, resting on the hall table. "Chloe!" Kitty's voice burst in Chloe's ear. "How are you?"

"Fine." Tears bubbled in Chloe's throat. She choked them down, not wanting to worry her friend.

"Roarke's finally been discharged from the army hospital near New York and I'm driving him home in my new car."

Chloe drew in a shaking breath. "I'm so glad. How is he?"

"I'll let you talk to him." Muffled voices.

Kitty came back on the line. "He says he's too tired to talk. I'll call you as soon as we get home."

Chloe hung up and stood waiting for her nerves to calm. Roarke was coming home. She hadn't lost him, too. A long-denied hope unfurled its soft petals within her heart. *Come soon, Roarke, please. I need to see you, to touch you and be comforted.*

"Why did you call Chloe?" Roarke growled.

Kitty stared at him. "Because she's one of your oldest friends and she's been concerned about you."

"You're matchmaking again and I won't have it." Roarke hunched up one shoulder. When Kitty had looked at his scarred face, her horrified expression had decided him. He knew what he had to do.

"I'm not matchmaking." Kitty flushed red. "I'm just trying to make you happy."

Make me happy? Roarke looked at his sister with disbelief. Words failed him. He closed his eyes.

"What is it, Roarke? I want to help." His sister led him to her jaunty roadster parked on the busy street.

You can't help me. No one can. He got in, refusing to look at Kitty. "Where are you driving me?"

"I thought we'd head home."

"No, take me to a hotel." He stared at the car's floor.

"Mother and Father wanted to come and pick you up, but you said you only wanted me. They're waiting for you at home." Kitty touched his frozen arm gingerly, as though it might be rigged to detonate. "I don't understand. Why didn't you want them to come with me? We've missed you terribly."

"They can come to New York to see me. Start the car. Let's get . . . somewhere." Pedestrians kept looking at them as they passed by the car. He propped his elbow on the car and pressed his hand to his scarred cheek.

"Roarke, you're not making sense."

He refused to look at her, ignored the plea in her tone. "I'm not going home . . . yet." He sensed Kitty struggling with herself, holding back questions. He didn't help her. Couldn't help her.

"If that's what you want, fine." She started the car and off they went, merging recklessly into traffic. "The Waldorf isn't far."

"No, take me somewhere we've never stayed or had lunch." He knew he was being obtuse, confusing to his sister. But how could he help her when he felt all mixed up and turned on end himself? They soon arrived at an unfamiliar hotel near Central Park. Roarke averted his eyes as Kitty checked them in to two adjoining rooms. But from the corner of his eye, Roarke caught the shocked stares of people walking through the elegant green-marble and polished cherry-wood lobby, and those of the desk clerk and the bellhop. His neck warmed with embarrassment.

At Kitty's side, he entered the elevator. The operator stared at Roarke's scarred face and his arm in a sling. Roarke resisted the urge to pull up his collar or lower his hat. He'd have to face this for the rest of his life, so he might as well get used to it. If only this was just about his stiff arm and the scars on his face . . . He shut his mind down, forcing himself to concentrate on the brass half circle that displayed the ascending numbers.

Chloe waited three days after Kitty's phone call, letting the McCaslins have Roarke all to themselves. When she couldn't wait any longer, she asked to be driven over to see him.

As the car pulled up to the front door of the McCaslin home, Chloe chewed her lower lip. What would it be like to see Roarke again? Should she have called ahead? She would have if she could have made herself complete the call. But she'd found herself suddenly reluctant to make contact. What had kept her lifting and then putting down the phone?

She was still in deep mourning; a knee-length black veil trimmed in black silk crepe hung in front of her. It made her world appear darker as the driver opened her door and she approached the silent house. She'd expected to see the cars of friends who'd be inside welcoming Roarke home. But the draperies were all drawn and no cars were parked in front. *Something's wrong.* She didn't even have a chance to touch the door bell before the McCaslin housekeeper flung open the door. "Honey, we don't know what to do."

"What's wrong, Maisie?"

"It's Mr. Roarke, Miss Chloe. He won't come home."

"He won't come home?" Chloe echoed, dumbfounded.

"The mister and missus gone up to New York City. He

stayin' at a hotel there. He tell his mamma and daddy he won't come home."

Chloe couldn't move, reeled with shock. "Why?"

"We don't know." The housekeeper was wringing her plump hands. "His parents are tryin' to get him to come home."

"Does he need extra care for his injuries? Maybe he needs to stay near the army doctors for extra treatment."

"I don't know 'bout that. But we're worried, Miss Chloe."

The breeze fluttered her black veil. She felt numb, empty. Then she realized—she'd been looking to Roarke to help her unearth the courage that had failed her, to help her start again. But he wasn't coming back to her. Just like Theran.

Gray, rainy late September was closing in on Chloe. Outside the window, the weathered black-eyed Susans were sodden and bent over. Turning away, she tried to think of something to do with the evening yawning before her. Upstairs, her mother was giving Bette, now over six months old, a bottle. Chloe trailed aimlessly from room to room, staring out windows at the dreary weather, straightening antimacassars and picking up lint. Over a year ago, she'd met Theran and run away and married him. All in vain. She was home now, but somehow her mother had usurped her role.

That thought gave her pause. *Why did I let this happen? Bette is my daughter and she should be my responsibility.*

Suddenly angry at her mother, Chloe stalked up the stairs to the nursery. When she got there, she took a breath and forced herself to walk calmly into the room. She was ready to confront her mother, but she was going to do it on her own terms. She opened her mouth to speak.

Her mother held a finger up to her lips. Chloe halted as Jerusha lifted the sleeping baby from her grandmother's arms and carried the child toward the antique crib that had been "updated" with an abundance of lace and pink satin. Chloe stepped in front of Jerusha. "Let me," she murmured. With painstaking care, Jerusha settled the baby into Chloe's arms.

"Now what are you doing that for?" her mother chided sharply. "I just got her asleep."

As though carrying delicate eggs on top of a feather, Chloe cradled the baby close. But as gentle as she was, Bette's little face screwed up and she began to wail. Deflated, Chloe held back her own tears. *Why does my own daughter cry whenever I take her?*

Her mother made a sound of irritation. Without a word, Chloe handed Jerusha the baby and escaped from the room.

At the foot of the staircase, her father was waiting. "Sugar, I want a word with you."

Chloe paused across from him. He looked unnaturally serious. "What is it?"

"I need you, honey." He took her hand.

Tears nearly burst from Chloe's eyes. *Someone needs me. But does it have to be Daddy?*

CHAPTER ELEVEN

*H*er father led her into his small den, a domain she'd previously only peered into but always avoided. She looked around at comfortable leather chairs, a mahogany desk, and a brick fireplace. Two lamps illumined the room done in navy and white. The effect was altogether welcoming, but the walls seemed to close in around her. Already occupying one of the commodious chairs facing the desk, was Jackson. He rose. "Miss Chloe."

Chloe's nerves tingled to life, warning her. Jackson wouldn't be here unless this was about politics.

"Have a seat, sugar." Her father waved her to the chair beside Jackson as he sat down behind his desk.

Chloe lowered herself onto its pillowy softness, her caution increasing.

"Chloe, you're a woman now." Her father leaned forward and folded his pudgy hands on his desktop blotter.

Chloe held her peace. What did her father want from her?

"It's time I treated you like an adult, not a little girl." Looking down, he appeared to be straightening the creases in his trousers.

She folded her hands primly, resisting her father's flattery. "What do you want, Daddy?"

He chuckled. "My girl's got all her wits about her. I told you that, Jackson."

Jackson nodded, his sallow face serious.

Chloe didn't respond. She focused on her hands in her lap. *Be on guard.*

"I have a job for you if you'll take it," her father said without preamble.

"A job?" Chloe ransacked her mind as to her father's motive. "What kind of job could I do?"

"You know I didn't win the election last November." He looked down again as though avoiding her eyes.

She nodded, analyzing her father's tone. He didn't sound angry or put upon, just matter of fact.

"Now another opportunity to serve my country has presented itself." His voice was low and neutral.

Jackson cleared his throat. "The Democratic Party is at low ebb, Chloe. President Wilson is fighting a strong Republican Congress and he needs help. This war has brought needs—expensive ones—to the fore, and Republicans hold the purse strings. And they don't want to loosen those strings. Our troops require things and the Republicans won't appropriate the money to get what's needed."

"I see." Chloe didn't completely, but she did grasp the bare meaning of what Jackson had said. "What is the party doing about that?"

"Our party needs someone to move things along." Her father made a motion with both hands as if pushing something forward. "I've been offered the chance to be a lobbyist in the US Congress."

"What's a lobbyist?" Chloe watched her father's eyes, looking for a hint of what he was pulling.

"A lobbyist talks to people, lays the groundwork for co-operation." He folded his hands in front of his lowest vest button, which strained against his paunch.

"A lot of politics happens behind the scene," Jackson explained. "Congressmen often have to deliver to their constituents projects that will bring jobs and money into their districts. But congressmen also have to keep the larger needs in mind. A lobbyist brings these sometimes opposing sides together so they can negotiate in private."

"Like what's happenin' here, Chloe, in our own county." Her father slid forward on his chair, making the leather creak. "You know times are hard. Farm prices are fallin' and at the same time the cost of things is risin'. Our croppers are going to have a hard time next spring what with the high price of seed and everythin' else. Francy has been glad to wet nurse your little girl 'cause her family needs the money."

"What do you want, Daddy?" Chloe resisted. *It can't be this simple.*

"I'm rentin' an apartment in D.C. at a good address. I'm goin' to start entertainin' people—influential people—there and try to lay the groundwork to do what I can to get what the troops need, what our people need."

"What do you want with me, Daddy?" she repeated, her distrust waning dangerously. This was her father. She couldn't trust him, could she?

"I need a hostess." He stood and walked to the mantel. "A lady. A woman with style who knows how to decorate the apartment and entertain the influential people who will be comin'. I need you, honey."

Chloe knew he was referring to the social elite, the ones called "cave dwellers" in Georgetown, the cream of Washington, D.C. society. And of course, she'd be acceptable to them with her mother's family background. But she shook her head and sat up straighter. Rain shushed against the windows. "But Mother—"

"Your mother has refused," Jackson put in.

"She's never been interested in helpin' me." Her father looked at her. "You know how she is. Only thinks about her own comfort. She's the grand lady. No one else counts."

Chloe looked at this man who was her father. His intent gaze was unusual. For once, he looked like . . . Like what? The usual glow of self-aggrandizement didn't light his eyes. But could she believe what she saw? She studied him and then turned to view Jackson. Both men appeared serious. "You say the Republicans aren't supporting our troops?"

"That's the Democratic Party's most pressing concern." Jackson leaned toward her on his elbow. "We can't send our men over there to risk their lives but refuse to give them the food, medical care, and weapons they need."

"I didn't know . . ." This was all so new, unexpected.

"Well, sugar, why should you?" her father asked, lifting one palm. "You've lost your husband. You got a baby who's sick and needs constant care. You been thinkin' about her. And I been watchin' you, not knowin' how to help you through this, how to give you somethin' else to think about. This would give you a chance to do somethin' good."

"But there are larger issues." Jackson rubbed his chin. "You could be serving your country as much as your husband did."

"I didn't know," she repeated, still distrustful. And who was she anyway? Since Theran's death, she'd failed at everything she'd tried. "I . . . what can I do?"

"Come to D.C. with me, sugar." Her father came to her and took her hand. "Take your place in Washington society. Help me smooth the way for the political deals that must be made to take care of our boys overseas and our people here at home. I need you. I really need you."

Chloe sat very still. Her father's voice was completely devoid of his usual coaxing, politician quality. For once in his life, he sounded sincere. His hand held hers, gentle yet firm. She frowned. Had her father changed? Could she trust him?

"I need to know your answer," he said.

"I need time to think," she stalled.

"Of course you do," Jackson replied quickly. "But we need to know soon."

Rising, Chloe nodded. Her father hurried ahead and opened the door for her. She walked into the hall, her mind reeling with new ideas. Maybe her father had been truly touched by her losing Theran. Maybe losing an election for the first time had made him reconsider what was really important.

As she reached the bottom of the stairs, she heard Bette starting to yowl. Chloe closed her eyes and clung to the railing. She knew she should hurry upstairs and take care of her child. But she also knew that her touch would only rouse her to greater fury. Somehow she hadn't been able to overcome her child's preference for her grandmother's touch. *Bette hates me. It can't be her fault. She's just a baby. It must be me.*

Somehow everything was Chloe's fault. She'd married Theran and he'd died. She'd had Theran's child and the child hated her. Roarke had gone to battle, been wounded. Though he'd not said anything to her before he'd left for war, she'd known he wasn't the kind of man whose feelings changed easily. Did he still love her? If so, why did he refuse to come home and tell her? Or was it that he had changed his mind and didn't want to hurt her? Chloe bent her forehead to the cool, carved railing and wept hot, painful tears. *It's all wrong. Everything's wrong and it's all my fault. It has to be.*

Washington, D.C., late 1918

*T*hough Theran had been gone for nearly a year, Chloe could not bring herself to put off mourning. After the first six months of her time of loss, she should have moved to white mourning; still she'd clung to her black veil. But now in D.C. she moved to white mourning. She wore a knee-length white chiffon veil with white silk crepe trim attached to her stylish new navy hat, which matched her suit. Today she had ventured out alone for the first time since she'd come to Washington to help her father. He was in a meeting at a restaurant near the Capitol, lobbying for better food for the troops. He'd told her that after what had happened to Theran he was making this his main effort.

Chloe emerged from her father's Cadillac and asked the chauffeur to wait for her. "I don't know how long I'll be," she said. The uniformed and gloved black man stood stiffly by the car. Disconcertingly, he reminded her of Frank Lawson. Minnie had written she was still dating Frank in New York City. Would this man even believe her if she told him she'd lived in Harlem? That she'd marched with the NAACP? Would he care? The life she'd lived those months in New York City felt long ago and far away.

She mounted the flight of steps of the immense stone house on Sixteenth Street called "Henderson's Castle" and then rang its bell. She smiled at the liveried Negro butler who opened wide the door.

"I'm here for the dancing," she murmured and handed him her ivory calling card.

He glanced at it. "Thank you, Mrs. Black. Mrs. Henderson hoped you would attend today."

A uniformed footman came forward and bowed for her to precede him. The house looked as if it had been decorated to imitate a nobleman's home, with oak-paneled walls, plush maroon carpet, and a crystal chandelier sparkling overhead. Chloe walked the long, carpeted hall, going over in her mind what she'd heard about these informal dances held every Monday afternoon by the widow of a famous Missouri senator. Mrs. Henderson was a powerful, influential force in D.C. society and politics. A lot of deals were struck in this house during parties and dinners.

Her father had arranged for Chloe to be invited today. She hoped she would make a good impression. He needed this contact and it was up to her to make good on it. It was a new feeling, a good feeling, to know her father needed her. And she was doing something for her country.

She stepped into the large, second-floor ballroom. A knot of men and women in afternoon dress milled around one end. In front of them a dainty white-haired woman sat on an imposing chair with her little feet on a step stool. She wore powder-blue bedroom slippers with pom-poms instead of shoes. The blue slippers went with the room's floor-to-ceiling royal blue draperies, which were partially opened, revealing a wall of French doors and a balcony beyond them.

Chloe walked across the expanse of polished maple to the lady. "Mrs. Henderson, ma'am." Chloe suppressed the sudden urge to curtsey to the queenlike woman.

"You're that young war widow from Maryland, aren't you?" the lady said, holding out her hand.

"Yes, ma'am." Chloe shook the small, wrinkled hand and stared into the petite woman's sparkling blue eyes. She couldn't think of a thing to say. Her nerves hopped and skipped.

"I'm so glad you've come." The lady smiled, unabashedly assessing Chloe.

This didn't upset Chloe. After all, she was used to being on display and she'd survived her own debut under the eyes of dragons just like Mrs. Henderson, hadn't she? She lifted her chin a bit. *Maybe I can do this.*

"I know you're still in mourning, Mrs. Black, but I think these informal dances make the formal occasions so much more enjoyable." The older woman gave an impish grin. "A lady learns from which partners she should accept an invitation to dance and which ones she should refuse—to save her toes."

Chloe still found she couldn't speak, but she smiled.

"And which category do I fall in, Mrs. Henderson?" A tall blond man stood opposite Chloe. He inclined his well-shaped head toward the older lady.

Mrs. Henderson patted the man's arm in a playful gesture. "Drake, you are most definitely a desirable partner."

He bowed in mock gratitude to the grande dame in bedroom slippers. "Would you introduce me to this lovely lady then?" He turned his eyes on Chloe. They were intense in spite of his lazy voice. She hoped her veil hid the faint blush he caused her.

"Of course. Mrs. Chloe Black, may I make you known to Mr. Drake Lovelady?"

Chloe looked startled at the man's name.

He grinned and took the gloved hand she'd offered him. "I know. My *interesting* name got me into a lot of trouble at school. But now I just enjoy the look ladies give me when we're introduced."

Chloe felt a deeper crimson blush stealing up her throat. Once more, she hoped her veil would hide it, but doubted it.

"That's enough, you scamp," Mrs. Henderson taunted. "Please," she called to the musicians at the end of the ballroom. They began to play a popular melody, "A Pretty Girl Is Like a Melody." With a nod of request, Drake led Chloe to the dance floor and without a word began dancing with her. After a few minutes, Chloe's blush faded away and she began to relax.

"That's better," Drake murmured. "You are too lovely a lady to doubt her ability to attract a man's attention."

"I'm not trying to attract any man's attention," Chloe said, suddenly bristling.

"You lost your husband in France?"

Chloe nodded, unappeased.

"You have my sincere sympathy." Then he fell silent, merely leading her expertly around the floor.

His tone had been perfectly sincere and respectful. In admission of this, Chloe relaxed again and began enjoying the dance. She glanced up at Drake's face. He was handsome, with slicked-back golden hair and sky-blue eyes. His attraction, however, emanated from his personality. He seemed to be a confident man who would be at ease in any situation.

"I've been refused for military service," he murmured.

She looked up, surprised. Did he think she would disdain him for this? "I'm glad."

He lifted an eyebrow.

"I mean," she stammered, "I hate this war." There—she'd placed her foot in it now. But she was tired of putting on a show. Everyone she met seemed to think she should glow with patriotic pride when she explained the reason for her widow's weeds. She couldn't have felt more differently.

"You must have loved your husband very much."

"I did." She looked away, unable to think why he'd said this. She took a misstep in the dance and Drake expertly drew her back into stride.

"Your father is new here."

"Yes, he lost the Senate election and has come to help our troops by lobbying for them."

Drake gave her an unreadable look. The music ended. He bowed. "You are a delightful partner, Mrs. Black. I hope you will grant me another dance today."

She smiled, a bit uncertain now that the dance had ended. She had no idea what she should do next. Why did her father think she could help him in this way? "Of course," she managed to say.

Then another man came forward and introduced himself. The next melody started and Chloe began to dance with her new partner. But her gaze flickered often to Drake's golden hair as he danced nearby, always within an arm's length of her. Was he staying close to her on purpose? The sensation of having a man admire her again stirred her blushes. And her guilt. She'd come to help her father help the troops, not to attract men. The connection between dancing with handsome men and helping the US troops seemed incongruent, silly. But then what did she know?

A week later, Chloe woke in her old bedroom at Ivy Manor just after dawn. In the dimness and silence, a child was crying. Chloe blinked. *It's my child.* But she didn't immediately rise. Her limbs seemed heavy and insensate, like logs.

For some reason, in that moment between dreaming and waking, Roarke's face floated before her sleepy eyes. She must have been dreaming of him, she realized. At that, her heart twisted painfully. *I can't think of that now.* She'd come home to make another last-ditch attempt at forging an attachment with her daughter. She turned on her side and made herself leave the warm nest. Her daughter needed her. Didn't she?

Tying her blue-satin wrapper around herself, Chloe lurched toward the nursery at the end of the hall. Her mother was already bending over the crib, crooning to Bette, "What's the matter, sweetheart? Is your tummy hurting you again?"

Chloe watched in helpless chagrin as her mother picked up Bette. Her daughter was almost nine months old now.

Chloe tried not to think of how few of those months she'd spent caring for her. She hung back in the shadows by the door, dreading the coming struggle. In the room lit with one shaded lamp, her mother carried the fretting child to the black-walnut Windsor rocking chair by the fireplace. She sat and began rocking her.

Chloe forced herself to approach her mother with a careful politeness. Her arms crinkled with gooseflesh at the early morning chill. Or was it fear? *It's now or never. I have to make this work. I have to claim my daughter once and for all.* "You should be getting your sleep. I'll do that, Mother."

Her mother grimaced. "Chloe, you'll just upset her more."

This response was all too familiar. Chloe kept her temper under tight control. "Bette has to get used to me sometime. I'm her mother." Still, Chloe felt more like a petulant child than a maternal figure. Something had to go right soon or what would be the point of trying?

Her mother huffed and shoved Bette into Chloe's arms. Bette instantly screamed her displeasure.

Chloe ignored the other woman's rudeness, though her nerves tightened like violin strings. She began crooning softly to her baby and pacing, her blue-satin slippers flapping on the maple floor. Her daughter twisted, almost forcing herself out of Chloe's arms, and shrieked louder. Chloe patted Bette's diaper-cushioned bottom and sang to her some half-remembered tune her Granny Raney had always hummed. Her daughter stiffened like an ironing board in her arms.

All the while in the background, her mother rocked the chair in a rapid tempo; with each downward dip, she tapped one angry toe on the floor, and each toe-tap and creak of the chair scolded Chloe. Was Bette responding to it, too? Chloe felt her heart beating like a fast train over uneven railroad tracks. *What am I doing wrong? Why can't I do this?*

Minutes passed. Bette finally calmed slightly, though she still mewled and her breath caught in sobs. Chloe tried to take a deep breath, but couldn't. Her lungs were tight with tension and hurt.

Jerusha slipped inside the nursery with a baby bottle in her hand. The black woman paused at seeing both Chloe and her mother there. "Here's her mornin' bottle."

Chloe held out her hand for it.

Jerusha, looking confused, halted on her way to Chloe's mother, looking back and forth between the two women.

"I'll give it to her," Chloe said, sounding stiff to her own ears. Jerusha handed her the warmed bottle and slipped away while Chloe lifted the rubber nipple to Bette's tiny mouth and nudged it against the closed lips. Rather than accept it, Bette stiffened and batted both hands at the bottle. Chloe hadn't been holding it tightly enough and the little hands knocked the bottle sideways. Chloe lost her grip on its slippery, wet sides and it flew against the wall, knocking the nipple off and sending milk flying.

"Chloe!" Her mother leaped up. "Jerusha!"

Bette squalled louder than ever and Chloe struggled to calm her. As Jerusha rushed in, saw the milk splattered on the wall and flowing over the floor, and ran out again, Chloe began to cry herself. *I can't do this!* she screamed to herself.

Suddenly Bette stiffened and then began to jerk. "What's wrong?" Chloe gasped.

"Convulsions, again!" her mother exclaimed, "Call the doctor!"

The next two hours were a bad dream. Bette's face turned blue and then white. Chloe watched helplessly as the doctor arrived and hovered over her daughter and Jerusha applied cold compresses to the baby's face. Finally Bette began breathing normally again.

Chloe sat down then in stunned horror. Seeing her confusion, Doctor Benning came over and took her hand. "Bette has these spells off and on. I don't know if it's epilepsy or not. And she might very well outgrow these seizures."

"She's had these before?" Chloe couldn't believe it.

"Didn't your mother tell you?" he asked.

"I didn't want to worry Chloe," her mother snapped. "She's had enough to deal with losing her husband. Besides, they always happen after the child's been upset, after Chloe's tried to disrupt the child's schedule."

In disbelief, Chloe looked at her mother, trying to divine the true meaning of these words. Was she saying it was Chloe's fault her daughter had these spells? Her mother averted her eyes.

"It's important that the child live in a calm household." The doctor's voice became stern. "This battle between you two over this child must end. Or the consequences for Bette could be severe." He stalked from the room.

Chloe stared at her mother and then over to Bette, who lay still shivering in Jerusha's arms. Chloe went over the facts: *My daughter needs quiet. I can't stand to watch my mother constantly remind me that my child prefers her. I have no money of my own. How can I take Bette away by myself?*

Her mother lifted Bette out of Chloe's arms. "You're always upsetting the child. And you're not needed. I'm the grandmother. I'm the one who should be taking care of this child."

The words were like poisoned darts and each one hit the bull's-eye. Dazed, Chloe walked from the room onto the landing. Distantly she heard the phone ringing downstairs, and Haines answering it. Blinded by impotent tears, she opened the door to her room, where she could hide from her child, from her mother, from everything.

"Miss Chloe, it's for you," Haines called up to her.

Wiping her eyes, she hurried down the steps. Who would be calling her at this early hour? For a moment, the hope that Roarke had come back to Maryland opened its petals. "Hello?"

"Chloe, sugar, I'm sorry to wake you."

It was her father. Chloe quelled the instant disappointment. Of course it wouldn't be Roarke. Where had that crazy idea come from?

"But I need you to come to D.C. today," her father went on. "Can you?"

The invitation whispered a reprieve. "Yes," she said without a second of thought. "Yes."

"Great." Her father sounded pleased. "I need you to plan an open house for the end of this week. Something's come up and I need my hostess. You're becomin' a real help to me, sugar."

"I'll be there as soon as I can, Daddy." Hanging up, she thought about the stylish apartment in D.C. she'd decorated, her father's work, the interesting people she'd met. She closed her eyes and then opened them. She mounted the stairs. Pausing to look downward, she said, "Haines, I'll be leaving for Washington after breakfast. Ask Jerusha to pack for me, please."

Haines nodded, staring at her with sad, serious eyes.

I should have known that nothing would ever be right after Theran's death. He was my one chance to be different and that chance died with him. What did a person do when everything that could go wrong did?

Would her daughter ever understand that she'd left her here to protect her, not reject her?

CHAPTER TWELVE

New York City, May 1921

The prospects for both disaster and humiliation this
evening held threatened to overwhelm Chloe. For the
first time since they'd parted at the end of 1917, she would see
Roarke. Would he still be her friend? More than a friend? Or
would he merely take the opportunity to reject her in person?

It was just after seven in the evening when she took a deep
breath and entered the tiny foyer of Kitty's apartment in the
Village. Kitty had passed the New York Bar and had been
practicing law for over a year. The young attorney had decorated her apartment in the latest style with sleek, ultra-modern
furnishings—a lot of gray and white. Several original cubist
oils hung on the walls.

Kitty squealed in welcome. She wore a crimson silk dress
in the popular Oriental style with a mandarin collar and cap
sleeves. The long, slim skirt was audaciously slit up both sides
to her knees. The scarlet dress was the perfect counterpoint to
the gray-and-white background.

In contrast, Chloe had chosen to wear a severe sleeveless
evening dress of ebony satin with a matching cape. Around

her short blonde hair, she wore a black bandeau spangled with jet beads. Long black gloves and daring high heels completed her ensemble. Dressing in the forefront of fashion had become Chloe's signature, her hobby. Now she let Kitty embrace her and hoped her nervousness didn't betray itself.

"It's about time you came back to the big city." Kitty shook a finger at Chloe. "I've called. I wrote you scads of letters. Why wouldn't you come?"

Chloe had expected this question and had practiced many plausible replies. But all of them deserted her now. "I don't know."

"Why did you move to D.C.?" With a quick movement, Kitty looked into the hall mirror, finger-combing the waves of her bobbed hair into place. With her little finger, she applied her lip rouge, the same red as her dress. "If you weren't going to stay at Ivy Manor, why not come back to New York?"

Chloe had no appetite for explaining her motives for leaving her home and her child in the care of her mother. "Kitty, you don't understand."

"Enlighten me." Kitty put down the rouge pot and turned to Chloe with hands propped at her slender waist.

Impossible. Chloe shook her head and changed the subject. "Tell me about Minnie."

"The divine Mimi's the most beautiful woman in the chorus line." Momentarily diverted, Kitty babbled on about the musical Chloe's former maid was currently involved with. As Kitty talked, something in her friend began to disturb Chloe. Kitty's trademark cheerfulness harbored a trace of . . . what? Frenzy? Volatility? For what reason? *Kitty, you have it all. What could make you unhappy?* But maybe it was just Chloe's imagination.

"I can't wait for you to see Minnie tonight. It's so exciting." Kitty danced a jazzy step and through the slits revealed pale silk stockings.

"Then what are we waiting for?" Chloe trembled with an exquisite premonition of disaster.

Kitty pouted as she donned long, transparent red gloves. "You just don't want to be alone with me, so I can make you tell me the truth about why you didn't move back here."

"I don't like to be late to the theater." Chloe shrugged and faced the hall mirror. She had known this trip to New York City would be a precarious venture. But she hadn't been able to refuse Minnie's invitation. Or resist a chance to see Roarke again—whatever the cost. She opened her purse and took out a round, eighteen-karat-gold compact and matching lipstick tube, a gift from her father for her trip to New York City and a characteristic but unnecessary reminder from him of why she should return to him. Her father never understood that she didn't care about money and what it could procure. He hadn't bought her, no matter what he thought. She powdered her nose and in an effort to overcome her own nervousness, focused again on her friend's agitated behavior. *What are you holding back from me, Kitty?*

"Why haven't you asked me about Roarke?" With arms crossed, Kitty stood behind Chloe.

"Let's go down and have the doorman hail us a taxi."

"You're not acting like yourself," Kitty muttered.

Chloe made no reply. Kitty was acting different, not she. But she knew if she asked Kitty what was wrong Kitty would evade a direct answer. So she ignored Kitty's comment and touched up her lip rouge and straightened her hair. Her reflection in the mirror showed a cool, well-dressed blonde—just the illusion Chloe wanted. She'd left off her mourning veil two years ago. Back now in New York City and dressed to the nines, she felt unusually vulnerable to life's careless cruelty. So much could be gained tonight. So much lost.

"You do look divine though." Kitty threw her arms wide. "All that pale skin against black satin. You'll be turning heads. Why don't men go for perky brunettes like me?"

Chloe turned toward the door. "I think you're very attractive, Kitty."

Kitty shrieked with laughter. "Only you would take me seriously. Let's go."

Kitty's unnerving giddiness made Chloe feel a hundred years older than her lifelong friend. She'd put off her widow's weeds, but she couldn't put off all the loss Theran's death had brought her. Maybe tonight she could start again. She'd braved New York City, the city where she'd married Theran, because Roarke would meet them sometime tonight. He'd promised Kitty and that promise was what had brought Chloe to the city. Something inside her felt as if this were her last chance to reach Roarke. And Roarke was the one who could help her find her feet again.

The taxi ride to the theater passed with Kitty's incessant chatter. Chloe provided monosyllable replies, heightening the contrast between them. Then they were there.

And Roarke met them at the entrance under the glaring marquee lights.

"Roarke, she came," Kitty crowed.

Chloe's pulse raced. After all this time she was finally seeing one of her dearest friends—one who had sacrificed his own feelings to help her when she most needed it. It had been too long. Amid the milling theatergoers, she devoured what she could see of Roarke's outline. Then he stepped out from the stark shadows.

Chloe took in a sharp breath. His face had been flayed across one cheek, as though gouged by a hand with razor-sharp nails, and left to heal that way. One eyebrow looked as if it had been raked with a garden tool. Its sparse hair stuck out every which way. And he looked grim.

"Roarke, it's so good to see you." She leaned forward and kissed his unscarred cheek. Then she wondered if she'd said and done the wrong thing. Her heart fluttered. It was good to see him, but not disfigured and so somber. She wanted to tell him that his scars didn't matter. She longed to sit close to him and hold one of his strong hands. Instead, she held out one of her own.

He nodded, but didn't take it. His stiff arm remained crooked under his evening coat. "Chloe, good to see you." However, he didn't really look at her and his voice was flat, so the sentiment rang hollow. In an instant Chloe's elation plummeted. She let her hand drop. "I'm glad you came, Roarke." *Please don't shut me out. I need you.* She tried to gauge his emotion, but his face remained shuttered.

"Well, *then*, escort us." Kitty took his normal elbow. "Go ahead, Chloe, take the man's arm." When he didn't offer his damaged arm to her, Chloe hesitated. "He's become more and more the strong, silent type and something of a recluse," Kitty went on breezily. "But not tonight. Not for your first visit to New York since . . . since . . ." Kitty suddenly became flustered.

"Since Theran died," Chloe supplied. Should she tell them that by now she could think of Theran without bursting into tears? A blank silence enveloped them. Shrill voices of women greeting each other and the street noise of auto engines and horns flowed around. Someone had to do something and now.

As if it were a delicate Fabergé egg, Chloe took Roarke's stiff elbow and hoped she wasn't hurting or embarrassing him. "It is good to see you again, Roarke," she repeated the polite phrase. Why hadn't finishing school prepared her for this situation?

"You look lovely, as usual, Chloe. How's your little girl?"

Chloe tried not to take this as a slap to her face. How would Roarke know that she ached always for her child? She still visited Ivy Manor every few weeks. Over the past few years Bette had grown into a quiet, sickly child who treated her like the stranger she was. "Fine," Chloe lied, "Bette's fine."

Looking at neither Kitty nor her nor anyone else, Roarke led them through the gilded lobby, crowded with chattering men and women in evening dress, and then up the red carpeted stairs to their box. Chloe willed away the hurt his question about her child had stirred up.

And she tried not to react negatively to the wooden, silent man beside her. She supposed he was self-conscious about his bent arm and scarred face. That was understandable, but why had he avoided his home and friends for over two years now? It couldn't just be because of these physical imperfections, could it? That just didn't feel right with Roarke. He wouldn't act that way. Someone had to do something, find out what the matter was and make it right. But could she?

She'd hoped that if she finally confronted Roarke tonight, at last the ice jam between them would crack and begin to break. Their friendship would pick up where it had left off. So far she felt no softening in him. But she didn't give up hope. *The evening's just begun. I won't surrender so easily. God, help me bridge the gap with Roarke. I just want him to talk to me, look at me.*

Roarke seated them in the box, urging them to sit in the two forward seats while he sat behind them, shielded by the red velvet curtains that draped on either side of the box. The orchestra began to play the jazz overture. The lively, syncopated music captured Chloe's attention and made her smile. Then the lavish, deep-red curtain swept open and the chorus line spread out in front of them, a glittering line of young very beautiful black women. They wore a rainbow of dyed ostrich feathers in their hair and beaded dresses. Chloe searched for and found Minnie—or should she say *Mimi*?

The musical play was a revelation to Chloe. She'd never seen an all-black cast before. How had it happened? She hummed along with "I'm Just Wild about Harry" and then "Love Will Find a Way." In no time the play ended and the audience rose in a standing ovation. Applause and shouts of *"Bravo!"* ricocheted off the high walls and ceiling. Chloe clapped with the rest, her gloves muffling her applause. For the space of a few hours, she'd forgotten everything but the dancing and singing on the stage below. She turned to Roarke and beamed. "Wasn't it wonderful?"

The poignant expression of longing on Roarke's face caught her by surprise. "Roarke?" She took a step toward him and reached out a hand. She was stunned when he stumbled backward and her hand fell short of his. His expression spoke of revulsion. She pulled back as if he'd cursed her.

"Let's go backstage," Kitty crowed heedlessly, "Minnie gave me passes."

Chloe let Kitty lead them out of the box and through the crowded aisles to the wings. Only rigid self-control kept her from tears. Though Chloe felt Roarke's resistance, she claimed the crook of his frozen elbow, trying to come up with some way to break through the man's repelling silence.

"I went backstage last time, too," Kitty enthused. "It's exciting to see all the costumes and everyone talking and giggling. After the performance, everything's funny, like everyone's tipsy or something." *How can Kitty rattle on so? Doesn't she see her brother's sadness right under her nose?*

Laughter, chatter, and squeals of delight bounced off the unadorned walls of the area backstage. Chloe felt like an intruder amid the colorful scene of sparkling costumes and stage makeup. Why had the Negro actors blacked their faces? She wanted to ask someone, but felt too awkward.

Then she caught sight of Minnie. "Chloe!" the other woman shrieked, "Chloe!" Her old friend, still in sequined costume, wrapped her long, tan arms around Chloe, hugging her close and weeping. "I've missed you so," she whispered into Chloe's ear.

Chloe wiped sudden tears from her own eyes. "You were wonderful. The show was great. I can't tell you how happy I am for you."

"I'd never have gotten here without you," Minnie whispered.

"Yes, you would have." Chloe squeezed her friend close once more with pride. At least Minnie had made good their escape from Ivy Manor.

"See those men over there." Minnie pointed to the right. "That's Eubie Blake and Noble Sisson. They wrote the play. Mr. Blake is from Maryland, too—Baltimore." Then Minnie looked up at Roarke. "Mr. McCaslin, sir, so glad to see you, too." She offered him her hand and he shook it.

"My pleasure, Minnie. You've done very well for yourself."

Minnie beamed at him. "I hear you're making lots of money on Wall Street."

"For other people, unfortunately," Kitty put in. "He's so good at being a broker and I don't have a penny to invest."

Frank Dawson appeared at Minnie's elbow. "I recognize this lady." He took Chloe's gloved hand and kissed it. "My compliments, Chloe. You are lovely as ever."

"It's good to see you again, Frank," Chloe replied, wondering if he and Minnie were still an item.

Roarke stared hard at Frank, but the black man only lifted an eyebrow. "As soon as Minnie changes, we're off to a blind tiger in Harlem. Would you like to join us?" Frank invited.

"What's a blind tiger?" Chloe asked.

"Blind tiger is another name for a speakeasy," Roarke replied with disapproval. "I think Chloe is fatigued from her journey—"

"This is a nightclub in Harlem," Minnie urged. "Come on, Chloe, you'll enjoy it."

"Roarke, I'm fine. Please, let's go." Impulsively, Chloe clung to his arm, not ready to admit defeat. *We just need some more time together. That's all.* "I'm too keyed up to go back to the hotel." There was a pause while everyone looked at Roarke.

"Very well," Roarke said with grudging grace.

Kitty heaved an audible sigh of relief. Chloe's own relief was less evident but equally as strong.

Within minutes Minnie had changed into a breathtaking, spangled emerald-green gown and Roarke was hailing them a cab. The five of them squeezed inside. Roarke and Frank perched on the drop seats, their backs to the cabbie.

While Kitty kept up the flow of conversation, Minnie covered Chloe's hand with hers on the seat. Chloe squeezed Minnie's hand in return. Hope blossomed again. Minnie had achieved her goal. Chloe would find a way to reclaim Roarke as her friend. *I must.* "I'm so happy for you, Minnie," Chloe murmured again.

"It's like a dream come true. And it all started that day Mr. Crowe picked you out of that crowded employment agency."

"I remember." But the events felt as though they'd happened to someone else not her. "I was sad to hear Madame Blanche went back to Paris."

"Me, too. But working for her made all the difference for me. Are you happy in D.C. with your daddy?"

Noting that Minnie had successfully rid herself of her accent, Chloe nodded. "For once, Daddy was honest with me. I think losing that election opened his eyes to what was really important. He helped the Democrats get what the troops needed and now he's working on making sure our boys come back to good jobs. I act as his hostess."

"I see."

Minnie didn't sound convinced, but their exchange ended with their arrival in Harlem. As the taxi sped on, Chloe caught a glimpse of Mrs. Rascombe's house and a wave of nostalgia swept through her like an ache, a need. She wished she could walk inside and sit down with her old landlady.

Minnie must have guessed her thoughts. "Mrs. Rascombe passed away during the flu epidemic in 1918. I went to her funeral. I meant to write to you."

Chloe blinked away tears, filled with sudden sadness, a sense of loss. "She was a good woman. Good to me."

The taxi pulled up in front of a drugstore. Roarke extended his good arm and Chloe took his hand and emerged from the cab. She looked around for their destination and was surprised when Frank led them into the tiny drugstore and to the rear and around the corner to a door. With a grin at Chloe's confusion, Frank tapped an "SOS" on it and it swung open.

Chloe let herself be ushered inside. Again, people in evening dress—both white and black—milled around. Loud voices and louder jazz hit her like a physical force. As they were taken to a table, many people greeted Minnie as "Mimi."

Chloe tried to take it all in—the raised voices, the boisterous music, the scents of food, the shrill laughter. It was too much of everything.

When they slid into a large corner booth, she leaned over to whisper into Roarke's ear, "Let's not stay long. I'd like to go somewhere quiet where we can talk."

Roarke acted as if he hadn't heard her.

She leaned closer. "Roarke, I've missed you. Can't we spend a few moments alone this evening?"

He didn't reply. He turned to Kitty and said, "I'm tired. Can you see Chloe home?"

Kitty gripped his bent arm. "Roarke, don't you dare leave—"

"I thought it was you."

Chloe instantly recognized the voice. Shocked, she looked up as Drake Lovelady stepped close to their booth. "Drake? What . . . I didn't expect to see you here."

Drake chuckled. "I called earlier today and your father told me you were coming up to see a musical and that an old friend of yours was in the cast. I decided I'd come up and see if I could spot you at the theater. I did and followed you here."

"Chloe, are you going to introduce me to this handsome man?" Kitty demanded archly, leaning her cheek on her hand and batting her eyes outrageously.

Chloe felt Roarke's body stiffen beside her. She glanced around the table, her gaze lingering on Roarke. "Drake Lovelady, these are my longtime friends." She made the introductions and everyone squeezed together in the large corner booth to make room for him beside Chloe. There was no way Roarke could leave now; the thought made Chloe glad.

As her friends eyed her speculatively, Chloe felt herself blushing with more than mere embarrassment. She didn't have a *tendre* for Drake and she'd never expected him to pursue her like this. She wanted to say to Roarke, "We're just friends." But saying that presumed Roarke would care that she had no romantic feelings for Drake.

The band started a lively melody for the newest dance, "The Charleston." Drake took Chloe's hand and drew her to her feet. "Let's show these New Yorkers how this is done."

Chloe glanced back at Roarke, but he was looking pointedly the other way. She allowed Drake to sweep her onto the crowded dance floor, where they began stepping to the lively tune. Drake had taught her and the others at Mrs. Henderson's informal dances just a month ago. Mrs. Henderson had been shocked at the wild movements of the dance, but had permitted it, saying it unfortunately suited the times.

Forcing herself not to keep glancing back at Roarke, Chloe counted the beats and kept her hands and feet moving wide and free. She had to lift her slim skirt a few inches to do this. Drake grinned at her and then pulled her close, cheek to cheek. Frank and Minnie danced nearby and called out to Chloe and Drake. A stranger had claimed Kitty and she waved happily at Chloe, dancing enthusiastically with a flirtatious expression. It was so "Kitty" that Chloe laughed out loud in spite of herself. The combination of the dance and the high-stepping tune were irresistible. Her spirits rose, in spite of her concerns about Roarke. She wouldn't give up. Sometime tonight she'd steal a moment alone with him. With that determination, she gave herself up to the moment.

But when the Charleston ended and the three couples, flushed and exhilarated, returned to the table, it was empty. Roarke had deserted her. Chloe felt her happiness drain away, leaving her shaken and wilting. There could only be one explanation. Roarke wasn't just abashed because of his bent arm and scars. It was obvious he couldn't stand to be near her.

Drake gripped her arm. "Your friend left us?"

Chloe nodded automatically as a door inside her heart slammed shut.

"I would never behave so foolishly," Drake murmured in her ear, "if you looked at me the way you looked at him."

Chloe couldn't speak. What had she done to send Roarke away? Why did he despise her? And, more important, how did Drake's comment make her feel?

Drake nudged her back into the booth, sat beside her, and lifted her hand to his lips. Frozen in a pain she couldn't name, she made no move to pull her hand away. Drake smiled at her. "Did I tell you how beautiful you are tonight?"

She glanced into his blue eyes. "No."

"Well, you are and I'm going to enjoy being the envy of every man here tonight."

She looked down at her lap, his fulsome compliment embarrassing her.

"You're so sweet, so innocent." He chuckled low in his throat. "*I* won't disappear on you, Chloe Black."

She merely shook her head and tried to look knowing and worldly like Kitty, but knew she'd failed. Her last chance to regain Roarke had failed, too. And it hadn't been only about regaining Roarke. She'd just lost herself.

Monday morning after he'd attended the theater with Chloe and Kitty on Saturday, Roarke strode through the crowded sidewalk of Wall Street. He entered the tall brick building where he'd worked for the past few years and rode up the packed elevator. He looked neither right nor left but kept his eyes on the changing numbers above the door. He'd learned not to look at strangers. If he didn't, then he didn't have to suffer their shocked stares or answer their stupid, prying questions.

The sympathetic look on Chloe's face when she'd seen his scars Friday evening would haunt him long enough without adding to it. But deep inside him, he carried a worse scar—the knowledge of his own failure. He was almost thankful for his ravaged face and stiff arm. People could attribute his refusal to go home after the war to that alone. And it gave him an excuse to shun casual socializing here. His scars made everything easier.

With his customary nod, he walked past the middle-aged receptionist at the entry to his company's well-appointed office.

"Mr. McCaslin," the receptionist called to him over the heads of other arriving brokers and staff. "Mr. Ward wants to see you immediately."

Ignoring the ripple of interest this announcement caused, Roarke nodded. He changed directions, heading toward the plush corner office. Ward's pretty young secretary, a stylish college graduate, rose and opened the door behind her, announcing him.

Ward, a graying but well-preserved senior partner, stood up and offered Roarke his hand. They shook perfunctorily and Roarke backed into the chair in front of Ward's very neat and highly polished cherry wood desk.

"McCaslin, I wanted to make it clear to you how impressed we are with your ability to bring in new clients and carry such a heavy work load."

Roarke murmured an appreciative comment. But his nerves tightened. He didn't want anyone's praise. His work numbed his mind and gave him a reason to get up every morning. That was enough for him.

"Today, you have an office of your own." With a stagy

smile, Ward indicated a brass key on the desktop. "You'll have your own stenographer also. You can choose whomever you wish from our steno pool."

Roarke made himself smile and tried to look gratified. He wondered what Ward would say if he told him the truth—that all Roarke cared about was doing a job that kept his mind busy. An office of his own and a secretary held almost no interest for him. On the contrary, he vaguely resented them. "Thank you, sir." He said the expected words. "I'll try to live up to your confidence in me."

"We were happy to hire you after you returned from the warfront, happy to show our support for a veteran," Ward continued. "But you have proved a wise addition to this brokerage firm. We hope you'll stay with us."

"I have no plans to go anywhere at this time." *I don't have the energy and I could care less where I work.*

"Good. Good." Ward rubbed his hands together. "Then you might as well go see your new office and drop down to the steno pool and take your pick of the stenographers."

Roarke stood, shook hands again, and received the key. It was so cool and small for something that brought such an increase in prestige. He paused by Ward's secretary and asked directions to his office. Ignoring the mild interest from a few of the other young brokers, he walked down the length of the blue-carpeted hallway and then unlocked the oak door near the other end. There was a small entry area next to his office with a small, gray metal desk, which had a typewriter and phone on it.

He walked through a door at the far left and entered his office proper. It was comprised of a small, freshly cleaned window, an oak desk and file cabinet, phone, ticker-tape machine, and a leather office chair and a matching chair for clients on the other side of the desk. The floor was carpeted in gray and the walls had been painted white. A few landscape paintings adorned the office. He settled in his leather chair and tried to feel something beyond what he usually felt upon coming to work. He didn't and gave it up.

He walked back down the hall to the plump, widowed receptionist. "Mrs. Grimes, I'm supposed to choose a stenographer from the pool for myself."

"Yes, sir, that's what I've been told." She eyed him as if trying to read his purpose for mentioning this.

"I don't know anything about choosing a stenographer." *And I don't want to know.* "Do you know the pool well enough to recommend someone to me?"

The woman pursed her lips. "What were you looking for in a secretary?"

"Someone who is good at her job," he answered without hesitation. *Also someone who won't flirt with me or want to heal me with the purity of her love.* He'd learned to read the evidences of that crusading emotion in women's expressions—a moistening around the eyes or a simpering manner. And he avoided every woman who tried it on him. But for Mrs. Grimes, he translated this into something polite, saying, "She must have a serious demeanor."

"I can think of a few girls who fit those requirements," Mrs. Grimes said, still eyeing him.

"Good," he said, already turning away. "Send them up this morning and I'll interview them quickly and make my choice. I don't have much time to waste on this. I have customers to meet with before I go to the Exchange."

"I'll get the ball rolling right away, Mr. McCaslin." She reached for her phone. "I'll send them to you one at a time."

He thanked her and went back to his office. He found that someone had already moved boxes of his records and papers to the new office for him. He went through restoring order to his client files and setting up his desk to suit him.

The outer door opened and a woman cleared her throat. "Mr. McCaslin?"

He glanced up and saw the look he hated most. "Thank you, but you won't do."

The young woman opened and closed her mouth once, twice, and then turned and exited.

Roarke went on with his arranging things. Within minutes, another young lady stood before him, clutching a steno pad to her chest. He looked at her face. He read the way she sized him up and the look of determination in her eyes and her firm chin. "Your name, please?"

"I'm Talbot, sir. Miss Edna Talbot. I take dictation at 118 words a minute and I type at eighty-three words a minute. Those are averages, you understand."

He assessed her. She was dressed neatly and with propriety. Her dark skirt fell far below her knees and she didn't look at him as if her love alone could save him. Edna Talbot looked . . . ambitious. Or driven to obtain his approval. She didn't want to redeem him. Clearly, she wanted him to elevate her from the steno pool.

That motivation he could understand and appreciate. "I'll give you a try. Make yourself comfortable out in your office and then come back and I'll run you through my list of clients and my immediate plans and strategies to make them a lot of money."

"Yes, sir." Talbot nearly saluted him.

This brought a rare grin to his face. He chuckled silently. Ambition was better than salvation as far as he was concerned. Especially since he belonged among the ranks of the damned.

*   *   *

An enormous wave of warm relief had deluged Chloe when she entered her father's apartment in D.C. on Monday morning, two days after seeing Roarke. Guilt followed the relief, but the relief won. No one here would reject her. No one here knew she was a failure as a mother. And her father needed her.

He'd left her a note on the dining room table. She read it and sat down immediately with the cook at one end of the expanse of polished mahogany table to draw up a menu for an open house for the wives of Democratic congressmen. After she'd thoroughly discussed finger sandwiches, *petit fours*, and buying a new and larger coffee urn, the phone rang.

Chloe stepped out to the hallway and answered it herself. They didn't have a butler in the apartment, just a cook and a maid. "Hello, this is the Kimball residence. Chloe Black speaking."

"Mrs. Black, this is Mrs. Meyer Hughes. Mrs. Henderson recommended I call you and invite you to join our group."

"What group is that, Mrs. Hughes?" Chloe tried to think if she'd met this lady, but couldn't bring a face to match the name.

"We are a group of civic-minded women who perform various charitable tasks in this city. We were wondering if you'd be interested in helping with a fund drive for the orphanage here. We hear that you are a war widow and the orphanage has been inundated by orphans of soldiers whose mothers have died or who can't support them. I'm afraid the flu epidemic of '18 alone took a terrible toll in the lives of many children, robbing them of their remaining parent."

Tears rushed to Chloe's eyes. The war had robbed her of her life, the independent life she'd tried to claim. At least she was an adult and hadn't ended up in an orphanage. But should she tell the woman that she wasn't good with children? She fidgeted with the telephone cord. No, of course not. After all, she wouldn't be asked to care for children, just raise funds for them, and the woman would tell her how to do that. "Yes, I'd be honored to help in any way I can."

"Wonderful. Do you have plans for Thursday afternoon?"

"No, nothing at this time. I've just returned from a jaunt to New York City."

"Then I'll pick you up on my way to the orphanage. Let's say around one that afternoon?"

"I'll be ready."

On Thursday morning, Roarke stepped out of the elevator, nodded to the receptionist, and walked into his new office.

Dressed in an unobtrusive navy suit, Miss Talbot was already there at her desk, answering her phone. "Mr. Roarke has just stepped in, Mrs. Creighton. He'll pick up momentarily."

Roarke liked the way Talbot had come early every day and the way she talked to clients as if he already had a corner office and she were presiding over her own roomy office instead of the postage-stamp area she occupied at present.

With a nod, he strode to his desk, shed his trench coat on the coat rack, and picked up the phone. Suddenly, as if a delayed reaction, he felt a spurt of satisfaction. He squelched it. This job wasn't about being successful; it was about having something to do every day. It was about having enough money to live completely free of the entanglements of family and friends. It was about survival, just as it had been on the front.

He listened with half an ear to Mrs. Creighton's "feeling" that a certain oil company's stock would explode soon and her query whether he should buy some for her.

Miss Talbot appeared in the partition, holding her steno pad like a shield. Today there was a new look in her eye that Roarke couldn't decipher. He could identify cloying sympathy and revulsion with practiced ease. But this was a more complex expression. With deliberation, he decided it was another form of ambition—Miss Talbot was sizing him up as a possible husband. Well, no harm in that. She'd learn soon enough he wasn't interested in marriage to anyone.

On Thursday afternoon, Chloe walked into the Washington Orphanage, which occupied a large, two-story house in a sad neighborhood. Though the entrance and foyer of the building were spotless, the orphanage smelled of urine and strong disinfectant. Miss Jones, a middle-aged spinster wearing an outmoded black dress, greeted them with a tense smile. "So happy you ladies made time for a visit today. Some of the children are waiting to greet you in our dining room." She led them toward the rear of the building.

Chloe heard a child crying somewhere above them. Her nerves tightened at this cue.

"Our infants and toddlers are on the second floor," Miss Jones explained, nodding toward the staircase.

Chloe felt the same panic she experienced when dealing with her daughter. But they weren't going to the second floor. Miss Jones had said so.

"I'd like you to give Mrs. Black a quick once-over tour today if you would," Mrs. Hughes said. "She's new to our work and needs a quick education on your orphan's home."

"Of course." The orphan director changed directions. And Chloe found herself being led up to the second floor. She wanted to decline, but she couldn't; in this social situation, she had to follow the ladies. She'd just have to keep her distance from the children. They'd already been orphaned. They didn't need her upsetting them.

At the top of the stairs, the other two ladies preceded her into a communal nursery. Little ones lay in cribs and bassinets in the crowded room. Toddlers staggered around the unadorned wooden floor, grabbing hold of crib legs as they tried to walk. Two older matrons dressed in drab gray uniforms rocked babies while keeping an eye on the unsteady toddlers. The little ones of both sexes all wore the same clothing — shapeless, unironed and stained cotton dresses.

Chloe hung back near the entrance. The dingy room excited her sympathy but she was terrified of the children's reaction toward her.

"Come in, Mrs. Black," Mrs. Hughes encouraged.

Chloe took a few hesitant steps into the room. Three toddlers headed toward her in their jerky, uneven gaits. She took a step backward. But one, a little boy with black hair, ran faster and caught her around the knees. He squealed with triumph. Chloe couldn't describe what she felt. *He came straight to me.*

Within seconds, the other two, both little girls, had joined him, clinging to her skirt. Chloe felt them swaying, their balance uncertain. One of the matrons hurried forward. "I'm so sorry. Are they wrinkling your dress?"

Chloe looked down at the three happy little faces beaming up at her and shook her head. As if in a dream, she stroked the silken, baby-fine hair of each one in turn. "No, they're all right." *More than all right.* "What is this little boy's name?"

"Jamie. Our little Jamie."

The toddler looked up and squealed with obvious pleasure at hearing his name.

"Hi, Jamie," Chloe murmured.

The child tightened his hold on her. Didn't he know she

wasn't good with children? *Or maybe only my daughter hates me.* Unable to contain herself, she burst into embarrassing tears.

Within moments, Mrs. Jones had settled Chloe with Jamie on her lap into one of the commodious wooden rockers. Chloe had babbled some incoherent explanation the orphanage director seemingly ignored. She and Mrs. Hughes had then left to follow the planned program. But Chloe had stayed behind, rocking Jamie, letting him cuddle close to her, fingering his black hair and whispering soft words to him. Finally, the little one had fallen asleep in her arms and Chloe had reluctantly relinquished him to one of the matrons.

Now Chloe walked down the stairs to the main floor. Mrs. Jones was waiting for her at the bottom. "Thank you, Mrs. Black. That was a lovely thing you did. I know you're a busy lady, but we can always make use of someone who likes to rock and mother our little waifs."

Chloe didn't know what to say.

"Would you like to visit us? We always need volunteers."

Before she could stop herself she replied. "Yes." *Yes!* Her failure with her own child would always sting. But the satisfaction she'd felt holding Jamie had poured over her heart like warm oil over irritated skin, soothing and easing her loss.

"Late afternoons are best," Miss Jones continued. "Our staff welcome breaks then."

"I'll come back." Chloe blinked away tears. Why couldn't holding Bette be easy, like holding Jamie?

"How about Monday?" Mrs. Jones invited.

"Yes." Chloe looked around. "Where's Mrs. Hughes?"

"She had to leave with regret, but I believe . . ." Mrs. Jones motioned toward the entrance.

Drake Lovelady stood outside in the late afternoon sun.

Shaking her head in surprise, Chloe walked out to greet him. "Drake, how did you know?"

He swept off his hat. "Your estimable maid told me where you were and I just happened to be going this way and thought you might be glad to see me."

She took a deep breath. "I am."

He answered with a slow grin. "May I squire you home, then?"

"Please."

He walked her to his shiny black Cadillac and drove her away. As he inquired about her day, she wondered if Drake Lovelady liked children, and then wondered why she should care. Unbidden, a song from Minnie's musical played in her mind, "Love Will Find a Way." But after all was said and done, it was just a song.

Wasn't it?

Part Two

CHAPTER THIRTEEN

Washington, D.C., March 1929

At the Washington Auditorium, the well-known orchestra played on and on. Chloe moved in time with a youngish tuxedo-clad senator from California. Nearby Drake danced with a well-padded matron, the wife of a Supreme Court judge. Chloe wore her signature color in evening wear—ebony. Her French gown was cut slim and beaded with black jet. For the occasion, Drake had given her long, art deco platinum-and-diamond earrings that dangled from her ears. Her father had scolded her for accepting such an expensive gift from a bachelor. But she'd only laughed at him. Drake had money to burn and she liked the earrings.

Chloe's head felt fuzzy, although not with alcohol; nothing could be drier than the charity ball in honor of Herbert Hoover's inauguration. Rather, her thoughts were focused on earlier that day. She'd spent the afternoon at the orphanage as she'd done twice a week for the past few years. If she could have chosen, she'd have preferred spending this evening rocking the toddlers and soothing them before they went to bed. She shut her mind to memories of small hands clasping hers and the feel of a child in her arms who wanted to be there. Ten-year-old Jamie was too old to be rocked now. But when at the orphanage, she always spent after-school time with him.

The waltz ended and the next dance—the Charleston—began. Drake claimed her and she accepted without demur. Overhead, the glittering chandeliers almost hypnotized her as she unconsciously went through the motions of the dance. Jamie's face kept coming to mind, the way he always looked crestfallen when she had to leave. He'd never asked, but his expression always asked, "Please take me home." What was she going to do about Jamie?

Finally, the dance ended and she took Drake's arm, feeling suddenly desperate without knowing why or how to stop it. "I need air."

"I need more than that," Drake murmured into her ear, his breath fanning the hair over it. "Let's get out of here." She nodded. "Meet you a block away." Drake didn't wait for her answer, but was already heading toward the exit, shaking hands and smiling his way out of the room. At social functions, she and Drake rarely arrived or left together. She wondered if their ploy fooled anyone. She hoped so; she didn't want any gossip about their having an affair. Because they weren't having one. *What are we having?* Chloe shook away her thoughts. Thinking didn't help. It only made a person sad. Better to keep busy and amused. Drake could be very amusing.

She claimed her fur wrap and sauntered into the chilly night. Strolling down the crowded street, she glimpsed Drake's sleek Lincoln at the corner and approached it. He hopped out, swept her inside, and they were off.

"You should be flattered," he murmured.

"By what?" She watched the city lights flicker by.

"By being invited to the Republican charity ball, of course."

She laughed on cue. "You know you arranged it. The invitation to me was to please you."

"A man has to protect himself from an evening without at least one good dance partner." He flicked his fingers through the hair over her ear, teasing her.

She shook her head and laughed again, though she felt no real amusement. Drake had connections. Any man who gave as much as he did to the Republican Party would. She pushed politics away as she enjoyed the feeling of being swept away from duty in such a dashing car. She didn't ask where they were going. She knew. Within minutes, Drake knocked at a discreet dark-green garden apartment door. A panel slid open.

"Hot mama," Drake muttered the password.

"That's Jake." The panel shut and the door opened.

Chloe passed through first with Drake at her heels. Raucous laughter filled her ears. Tony's speakeasy was the most popular in D.C. and catered to the Washington elite. Sauntering languidly, very aware of the way Drake and she looked together, Chloe nodded at someone at almost every table.

"Mostly Democrats here tonight," Drake pointed out.

"The few of us that are left," Chloe quipped. Harding-Coolidge prosperity had lured most Americans to the rival party. Hoover had won easily over Al Smith.

Drake seated her at the small table they'd been led to and signaled to the waiter. "A whiskey and soda for me and club soda with a twist of lime for the lady." The formally attired waiter nodded and went off to the bar.

"When are you going to drop being Carry Nation's daughter?" Drake shot his cuffs and leaned his elbows on the crisp, white-clothed table. Tony's tried and succeeded in appearing to be a successful dinner club.

"I stopped carrying my hatchet, didn't you notice? It clashed with my gown." Chloe hadn't picked up the cocktail habit that had risen with Prohibition. Somehow Bette and the Eighteenth Amendment had stopped her mother from drinking. But her mother's former overindulgence with alcohol made Chloe wary. Then, too, just because this was a speakeasy that catered to a high-class clientele didn't mean the liquor could be trusted one hundred percent. She knew of two men who'd gone blind from wood alcohol, colored to look like Scotch, at another exclusive D.C. speakeasy.

Their drinks arrived. Chloe was stirring her swizzle stick in the bubbling soda when a woman in a very short, very tight, fringed red dress with many strings of beads bouncing around her low neckline stumbled over to their table. "Drake, honey. You didn't call me." The woman slid onto Drake's lap with a high giggle.

He smiled, but Chloe noted chagrin in his narrowed eyes. "I think you've had a few too many, Marvel."

The woman gurgled. "Haven't we all? Except for the chaste and dry Miss Chloe."

Chloe couldn't stop herself from speaking in frosty disdain. "Have we been introduced?"

Marvel shrilled with laughter. "No, but everyone knows you or about you! Your father's Quentin Kimball and your mother's a Carlyle of Maryland. You don't drink. You don't smoke. And you don't—"

"That's enough," Drake snapped. He stood up, dragging Marvel up with him; her red fringe splaying across the white front of his shirt. "You're becoming a dead bore." He marched the woman back to the disgruntled-looking escort she'd abandoned.

Marvel tried to resist Drake, but couldn't. Still, she glared back toward Chloe. "She's a case of neurotic inhibition all right," Marvel squealed. "Freud would have a heyday with her." She laughed shrilly, drawing even more attention to them.

Drake's face turned brick red and his mouth twisted downward. For a moment, Chloe feared he would slap the woman. "You're making a scene, Marvel," he said in a tight voice, "and I hate scenes. Now be a good girl and sit down."

"Hey," the other man objected, "Marvel can do better than hang around with you, and she's got a right to say what she thinks. I ought to darken your headlights, bud."

Tony, the small, olive-skinned proprietor, appeared at Drake's elbow. "Is there a problem?" Tony's ex-boxer bouncer, looking like an ape in his formal attire, lurked in the background.

"No, I think these two were just leaving." Drake looked pointedly at Marvel's date.

The stranger took the hint, but without grace. Grumbling, he grabbed Marvel's arm and stomped out the door.

Drake returned to Chloe. "I apologize for that." He sat down across from her again. "Marvel doesn't carry her liquor well."

Chloe felt embarrassed for and scornful of Marvel at the same time. The woman should have known Drake wouldn't tolerate such a déclassé scene. But then Drake was still somewhat a mystery to her as well.

"Why do you stick with me, Drake?" Chloe couldn't stop the question from slipping out. It had been going around in her mind for years now. Ever since they'd met at Henderson's Castle in 1919, Drake had hovered at her side. The one time three years ago when he'd asked her to go away with him for a weekend, she'd declined. She'd expected him to drop her then, but he hadn't. "Why, Drake? Please tell me."

"Haven't you guessed . . . yet?" He sipped his cocktail.

So he had an agenda for her. What? "Tell me."

He stared at her and without his usual savoir faire. "I intend to marry you."

Of all the replies he could have given, she'd never expected this one. Shock shimmered through her, but she replied without hesitation, "I'm never going to marry again."

"Especially a Republican?" he asked with a rueful grin, obviously not taking her at her word. Drake's suave mask had snapped back into place.

He couldn't have spoken in earnest. His arch comment hurt her. "You're not being serious." *I never thought you'd make fun of me, Drake.*

"Oh, but I am completely serious. I decided to marry you years ago."

She knew from gossip that Drake usually acted the rake. So why did he always play the gentleman with her? She decided to take a chance, ask for the truth. "Did you decide that when I refused to go away with you to Martha's Vineyard?"

"Before that. I didn't expect you to accept my invitation." He swirled the amber liquid in his short glass.

"Then why did you ask?"

"Just to make sure I was right," he said lightly. But then he took her hand and his expression became serious. "I need a wife I can trust. A wife who will give me an heir that I can be sure is really mine. A wife who will make me the envy of other men."

"You don't want much, do you?" She made her voice light and teasing, but her heart throbbed in her ears. She'd hoped Drake was her one friend. Not once in their years together had she ever felt any other attachment to him. *How do I get out of this?* She drew her hand from his.

"I'm making you nervous, aren't I?" he asked with a repentant smile.

She looked away. The Negro jazz trio that played each evening was gathering in the corner. "Me?" She shook her head and smiled falsely. "I don't have a nerve in my body."

"'Ask me no questions, I'll tell you no lies,'" Drake said.

Chloe couldn't decide if he were mocking her or himself. She sipped her cold club soda. The trio began playing, "The Man I Love." Setting down his drink, Drake offered her his hand. She rose and he led her to the small dance floor. She let him draw her close and move her effortlessly around to the music of the fox trot. His embrace wasn't seductive or suggestive. He never tried to kiss her while they danced. He just seemed to enjoy dancing with her. Drake Lovelady had become such an integral part of her life that Chloe had ceased to wonder why he was there. Could he really want to marry her? Did his reasons make any sense?

The song ended and they sat down. The police commissioner waved to them from the next table and several Democratic congressmen nodded from farther on. She saw their speculative glances and wondered how many people watching them here tonight expected her to marry Drake. *I'll never marry again.* She was absolutely sure of this, but didn't know why.

Just then her father and a pretty young redhead in a flashy green dress entered the speakeasy. He settled the woman at a table distant from them. Chloe knew why he did this. He didn't want to introduce her to one of his many women.

Then he came over to shake hands with Drake and pinch her cheek. "Chloe, tomorrow mornin' you talk to Jackson. He's set up somethin' for you to do in the afternoon. It's a public relations outin' featuring the wives of Democratic congressmen. I want you to go along and get into any photos the press take. They always put you front and center 'cause you're the prettiest Democrat in town." He chuckled.

Chloe nodded, keeping her eyes from shifting toward her father's date, who looked much younger than Chloe. Once again she tried to put her father's philandering out of her mind. Why should she mind? Her mother evidently didn't.

He turned to go. "Oh, I just heard from your mother."

Chloe looked up, foolish hope zinging to life. "Yes?"

"She called tonight to tell you Bette just got over the measles."

"Measles?" Foolish hope died instantly—to be told news about her daughter secondhand by her father! Hot shame flooded Chloe.

"Your mother said she didn't want to worry you," he explained, "so she waited till the crisis passed."

Chloe nodded woodenly. She'd seen her daughter a month ago at her child's eleventh birthday party. Bette had stuck close to her grandmother and stared at the ground every time Chloe addressed her. The worst of it was that it reminded Chloe of the way she'd behaved as a child around her absent mother. She'd been raised by her grandmother and Minnie's. Mrs. McCaslin long ago had called it the Carlyle tradition. But it was more like a curse. Would every generation see trouble between mother and daughter? Would there never be peace?

Her father went back to his date. Drake asked Chloe to dance again and she rose with a smile. She could lose herself in music and laughter, couldn't she?

"Don't be sad," Drake murmured. "We're doing the best we can. Even Solomon said it: 'Eat, drink and be merry for tomorrow we die.'"

Chloe chuckled, as she was supposed to. "Why not?"

* * *

About one in the morning, Drake drove Chloe home. She'd begged off from going to another speakeasy that included a casino. She couldn't bear another dose of fun tonight.

Drake handed back her key after he'd unlocked the front door and then drew her gloved hand to his lips. "Good night, princess."

She didn't like his nickname for her, but she merely nodded and walked inside. She shut the door and locked it. Drake's unexpected proposal had destroyed her peace. Was she frightened at the thought of marrying again or of the idea that she might marry Drake not from any feeling of love but rather because he'd finally worn down her resolve?

The phone in the hallway rang. The sound sent waves of fear through Chloe. Who would be calling at this hour? Had Bette had a relapse or complications with measles? Chloe jerked the phone to her ear. "Yes?"

"Chloe, is that you?"

Roarke McCaslin's voice rushed over the phone line to her, clear and unmistakable. The unlooked for voice set off a gale of sensations and weakened her knees. She leaned against the wall. "Roarke?"

"It's Kitty. Chloe, she's in critical condition."

"What's wrong?" Chloe had trouble drawing breath.

"Bad booze. The doctors don't know what . . . what the outcome will be. She told me not to call our parents, but she wants you, Chloe. She told me to call you."

"Where are you?" Chloe's hands shook as she pulled the note pad and pen to her on the hall table.

"A private hospital in upper Manhattan." He gave her the name and address.

"I'll leave right away."

"I don't know what you can do for her."

"I can be there." She hung up. For a moment, she held her

face in her hands. This couldn't be happening, not to Kitty. Kitty had continued her law career in New York City. Chloe had lunched with her whenever she shopped on Fifth Avenue. But their lives had become so different and Kitty had seemed progressively . . . unhappy, dissatisfied under her almost frantic gaiety. Every meeting had depressed Chloe. Now this.

In the end, Chloe had her chauffeur drive her to New York. It took the rest of the dark hours and into the next day. He delivered her to the hospital in mid-morning. Once there she sent him away to reserve a room for her at the new Benjamin Hotel and told him to drive home after doing that. She'd use public transport in the city. He tried to remonstrate that her father wouldn't like that, but she ignored him and went through the entrance. The hospital was small and smelled, as all hospitals did, of formaldehyde and Lysol and other odors Chloe couldn't distinguish and didn't want to. With the help of an aide, she found Kitty's room . . . and Roarke. He sat in a chair by the bed. His face looked flattened, as if all hope had been lost.

Fear like a specter rose in her. Was Kitty going to die? Roarke's name was all Chloe could say. At the sound he stood up and stared at her. The sight of him gazing at her coursed through her like warmed wine. She couldn't move, could barely breathe. Over five years had passed since she'd seen Roarke's face. Chloe quashed the urge to throw her arms around him. His expression was easy to read. *He doesn't want me here. Don't embarrass him or myself.*

"Chloe," he murmured.

To escape his relentless gaze, she looked to the bed. Kitty lay very still, her eyes shut. Her skin was sallow and her face looked puffy, unnatural. "How is she?"

Roarke visibly pulled himself together. "Not good. The doctors think she got some wood alcohol in a cocktail some-place. They think it's damaged her liver. That's why her skin's turned yellow and she's holding fluid."

This can't be happening. "What are they doing for her?" Tears crowded her throat. She pushed them down.

"There's not too much they can do." Each stark word obviously cost him. Roarke slumped back into his chair and lowered his head into his hands. He looked like he wanted to lie down and die.

She resisted the urge to kneel beside him and smooth back his tousled hair.

"They're giving her a diuretic, trying to get the bloating and toxins out of her system and they've catheterized her to move this along."

Chloe approached the bed and took Kitty's flaccid hand. "Is she . . . asleep?" She couldn't bring herself to say the word *coma*.

"She's weak. She comes and goes."

Kitty's eyes fluttered open. Her mouth tried to form a word. Chloe reached for the bedside table where a metal pitcher of water and a glass with a straw stood ready. She poured a small amount of water. Before she could do it her-self, Roarke was up opposite her, lifting Kitty's head. Chloe slid one hand into Kitty's hair. Her hand brushed Roarke's. Sparks darted through her hand and up her arm. She concentrated on the task at hand. She gently nudged Kitty's lips with the straw. "Take a sip, Kitty. Then you'll be able to talk."

Kitty obeyed and drank one, two shallow swallows. Then she leaned back against Roarke's arm, looking up into Chloe's eyes. "You came."

Chloe clutched the glass with both hands then. "As soon as I could get here."

"Glad." Kitty looked as if saying those few words exhausted her. Roarke lowered his sister's head. She rolled it against the pillow, restless, pained. "Roarke here . . . alone."

"I'm here now." Before she dropped it, Chloe put the glass down on the bedside table. "I won't leave until you're well enough to go home."

"Might not go home. So weak." Kitty shut her eyes.

Chloe felt electric shocks flash through her. *Kitty, you can't die. You can't leave me . . . us.*

Roarke and Chloe's eyes met and held. "Chloe, I . . ." He faltered and turned. Chloe looked away.

A slim, young doctor followed by an older, stout nurse walked into the room. "I'm just making rounds. Has she been conscious at all?"

Roarke turned to him. "She just spoke a moment ago."

"Good. Her heart's strong. That's a plus. But her liver has suffered damage. The good thing about livers however is that they can right themselves if given time."

"How long . . . When will we know?" Chloe ventured.

"I honestly don't know, madam. She's young and strong and that may be enough to counteract the damage done to her liver. But we'll just have to wait and see."

Chloe wanted to shake a better answer out of him. But she refrained from asking anything more. This wasn't his fault. The doctor and nurse left them, already discussing the next patient. "How long have you been here?" Chloe glanced at Roarke and then away.

"All night."

"Do you want to go home for a while? Take a shower, eat breakfast?" They both kept looking at Kitty. Were they fearful of what their eyes might find or reveal if they dared look at each other?

"No, I can't leave."

She didn't press him. But they weren't speaking like people who had been parted for years. Unlike that night at the theater, their time apart now melted away as a vapor. Did Roarke even remember abandoning her to Drake that night in Harlem? Probably it had meant nothing to him. After that, he'd never called and she'd never had the nerve to call him. "I can't leave either."

He stretched his arms over his head. "But a cup of coffee might help. Will you stay with her while I get one and call my office? I'll try to bring you back one, too."

"Sure. That would be good."

Roarke left, promising to return soon.

Within minutes, Minnie walked into Kitty's hospital room. Feeling as if she were in a dream, Chloe stood. Minnie hugged her tightly. "Chloe, you look prettier than ever," she murmured, appearing loathe to look at Kitty.

"And vice versa." It had been nearly six months since she'd met Minnie for coffee in the Village. Chloe gazed at Minnie with new eyes. Today, her old friend looked the picture of success—marcelled hair, fur coat, a designer dress in royal blue, scarlet lipstick, and expensive perfume. Minnie had become everything she'd wanted. For one awful second, Chloe wanted to claw her old friend's eyes out. She doused the flash of virulent envy. What she'd done with her own failed life wasn't Minnie's fault.

Minnie drew the other chair in the room nearer to Chloe's and sat down. "This is tough."

Chloe tried to get her mind to settle down. After many years of sporadic and casual contact, Kitty and Minnie, as well as Roarke, had come together now that one of their lives hung in the balance. She knew she'd been the one to distance herself from Minnie and Kitty. But Roarke had caused it. "Did Roarke call you?"

"No, I called Kitty's office and her secretary told me."

"Why did you call her office?" Chloe sat down on the edge of her chair.

"Because if you recall, she's my lawyer, silly." Minnie finally glanced at Kitty.

"Sorry." Chloe realized they were both speaking softly, as if at a wake. She swallowed down the fear.

Minnie shrugged. "Kitty was supposed to go over a new contract along with my agent."

Somehow it was both wonderful and dreadful to be reminded that Minnie needed an agent and a lawyer. *Of the two of us, Minnie, you did best. I'm glad for you.* But envy over Minnie getting what she wanted while Chloe hadn't still pinched. Maybe that explained the infrequent, brief meetings over the years.

"Kitty always takes too many risks." Minnie sounded grim.

Chloe didn't quite know what risks Minnie meant. Once before Minnie had mentioned that Kitty went too far and too fast with men. But Chloe didn't want to bring that up now. She bowed her head. "I feel so helpless."

Minnie nodded, clutching her black purse with black-gloved hands. "This year would have been your twelfth wedding anniversary."

If anyone else had said this, Chloe would have been resentful. But she understood; her wedding anniversary had been Minnie's day of emancipation as well as hers. Minnie and she had been innocents together long ago. An impression from their past flickered inside Chloe. Once more she heard Minnie giggling beside her in the darkened bedroom upstairs at Mrs. Rascombe's so many years ago. "I remember."

"Me, too. What I still can't believe is that you ended up

in Washington with your father. You've never told me why."
Minnie looked straight into her eyes.

Minnie's question floored Chloe. She wasn't prepared for this level of honesty, not for speaking the truth out loud. It had been too long since Chloe had done that with anyone. She shook her head. "Minnie, I . . ." She shrugged and looked at Kitty.

As if on cue, Kitty opened her eyes and whispered, "Minnie, I thought I heard your voice."

Minnie reached over and took Kitty's hand and teased, "What are you doing here, Kitty? I know you like handsome doctors, but couldn't you think of an easier way to meet some new ones?"

Kitty chuckled weakly. "I do have a cute one. I'm going to get well and then he better watch out."

Suddenly, Chloe couldn't stand the little room any longer. Kitty and Minnie were still in each other's lives, while Chloe was not. "I'm going for a little walk, now that Minnie's here," she excused herself and walked out of the room without a backward glance.

Minnie knew her too well, that was the problem. She'd finally asked point blank why Chloe had ended up in Washington with her father. Chloe had gone there ostensibly to help the troops. But the war had been over for years now. She'd told herself that she stayed so her daughter wouldn't be the center of her grandparent's war. But the real answer was she'd had nowhere else to go. For a few seconds when Minnie had come in, Chloe had felt the old call to her former self, that naïve child who'd run away to marry a dashing soldier and the innocent who'd become a model on Fifth Avenue. But it had waned almost immediately. Minnie and Kitty had gotten what they'd wanted. She hadn't. *Our lives are what they are. I'll be thirty next year. It's too late for me.*

*　*　*

Toward the end of the day, a young woman entered Kitty's room. Roarke rose. "Miss Talbot."

Chloe and Roarke had been sitting in total silence most of the afternoon. Each moment that passed had brought back the gap between them. Now Chloe looked up from the bedside chair. She found Miss Talbot studying her from under a very severe brown-felt hat. There was something repelling in the other woman's perusal of her and Chloe lifted one eyebrow.

"Chloe, this is Miss Edna Talbot, my secretary," Roarke made the introduction. "Edna, this is . . . Kitty's good friend, Mrs. Chloe Black."

Chloe only nodded. She didn't like Miss Edna Talbot. She'd heard of taking an instant dislike to someone, but it had never happened to her before. Why now?

"A pleasure, Mrs. Black," Miss Talbot said, not sounding pleased at all. Then she turned to Roarke. "I had some papers that needed your signature and couldn't wait indefinitely."

"Sorry you had to make the trip here." Roarke took the papers from her.

"Mr. Ward said he hopes your sister will be well soon."

"Which means he doesn't want me to take off any more time."

"Roarke," Chloe said, "I'm not leaving New York until Kitty's better." It was uncomfortable being alone with Roarke and trying to act as if it didn't bother her. "Why don't I sit with her during your work hours and then you come in the evenings?"

"No, I don't want to leave her."

"Roarke, the doctor said this will take time." Chloe leaned toward him. She'd say anything for a reprieve from Roarke's brooding silence, from Miss Talbot's disapproving stare. "I'll call you at the office if anything develops. It's not that far, only a short taxi ride."

Roarke stared at her, his face showing his struggle. "You're probably right."

"I'm here to help. Let me," she pleaded.

Roarke visibly pulled himself together and nodded. "Okay. Edna, let's go back to the office and see what we can do in the final hours of the office day." He waved the secretary out before him. Just as she passed through the door, Miss Talbot looked back at Chloe. Again, she was sizing up Chloe and this time Chloe recognized the expression. Edna Talbot was assessing Chloe as a rival—a rival for Roarke. At this absurdity, Chloe didn't know whether to laugh or cry.

That evening, Chloe walked through the door of her room at the Benjamin. She kicked off her shoes and began unbuttoning her dress. She just wanted to take a bath, wash off all the bad odors from the hospital, and then order room service. But first she paused at the bedside phone. Within minutes she'd arranged a call to D.C. to her father's house. The maid answered.

"Hello, Mavis. Is my father there?"

"Yes, ma'am, here he is."

"Chloe, how's the McCaslin girl?" her father boomed.

"Not good at all. She's all puffy and yellow."

"The doc's sure it's from bad booze?"

"I'm afraid so. He suspects liver damage."

"That's awful, sugar. I always liked Kitty."

Chloe didn't appreciate his tone. He spoke of Kitty as if it were a foregone conclusion that she would die.

"You got a call this afternoon, honey, from the orphanage."

"Oh, no." Chloe sank onto the bed. "Oh, no. It was Jamie's birthday and I forgot to call and tell them I'd been called out of town."

"The maid told them where you were and Miss Jones said not to worry, just visit when you returned. She said Jamie was askin' for you. Sugar, do you think it's right to keep so . . . close with an orphan?"

She'd had this conversation with her father before. Contrary to what he always said—that he didn't want her hurt when someone adopted Jamie—she knew he was afraid she might want to adopt the boy. Her father didn't want "someone's brat" as an heir.

"Don't worry about me," Chloe said automatically, glancing at the bedside clock. It was only a little after seven. "Daddy, would you please ask Jackson to check my appointment book and call everyone I was supposed to meet with this week and give them my regrets?"

"Already done. Stay as long as you need to, honey. But remember I count on you. I need you here."

She ignored this statement. She wondered at times if her father really needed her. But wasn't it too late now to go over this? She'd been in D.C. over a decade.

She shook herself back to the present. "Thank Jackson for me." She knew her father wanted to talk longer, but she cut him off. "I'm so tired and hungry. I'll call you soon. Bye."

She dialed the operator again and put through a call to the orphanage. After a brief exchange with Miss Jones and a long wait, Jamie's uncertain voice came over the line. "Mrs. Black?" His voice sounded small and sad.

"Jamie, yes, it's me. I'm so sorry I didn't get to come today. I'll make it up to you, I promise."

"Miss Jones says your friend is sick."

"Yes, she is, dear, and I have to stay with her and help her get better."

"Are you coming back?" Again fear etched each word.

"Yes, as soon as I can, dear."

Silence.

"You believe me, don't you, Jamie? It can't be helped."

"I know. I just miss you."

"I miss you, too." Chloe felt her throat closing up.

"Miss Jones says this call is costing you lots of money and I should hang up."

"Good night, Jamie. I'll see you soon."

"Bye."

Chloe put the receiver back in the cradle and wrapped her arms around herself. Why did she feel closer to an orphan child than her own daughter?

The phone in her hotel room rang in the dark hours of the morning. Chloe groped for the receiver and pulled it to her ear. "Yes?"

"Chloe, come back to the hospital." Roarke's voice sounded hoarse with emotion. "The security guard will be watching for you and let you in. Use the main entrance."

"What's wrong?"

"The doctor thinks Kitty might not . . . not make it through the night. I know she'd want to speak to you . . . if she gains consciousness again."

"I'll come right away."

When Chloe reached the hospital, the cabbie walked her through the darkness to the dimly lit entrance. A uniformed guard unlocked the door for her and she slid inside.

"Walk quietly, miss," the guard said.

Chloe couldn't reply. But she made herself take soft steps

on the polished linoleum, not letting her heels click. The hospital felt like a huge, dangerous beast, fast asleep, that she mustn't wake, mustn't anger, mustn't let loose on Kitty.

Chloe paused outside Kitty's door and looked in at Roarke sitting beside his sister's bed. A thought, a sudden wave like a hurricane tide, swept through her. Though he sat within feet of her, she'd lost Roarke in the war. Tonight she might lose Kitty. But she might regain Roarke—if she dared. *No, impossible.* She stood rooted to the spot, confused yet emboldened. "I'm here."

Roarke stood up, bumping the chair.

She walked over to him, not keeping the bed between them as she had earlier. "Roarke." She halted in front of him.

He appeared to pull inward, away from her. Did he sense her yearning to reach him, reach for him?

"What are we going to do without her?" Chloe spoke the words her heart pounded with.

"Don't say that," he muttered. "I can't lose her."

Like you lost yourself? Lost me? "Roarke, why do you . . . Why have you . . ." She pressed her lips together. Would it work? Here, tonight, could she get him to break down the wall he'd erected between him and everyone, especially her?

CHAPTER FOURTEEN

"Why can't we talk like we used to?" It wasn't exactly what she'd wanted to say, caught as she was between opposing impulses. She was afraid to reveal all that her pounding heart was clamoring to voice. At the same time, if she didn't speak now once and for all, she was terrified of losing Roarke forever.

Roarke gave an impatient toss to his head. "All that was years ago. It doesn't matter now."

Doesn't matter? "But it does. I lost you somehow." Long-denied truth gushed from her lips. "Why won't you let me in, or Kitty or anyone?"

He turned and gave her his profile. "This isn't the time or place to talk of the past."

"When will it be the right time and place?" She kept her urgent voice low, not wanting to be overheard by the nurses down the hall. Roarke stood only inches from her, as rigid as the Statue of Liberty. But this was Roarke, who'd always been so sensitive and kind to her. If she rested her cheek on his shoulder, would he fold her into his arm?

"There's nothing to discuss." His sharp words shoved her away. "You married Theran. You lost him and were changed.

I went to war. I came back different. Kitty is the only one the war didn't change, haven't you realized that by now?"

"Yes, I have realized that." Chloe drew closer to him, unable to stop herself. "That's why I can't bear to lose her. She's the only one who links me to the woman I was with Theran." Tears started in Chloe's eyes. She willed them away. "You changed. I changed. Why does that mean we can't be friends like we were?"

"I'm your friend, always will be," he said stiffly.

"How can that be when you won't talk to me?" She closed the inches between them. "Roarke, you're the one who knew me best."

He stood his ground, looking down at her. "You've changed. You said it yourself. You went to Washington with your daddy. You're not the Chloe I helped to run away to marry Theran."

She hated that he said these awful words aloud. *No.* "That's not true. Down deep I'm the same."

"How deep down?" he sneered. "I don't see it in you at all. We can't get it back, Chloe, or go back to where we were. We can't become young and innocent again."

"What has that to do with being able to talk to each other?" She touched his shoulder, and then flattered her palm against him, hungry for contact.

He shrugged off her hand. "I don't want to talk. That's the difference."

His dismissal stung. "Why?" Impetuously, she moved forward against him. His distinctive scent, so well remembered, was all around her. *Fold me in your arms, Roarke. I need you.* He moved back an inch or two. Desperate, fearless, she moved toward him once more, resting her head on his chest. *Don't pull away again, Roarke. Please.* "None of this makes sense."

"Don't you realize that's the normal state of affairs?" He plunged one hand behind her and grasped the back of her head. His fingers threaded in her hair, pulling her face upward to look into his. She shivered at his touch, even though it possessed a dangerous edge. Still, she pressed herself against him closer.

His eyes met hers. "You became your father's society hostess. I became a stock broker on Wall Street. Is that what we wanted in 1917?"

She shook her head. But fascinated by him, she ignored his words. With one finger, she traced his jaw line and then his lower lip. She felt him go rigid.

"So what do we have to talk about? Do you want to tell me about your steady boyfriend Drake Lovelady?" His harsh voice sawed into her. "I read the society columns, you know. Quite the dashing couple, you two."

"Stop it." Every word he spoke ripped her raw. She jerked away from him. *Don't speak to me this way, Roarke. This isn't you. It can't be.*

"Or are you tired of your affair with him—"

Chloe slapped Roarke's face. Her palm hit the deep grooves in his flesh and she recoiled, horrified at herself. Her breath came in gasps as if she'd just run the length of Manhattan.

Roarke flushed but said nothing.

"What?" Kitty moaned, opening her eyes.

Chloe looked down. "Kitty, it's me, Chloe." She dropped to her knees and took Kitty's hand. "Don't leave us." Chloe's voice shook. "I can't bear it."

Kitty fought for breath. "Not leaving you. Not leaving . . ." She lapsed into unconsciousness again.

Chloe pressed her forehead to Kitty's limp hand. "Don't give in, Kitty." *I'll die somehow if I lose you, too.*

A white-capped nurse entered, forcing Chloe to recall appearances. She rose unsteady, tears washing away her rouge and powder. What did it all matter?

Roarke stood motionless behind her. The fight went out of Chloe. She could do nothing but pray. She'd lost Theran, her daughter, Roarke. *Not Kitty, Lord. Don't take Kitty.*

The nurse finished checking Kitty and left.

"I'm sorry, Chloe." Roarke's voice was soft, hoarse. "I didn't mean to speak . . . harshly."

"I'm sorry, too." She made her way to the chair on the other side of the bed and collapsed onto it. "I guess I said things I shouldn't have." She felt nauseated. She'd gambled one last time and gone broke.

"They call us the Lost Generation," Roarke said with a sarcastic edge to his voice. He turned away and looked out the darkened window. He pressed his hands against the window frame like a man trapped in a cell. "We're not the only two who lost ourselves in the war."

"That doesn't help." She'd never again have the nerve to confront Roarke like this. It was truly over. Chloe's frustrated mind brought up the proprietary look in Miss Edna Talbot's face. Chloe wanted to use it in some way to slash Roarke, to pay him back for his snide remark about Drake. She resisted the urge. Only Kitty mattered now. Not lost love or lost hope. Just survival.

On the Maryland shore, late August 1929

S unshine shimmered on the white sand and blue ocean. Chloe stared out to the open sea as gulls squawked overhead and down the beach. Kitty and Jamie were with her.

Something was nagging at her mind, had been nagging for some time, as if she'd forgotten to do some task. The restless sensation had grown stronger day by day. What did it mean? Was it having Kitty with her? Or was it having Jamie finally, after all the years, staying under the same roof as she?

This morning, Kitty waded nearby at the edge of the surf, now and then picking up shells and washing them in the water. Jamie shadowed her and Chloe trailed them both. Chloe had buried herself under a wide-brimmed straw hat tied securely to her head with a vivid green-silk scarf. The wind played with its ends. She wore a pale-green cotton summer dress. Her only concession to the beach were her bare hands and feet.

Kitty, on the other hand, wore a royal blue bathing suit with a thin, red-striped cotton shirt covering her shoulders so she wouldn't burn. Sporting a peeling, sunburned nose, Jamie wore black swimming trunks and a white knit-cotton shirt. Nearly eleven, he was at that awkward age—all legs and arms—waiting to fill out. His head bent, he picked up shells and showed them to Kitty. Chloe felt like the grandmother along for the vacation with her daughter and grandson. But merely the sight of Kitty alive and walking on the white sand filled Chloe's cup. Her friend had kept her promise and hadn't left her.

Upon Kitty's release from the hospital, Chloe had insisted that she come home to D.C. with her. When summer had made the city unbearable, they'd escaped to the seaside together. They'd decided to bring Jamie along. In only a few visits to the orphan's home with Chloe, Kitty had fallen in love with the boy. Chloe felt shamed that she had never brought him before. But then she'd never been able to bring Bette. Mother didn't like the beach—too sandy. Still, Kitty's health had remained delicate and her spirits low. And Kitty had received several phone calls from a man. But she hadn't revealed who he was or why she became moody or weepy after each call.

"Look, Chloe." Kitty pointed downward "Another starfish."

Chloe nodded. Then she noticed farther up the beach a familiar blond man approaching them. She waved to him. "Drake!"

Drake had rented a nearby cottage, forgoing his own place on Martha's Vineyard. Since the night Kitty nearly died, when Chloe had failed to reconnect with Roarke, Chloe had given up being aloof with Drake. She wasn't going to have the life she'd wanted, she'd realized, so what was wrong with marrying Drake? Even if she didn't love him, he was a good friend and companion. *I could do a lot worse.* Still, she kept this to herself, not completely sure of her feelings.

"Come down to my place," he invited as soon as he was within calling distance. "Some friends have stopped for lunch. Come as you are. This is the beach, after all." Chloe nodded and started toward him.

"Do we have to have lunch with him again?" Kitty grumbled.

"Why not?" Chloe paused in front of her friend. "It will be an excellent lunch in amusing company."

"I don't know what you see in the man," Kitty muttered. "He's too Republican for me."

Chloe merely shrugged. For some reason, Kitty and Drake mixed like oil and water. She wondered if part of Kitty's reticence toward Drake had something to do with her mysterious male friend. *Who is the man who calls you, Kitty?*

Jamie looked back and forth between the two of them, troubled. Chloe smoothed back his wind-ruffled black hair and smiled into his serious face. "Miss Kitty and I aren't arguing. Don't worry."

The boy still looked concerned, but he nodded. Then he looked to Kitty as if for direction. Chloe pressed down the jealousy of being supplanted in Jamie's heart by Kitty. That was being small. It was just that when Jamie was with her, she didn't feel quite so unhappy. Did he do the same for Kitty?

Jamie was nearly the same age as her daughter and he hadn't been adopted and probably wouldn't be. She'd made sure he had what he needed so far and as he got older, she'd see to his education. But she wasn't even an adequate mother to her own child. Why harm Jamie by adopting him? Bringing him into her family wouldn't be doing him any favor.

Shaking off the sadness that thinking always brought, she started off toward Drake, who waited ahead for them. Kitty grumbled indistinctly for a few more moments but followed along with Jamie dogging her heels.

Drake kissed Chloe's cheek and also ruffled Jamie's hair. "Hey, kid, find any sand dollars?"

"No, sir." Jamie looked down shyly.

"Well, then we'll have to find you a substitute." Drake reached into his pocket and handed Jamie a silver dollar.

Jamie's mouth rounded. Holding out his sand-dusted hand, he showed it to Chloe. "Wow! A whole silver dollar."

Chloe chuckled. "You must thank Mr. Drake."

"A whole dollar." Jamie's large gray eyes widened. "Thank you, Mr. Drake. Thanks!" He turned to show the coin to Kitty.

"Buying more influence or just impressing Chloe?" Kitty taunted Drake.

Drake acted as if he hadn't heard her and took Chloe's arm, walking her toward his cottage and its wide screened-in seaside porch. "You always dress just as you ought, and beautifully."

"Oh, yes," Kitty piped up from the rear, "Chloe's always had style. She always looks good on the outside."

Chloe couldn't think why Kitty suddenly sounded bitter. Was it only because of Drake, or her own private troubles? "Thank you, Kitty," she replied as blandly as she could, not wanting to upset Jamie with any more verbal sparring.

"And I apologize for not taking note of your charms, Miss Kitty," Drake mocked her without a backward glance. "You've always been the quintessential perky brunette and a type much admired, I believe."

"Perky was attractive when I was twenty-five," Kitty said bitterly, "but will it still be when I'm thirty, next year?"

"Kitty," Chloe said with a forced laugh, "such strange things come out of your mouth sometimes." *What's wrong, Kitty?*

"Chloe, *you've* already fulfilled your primary purpose in life," Kitty retorted. "You've given your mother a grandchild. My mother called last night to ask me *once more* when I was going to *get married* and start giving *her* grandchildren."

Kitty's words sparked Chloe's irritation, but she merely passed it off. If Kitty only knew . . . Chloe stared up at the cloudless blue sky. "Why didn't you tell her that that was Roarke's job?" Little pins stuck into Chloe's heart at her own comment, and Edna Talbot's determined face flashed in her mind.

"I did, but it didn't do me any good."

Drake chuckled. "Lots of men like perky brunettes, Kitty. Why don't you snag one and make your mother happy?"

"I don't intend to marry. And no one intends to marry me."

Chloe tried to think of what could possibly have brought out this declaration. She glanced back at Kitty, trying to read her face.

Gleeful shouts of welcome interrupted their conversation, announcing Drake's visitors had made themselves comfortable on the porch. Furnished with white wicker and green-and-white-striped cushions and a large jute rug on the white narrow planked floor, it was picture perfect for the beach. The two well-dressed couples ensconced there already had cocktails in their hands. Through the introductions, Chloe put a smile on her face and clung to Drake's arm. The two men, who identified themselves as Cal and Jimmy, Chloe knew were sons of millionaires like Drake, and one of the women, Terry, was the daughter of a prominent Democrat senator. The other woman, named Katherine, looked and behaved as if she'd been on the stage. Gossip had it that Cal was keeping her in a style she wanted to become accustomed to.

Chloe greeted them with false enthusiasm. For some reason, today she felt unequal to playing her usual role of carefree flapper. She felt weighed down. Her restlessness intensified. She suppressed the urge to run away down the beach.

"Where's your white hood, Drake?" Terry sang out as she waved a newspaper in her hand.

Drake grimaced. "Another lynching?"

"No, a white mob of two thousand burned a Negro alive in Mississippi," Jimmy reported blandly. "Accused of raping a white woman."

Chloe shut her eyes and her mind to this horrifying image. No wonder she hadn't been reading the newspaper. Life at the beach seemed incompatible with keeping up with the daily news. All the news that year had been bad—gangsters gunning each other down in Chicago, the stock market experiencing jitters, now another racial killing in Mississippi. Who needed to read about such dreadful things?

"Oh, let's not discuss anything dreary," she begged as she settled herself into a cushioned wicker chair and crossed her legs. Her head ached with . . . what? A restiveness, an unhappiness she couldn't shrug off. There was a general round of loud agreement to this.

"Yes, what would forty thousand Ku Klux Klan members marching in Washington just a few years ago have to do with us?" Kitty asked sarcastically, flinging out her hands, dropping into a chair, and curling up like a cat. "We're the elite. We don't need to be concerned that the KKK lynches innocent people white and black all over the South, do we?"

"Ish kabibble," a very debonair Cal barked and waved his drink at her. "Have a drink and take it easy."

"Sorry," Kitty snapped. "Bootleg liquor singed my liver and my drinking days are done."

"Well, don't take it out on the rest of us," Katherine said, perching on the arm of Cal's chair. "Hey, I've seen you." The woman pointed at Kitty with sudden comprehension on her face. "You're that female lawyer who represents most of the Negro actors and actresses in New York. No wonder the KKK gets under your skin."

"The question is why doesn't it get under your skin?" Kitty's voice had turned mocking and subtly dangerous. The visitors shifted in their seats and glanced at each other covertly. Chloe stared at her bare feet on the jute rug—upset with Kitty, loathing herself.

"Kitty, it's a free country," Drake said. "The KKK disgusts me. And it can worry you if you like. It's a free country. To each his own."

"Chloe"—Kitty pinned her with her eyes—"why don't

we tell your friends about your living in Harlem and marching down Fifth Avenue with the NAACP in 1917?"

Chloe's face burned scarlet. Anger flashed through her. *Kitty, you have no right to meddle in my life.* Still, for appearance's sake, Chloe passed it off as nothing. "I can't think that anyone here would be remotely interested."

"You were a radical once?" Terry squealed with amusement. "Quentin Kimball's daughter marching down Fifth Avenue with Negroes! I can't wait to tell my father."

Chloe gripped the arms of the wicker chair with her hands. *Kitty, you nearly killed yourself with your wild ways and you dare to stand in judgment of me?* She stared coolly at Terry and addressed her, "I don't know why you think what I did is ludicrous. Or why it's yours or anyone's business."

"Terry, you're not amusing," Drake ordered. "Cut it."

Terry looked chagrined and pouted, but said no more. Chloe said nothing. She didn't owe these people anything.

Kitty turned to Chloe and continued as if she'd not heard any interruptions, "You're not the woman you were in 1917. But neither am I. I've been drifting too long." Kitty pursed her lips. "I have to make a decision. I've put it off long enough."

Cal started to say something, but Kitty cut him off. "Chloe, thanks for helping me get myself back this year. But now I think I'm ready to move on." She stood up and offered Jamie her hand. "Come with me, kid. It's time you had a family."

Chloe looked at her friend in sudden shock. Was she serious?

Jamie took Kitty's hand, looking confused. "Do we have to go back already? Can't Miss Chloe come with us?"

Kitty led the child off the porch toward the beach. "She can come any time she wants to. Let's go. I have a mother in need of a grandchild. Why shouldn't it be you?"

Kitty was taking Jamie from her, but Chloe couldn't seem

to move. In dawning horror, she watched Kitty march away without a backward glance. Jamie kept stopping, pulling on Kitty's hand, looking back longingly to Chloe, who could only sit there watching them leave. Finally, they were just two strangers far down the beach. A wave of sickening self-loathing crashed over Chloe.

Cal turned on the Victrola. The latest tune, "Happy Days Are Here Again," poured out. Drake pulled Chloe to her feet and began dancing with her. He held her flush against him and pressed his cheek against hers. Chloe didn't resist. Restlessness had become anguish. For once, she needed Drake and clung to him. Sobs kept trying to bubble up. The last remnant of her youthful hope had been ripped away. But why had Kitty done it? Was she just taking her own unhappiness out on Chloe? But even if Chloe deserved it, why had her oldest friend shot her point blank?

Chloe pressed herself closer to Drake. The moon had risen and shimmered on the waves lapping behind them. Both of them were barefoot in the sand. Drake had rolled up his white shirt sleeves and the cuffs of his gray Oxford bags. Chloe wore a thin shawl over one of her cotton summer dresses, trimmed with white eyelet. Its white skirt fluttered around her calves in the ocean breeze. Her bare toes dug in the cool wet sand as she rocked from her toes to her heels in time with a tune from a neighboring cottage. Raucous gulls still flew and hopped around in the sea foam. The waves lapped in an easy rhythm of their own. Chloe began to softly sing along with the melody on the breeze, "You Do Something to Me."

Kitty and Jamie had left over a week ago and Chloe had spent every day since with Drake. Acquaintances had come and gone, barely noticed by Chloe. Her eyes and Drake's had met often and it seemed that they shared a new understanding, a new intimacy. She'd come to the crossroads and she knew it. Kitty hadn't died, but she'd bailed out of Chloe's life, too. And she'd taken Jamie with her. The unkindest cut of all.

"'You do something to me,'" Chloe sang softly, "'that nobody else can do.'" She lifted her mouth to Drake's. It was the first time she'd ever initiated a kiss with him.

The significance of this was not lost on Drake. With a sudden fierceness, he tucked her even closer to him. She could feel the buttons on his shirt pressing into her skin. She deepened the kiss and his hands roved over her back, caressing and gripping the soft cotton of her dress. He whispered her name. Chloe responded to his touch, a quickening, a heady rush of sensations. She panicked and almost pulled away—as she always had before. Tonight, though, she held herself still, letting the seductive vibrations he ignited roll through her. Did she love Drake? Could she marry him?

He nuzzled her neck and whispered, "Marry me, Chloe." His warm breath tickled her tender ear lobe. "Let's set the date. I've waited long enough and so have you. Marry me."

Chloe pressed her face into the space between his neck and shoulder. Though her heart beat a frantic warning, she breathed in the mingled fragrances of his faint perspiration and lime aftershave and rolled them around inside her like a vintner testing a new wine.

"Chloe?"

"Yes, I'll marry you." As though diving into chilled water, she shivered sharply once. Then she rested her cheek against Drake's shoulder.

"At last," he breathed the words with obvious satisfaction. "All good things do come to those who wait."

She didn't answer, merely stood on tiptoe and kissed him again. Into this kiss she poured all her longing for shelter and love. Drake answered it with a passion that left her shaken and clinging to him. Even if she didn't love Drake, she cared for him, longed for his touch. *He's good for me. I will love him. I married Theran even though I was still unsure. And it worked out.*

"I'll take good care of you, Chloe," Drake murmured, kissing the curve of her ear.

"I know you will," she whispered back, her wayward pulse rattling wild and free. "And I'll try to be a good wife . . . and mother."

"I already knew that." He began kissing her again, not the usual chaste kisses she allowed him. These kisses packed long-denied yearning and bone-melting desire. And she reacted. Within her, a sudden tropical surf swept her away in a warm, frothy surge. She clung to him, the only stable thing in this world anew with passion. *I'm going to marry Drake and give him a child.* What other choice or path did she have? To be her father's hostess till she withered away, a war widow from a forgotten war? *No.*

Voices far down the beach penetrated Chloe's mind, filling her with caution. Though alone, they were still in a public place. She turned her head. "Let's go in," Drake invited. "We're engaged now. Come with me. Stay with me."

Chloe did not mistake what his invitation meant. Her raucous heart cried out caution. "We aren't married yet."

"What does that matter?" He hugged her closer. "I've given you my word."

"I'm not like your other women," her voice snapped cold and hard, barely sounding like herself. She stiffened.

"Is that what's holding you back?" He took a step back, his face shadowed in the moonlight. "You're afraid I'll be like your father?"

"Yes." The truth, a secret long held, felt dragged from her

by force. She pulled away and dipped her toes into the cool water.

"I'll never insult you as your father evidently did your mother." Drake's voice hardened, too. "I'll never pinch the maids or get them pregnant. If you are mine, I doubt I'll need other women. But I won't lie to you." He pulled her spine back against his chest. "I like women, but I'll give you this promise. If I do ever carry on an affair, it won't be with a woman you know. And I'll be perfectly discreet; you will never know of it. You will never suffer because of it."

His words didn't surprise her. From what she'd seen of the men in her world, his offer was at least honest. She closed her eyes and leaned against him, wanting, needing to trust him before she lost everything that mattered, even herself. "I couldn't bear it," she whispered.

"I know I couldn't bear it if you were unfaithful," he replied, gripping her upper arms. "But I know you won't be. Some couples are foolish. They think that just because times have changed and sex is out in the open, they can carry on any way they choose and there won't be any consequences." His tone was dismissive. "I'm not so foolish. I've chosen a chaste woman, a woman of character, for my wife. And, Chloe, I won't throw that away or wound you carelessly. I promise."

A woman of character. Turning swiftly, she kissed him, pressing against him, wanting to reward him for this tribute to her chaste ways, to let him sweep her off her feet, convince her that, in accepting him, she'd made the right choice.

"I won't pressure you to spend the night with me. Your reluctance just proves that you are the woman I think you are. But name the date."

Deep in sensation, her mind hadn't been prepared for this question. She blurted out the first date that came to mind, "December first."

He chuckled. "Do I have to wait that long? What made you think of that date?"

His laughter rippled against her. "I don't know. Maybe because it's a month before my birthday and I'll just have enough time to plan a small wedding. You don't mind a small wedding, do you?"

"Are you kidding?" He chuckled again deep in his chest. "I hate big crushes in huge churches and everyone drunk at the reception. Let's just have family and a few close friends. Do you want to be married at your home in Maryland?"

"No," her reply popped out. "Let's marry in New York. And leave immediately for someplace faraway." *Let's run away together, Drake. Leave it all behind.*

"You make it sound like an adventure, princess. Very well. But I'm going to move the date forward a month to November first, then. Okay?"

"Fine." She kissed him again, stopping his words, not wanting to talk about it any more. She wrapped her arms around his neck and stood on tiptoe.

He pulled away an inch. "I love it when you do that, but you've got to stop now. Or we may have to move the date up again. I can't spend the next few months taking one cold shower after another." He grinned.

She felt lost again and rested her head on his shoulder, hiding her face from him.

He hugged her, kissed the top of her head, and tenderly stroked her hair. "Let's walk on the beach. If I take you inside, I won't be responsible for what might happen." He spoke lightly, but Chloe understood the honesty under his words. She felt the same way. The temptation to go inside with him and cast the die once and for all held her fascinated. But she allowed him to draw her along the edge of the flowing and ebbing waves. Better to wait and start off as she had with Theran. Then it would have the best chance to go right.

I can be happy with Drake. I will be.

A few days later, far into the evening, Chloe arrived at the apartment in D.C. That morning, Drake had been called to New York City for some board of directors meeting of his father's corporation. Leaving the beach had been wrenching to Chloe. The days after she'd accepted Drake's proposal had passed with kisses, red roses, and tender moments, always on the beach. More and more, Chloe felt she'd made the right decision. They'd even discussed Bette and how to bring her into their home. Maybe now the doubts would cease. When she married Drake, she'd reclaim her daughter and be able to go forward instead of just marking time.

She'd just changed from her traveling outfit into a new black satin lounging gown when she heard the front door opening and voices below—her father and Jackson. She walked out onto the landing to call down a greeting, but stopped when she heard her father's voice rumble up from below. "Well, tonight we break out the champagne. Drake's finally done it. Chloe's set the date."

Chloe stood frozen with her mouth open. Drake had called her father?

"This is what you've been waiting for, isn't it?" Jackson said, sounding unimpressed.

"Well, if I'm going to lose my hostess, it might as well be to a millionaire." Daddy laughed heartily and with a repulsive smugness. "Anyway, she'll be even more use to me as Mrs. Drake Lovelady."

CHAPTER FIFTEEN

*C*hloe realized that she'd stopped breathing. She gasped
for air and leaned back beside her door, suddenly weak.
She pressed her palms against the wall to steady herself. Why
had Drake called her father? Was it possible he had done so?
But who else knew of their engagement? She'd told no one.
Had Drake?

She hazarded a glance down the staircase. Her father and
Jackson had moved into the parlor on the first floor. She
heard their voices, but faintly. She tiptoed down the steps and
paused at the bottom of the staircase. She'd never eaves-
dropped on her father and Jackson before. *But maybe I
should have.* She tiptoed closer, relieved that the soft-soled
slippers she wore made no noise. The men hadn't closed the
door. She could hear Jackson speaking clearly from where she
stood.

"I don't know why you want to marry Chloe off." Jackson sounded vaguely disgruntled. *Why?*

"That's because you aren't greedy like I am," her father
said with brazen satisfaction. "I made my pile and bought me
a classy wife with it, but my money don't even come close to
a million."

"But your stocks have been doing well. And how will Chloe being a millionaire's wife help you?"

Her father barked one harsh laugh. "It sticks in your craw 'cause she never looked at you twice."

A silence. "I may admire Miss Chloe, but I know she sees me as merely an extension of you. Not a completely erroneous inference." Jackson's tone was sadly ironic. "I've never had any hopes that she would see me as more than your shill."

Jackson admired her, wanted her for himself? Chloe clutched the post at the bottom of the railing.

"Bein' my shill has kept you in freshly ironed shirts and sleepin' on a soft mattress with a pretty little mistress. I don't think you have anythin' to complain about."

"I'm not complaining," Jackson muttered. "I just think that your own daughter ought to count for more than a mere convenience to you."

"My daughter has been plenty inconvenient to me. Runnin' off to marry a poor New York soldier for starters. Having a cranky, sickly baby. Well, that turned out all right. Lily was happy at gettin' to take over the granddaughter. And *that* kept her off my back and let me have Chloe to myself. But I've had to take real pains to keep her here in Washington. Had to handle her with kid gloves. Make her think I needed her."

Chloe tasted bitter bile rise in her throat.

"Well, didn't you?" Jackson demanded. "She's been a wonderful hostess for you."

"You have me there." Her father's tone mellowed. "She's done me proud—more than that useless Carlyle I married, that drab scoldin' shrew. All I ever got from her was Chloe and the right to call Ivy Manor my home." His tone reverted to cocky. "But that was all I wanted, so that's okay, too."

"Miss Chloe deserves better from you." Jackson must

have stood up. The sound of a chair scraping the floor pushed Chloe to back up onto the bottom step.

"I don't get what you mean. I've given Chloe anythin' she ever wanted—pretty clothes, ponies, a fine education at one of the best finishin' schools, a fancy debut. She's had everythin' a girl could want or need."

"I meant that she loves you." Jackson's voice firmed.

Chloe swallowed a moan, which might betray her presence. The walls around her appeared to warp in and out as though an earthquake moved beneath her.

"What about it? A girl should love her daddy."

His callous words pierced her. Long silver needles slid under her skin.

"I see trying to explain to you what I mean is futile." The sound of the glass decanter being set down hard on a metal tray gave voice to Jackson's irritation.

"Now you got that right. Chloe as Mrs. Drake Lovelady will smooth a path for me to the other side of the aisle. I can make a lot more milkin' Republicans than reapin' the little that the minority party, the Democrats, have to offer."

Her knees turned to jelly and she lowered herself onto the bottom step.

"Didn't you learn anything from the Teapot Dome Scandal?" Jackson snapped.

Her father laughed unpleasantly. "I learned that mostly the ones who got the dough kept it. Even if they had to appear before some silly senators just tryin' to get reelected. And how many crooked deals never see the light of day? I'm just the man to be the go-between in transactions like that. I'll take my chances. And I'll thank my Chloe for puttin' me in the way of new business."

"I don't know if you'll have much luck with Drake Lovelady. He's no babe in the woods."

Waves of heat and cold rolled through Chloe. She clutched the edge of the step to keep from slipping farther down.

"It's a little hard to say no to your wife's daddy. And I'll keep my eye on him and take note of any little indiscretion he might not like Chloe to know about. Fortunately Lovelady does love the ladies." He laughed at his own joke.

"So you'll blackmail him," Jackson sounded grim.

Bending double, Chloe pressed her hand over her mouth.

"You are almighty self-righteous tonight. Have another shot of that good Canadian whiskey and drop this. Chloe ain't for you and if I told her that you was takin' up for her, she wouldn't even believe it." The floor creaked as he moved.

Afraid of being seen, Chloe fled soundlessly up to her room, where she closed the door behind her and then leaned against it. Her heart throbbed, pounded. In the low light, she stared at the violet-sprigged wallpaper, the pale blue satin bedspread, and matching draperies she'd chosen. She'd spent the earlier part of this year redecorating the whole apartment. She hadn't realized at the time that she was part of the setting she was creating for her father. In his script, she wasn't even a bit player with a line or two.

Her years in Washington had been a charade. She'd never thought her father had changed completely, but she'd thought . . . She'd believed a lie—that he needed her, finally loved her a little. But to him, she wasn't a person. She was no more than his trophy in the endless tug of war with her mother. They'd split the spoils, Bette for her mother and herself for her father. *And I let them, thinking it was a kindness to my daughter.*

She knew she should be weeping, or maybe filled with anger. But all she felt was shame and disgust. *I've been a fool, a stupid little fool.*

*　　*　　*

The next morning, Chloe splashed cold water on her face once more and applied powder, rouge, and lipstick to cover the traces of a sleepless night. Aching and empty, she walked down to the dining room for breakfast. Should she confront her father or hide her knowledge?

He sat at the head of the table, hidden behind the *New York Times*. As she read the title of the paper, she suddenly knew what she would do and where she wanted to be. But not why. "Good morning, Daddy." Her calm voice sounded artificial to her ears.

"Mornin', Chloe. Glad you're home."

Chloe waited to see if he would say anything about her engagement. He didn't. Of course not; he was too clever for that. "Thank you, Daddy."

"I got a call from that orphanage woman."

This caught her by surprise. Her pulse jerked in her veins. "Oh?"

"Yeah, she wanted to know if you knew Kitty McCaslin is havin' her parents adopt that kid Jamie."

Another hit below the belt. She passed a hand over her brow, smoothing away the tension. This was no more than she deserved. She should have adopted Jamie long ago and taken him and her daughter far from her parents. "I knew Kitty had taken him home to live with her parents."

"No doubt to make up for neither of the McCaslin kids getting married and givin' their parents any grandkids?" he said with a superior twist to his voice.

Chloe couldn't make herself reply to this. The pain of losing Roarke was a wound that had never completely healed. "I'm going," she dropped the bomb, "to make a trip to New York today."

The paper lowered. "Oh?"

At last, she'd gained his attention. "I have some shopping

to do, a dress to buy," she improvised, "and I think I might as well go up there and get it all done efficiently." What would going to New York gain her?

"Well, sugar, here you're barely home and now you're leavin' again. You know I missed you."

Is that right, Daddy? Should she say anything about her engagement? She'd waffled back and forth, but she realized she must or arouse suspicion. "You should be wishing me happy, Daddy. I've accepted Drake's proposal of marriage."

"Sugar!" Daddy beamed as if this were the first time he'd heard the news. "I do wish you happiness. You couldn't do better'n Drake Lovelady."

Or richer, right, Daddy? "Thank you. "I'm very happy." *I was very happy.* Her father got up and hugged and kissed her. Chloe wanted to bat away his hands. The touch of his lips on her cheek made her skin crawl. *Daddy, you should be on the stage like Minnie.* She took grim satisfaction in knowing that if she'd done nothing else of worth in her life, she'd gotten Minnie out of her father's sweaty palms.

Maybe it was Minnie she wanted to see in New York?

"I'm going to take the train," Chloe continued, "I can hire a car in the city or just use taxis."

The maid brought in fresh coffee and her father went back behind the paper. "Well, all right. How long will you be gone?"

The rest of my natural life if I can help it. "Not long, Daddy," she lied with a serene smile.

After breakfast and her father's departure, she called the New York number Drake had given her as the one sure to reach him. Within moments, he came on the line. "Darling, I'm so glad you called. I didn't think I'd get to hear your sweet voice today."

"Good morning." The urge to demand that he tell her the truth about whether he'd let her father know about their engagement chewed at her. Suspicion made her voice come out starchy. "I hope I'm not interrupting any business."

"The meeting is just about to start and then I'll be tied up most of the day. The stock market jitters have spooked Dad's board of directors. We've got to reassure them that prosperity is here to stay."

"I just wanted you to know," she said, "that I'm coming up to the City today." Was it Drake, then, drawing her to New York?

"You are? Wonderful. We need to talk over wedding plans with my parents. And let Mother draw up the engagement announcement for all the society pages."

"You haven't told anyone yet?" she asked as casually as she could.

"Just my parents. Darn. I've got to go. Where will you be staying? You know they've razed the Waldorf-Astoria to make room for the new Empire State Building, don't you? Why don't you stay with us at our New York apartment?"

"No, I'll let you know where I end up, Drake. Goodbye."

"I love you, Chloe. Don't forget that."

She hadn't gotten a clue from Drake's voice if he'd been in complicity with her father. Then she recalled her father's intention to use blackmail against Drake. But wasn't Drake astute enough to avoid such a pitfall? Perhaps one of Drake's servants had informed her father? That was more likely. She couldn't bring herself to believe Drake had been dishonest with her. He might be a sinner, but he was an honest sinner. The promise of discretion he'd made her after her acceptance of his proposal had proved that. But her father wanted to use Drake's propensity to sin against them both. And she couldn't let that happen.

The next evening, Chloe stood with her hand on the phone in her suite at the Benjamin Hotel. She'd just dialed Roarke's New York number for the eighth time. Each time she'd hung up before anyone answered. She lifted the receiver again. A knock on the door made her put the receiver back in its cradle.

"Chloe?" Drake's voice came through the door and she opened it to him. He kissed her hello and then frowned. "What's the matter, princess?"

She walked farther into the suite, done in maroon and green with a lot of glass and chrome. "Drake, I'm going to Paris." The plan had come to her when she'd reached New York yesterday.

On a whim, she'd had the cabbie drive her by all the places that had been dear or important to her when she'd eloped here in 1917—Theran's rooming house, Mrs. Rascombe's, the shop on Fifth Avenue, that little café in the Village that Kitty had loved. She'd even had the man drive her to the dock where she'd waved farewell to Theran. And there, a longing to follow Theran had swept through her.

Startled, Drake tried to read Chloe, but her eyes were shuttered. "Paris? Why?" he asked as though it were only of mild interest.

"I want to visit my late husband's grave."

Of all the things she might have said this ranked as the worst possible news. He walked over to the room's bar. From the stainless steel ice bucket, he added ice to one of the glasses waiting on the bar. Then he pulled out his sterling silver hipflask and poured whiskey onto the ice. He took a swallow. "Chloe, that's so macabre."

"No, it isn't." She turned from him and walked to one of the tall windows.

This on top of the awful day he'd had. Drake felt his lungs tighten. He thumped his glass down on the bar. "Why?"

"I need to go and close that . . . that period of my life."

His temper flared but he clamped down on it. He wouldn't let his frayed nerves endanger his engagement. "Are you sure," he said, his voice lazy, "you want to stir up the past?"

"I have to go to Paris and close the book of my first marriage. I should have done it years ago." She pushed the pale-green draperies farther open, scraping hooks against the rod. "I've never felt that Theran and I had a chance to say good-bye once and for all. There was just a memorial service, you know, not a burial."

It sounded plausible, but he didn't like the way she turned her back to him. He wanted Chloe more than he'd ever wanted any woman in his life. *I've courted you most of a decade.* The fear that he might still lose her churned through him. His temper snapped. "Have you called Roarke McCaslin while you're in town?"

"Why do you ask me that?"

"Tell me, Chloe—" He tried to pull back to safer ground, but his mouth was dry with longing for her. "I need to know if you've called him."

"Of course, I haven't." She wrapped her arms around herself. "I haven't seen him since Kitty was released from the hospital this spring. Why would I call him and why should you care if I did? He's just an old family friend."

Through the tall window, the garish night lights flashed into the room, glimmering on her white satin lounging gown, outlining her slender silhouette. In the low light, her skin glowed like ripe peaches. He imagined nuzzling her nape, breathing in her subtle floral perfume. Physical desire for this woman made his whole body clench. It drove him, lashed him to expose his need. "I recall how you looked at that 'old family friend' that night in '21 when I dogged you to that club in Harlem."

"I don't know what you mean."

Her calm reply drove him to the ropes. "You were in love with him."

"That's not true," she fired up, still not turning. "I've never been in love with Roarke. He's just . . . he was just such a special friend. Roarke always understood me better than I did myself. I just wanted him back that way, the way it had always been between us."

Maybe she was unaware of her feelings for Roarke. He should let it drop. Again, he couldn't stop himself. He came up behind her. "I'm sure that's what you believe, but that's not what I sensed." He turned her to face him.

Chloe wouldn't meet Drake's eyes. "I'm engaged to you. I will not break our engagement. I am a woman of my word. Do you believe me?"

He didn't say yes. Instead, he lifted her chin and reveled in her beauty all over again. Other women he tired of—they grew stale and clung. But not Chloe. Never Chloe. "Very well, make this pilgrimage if you must." He smoothed his hand over her soft cheek, feeling the delicate bones underneath. He slid his fingers up through the shingled hair above her nape. *You will be mine, Chloe.* He dipped into his inside jacket pocket and pulled out an antique red velvet ring box. "This was my grandmother's engagement ring." He opened the box. "It's for you."

Chloe hesitated.

"Are we engaged or not?" His voice sounded rusty, like an unoiled hinge.

She looked up then. "Have you spoken to my father lately?"

He stared into her eyes, trying to fathom the significance of this odd question. "No."

Chloe studied him.

Needing to brand her as his, he leaned forward and kissed her. He took his time, drawing all the sweetness from this woman he loved, needed, was desperate to have. "I've never loved any woman but you," he whispered.

In reply, she slipped on his ring.

Relief sighed through him. "I warn you, Chloe Black," he said, keeping his voice a whisper, but added a hint of steel, "you better come back for our November first wedding or I'll come and get you myself."

"You have my promise, don't you?" She looked him straight in the eye. "If anyone breaks our engagement, it will have to be you. I will not."

"Then we will marry on November first. In your absence, I'm sure my mother will be glad to make the arrangements for us."

Chloe stood on tiptoe and kissed him. She lost herself in the feel of his lips and the contrast of textures, her soft skin rasped by his new growth of beard. "Thank her for me," she said, her forehead resting against his chin, "I just need to work out some things for myself and then I'll become your wife—fully and forever." *And be free from Daddy once and for all.*

Sometime she'd have to tell Drake about her father's scheme to use him. But it could wait. She was sure now that Drake hadn't betrayed her to him. He had nothing to gain from doing so.

Her eyes looked over his shoulder toward the phone. How had he guessed she'd been thinking of Roarke? Did Drake fear Roarke? He shouldn't. She recalled the proprietary look in Miss Edna Talbot's expression. And the very capable Miss Talbot didn't look like the type who failed at anything. She would marry Roarke.

A month later in early October, Chloe sat in the back of the Paris taxi trying to get up enough nerve to emerge from the vehicle. Finally, when the driver started casting furtive backward glances at her, she gave in and got out. She paid off the cabbie and entered the shop that bore the name in gold letters on the show window: "MENER LA MODE." Under this in the same gold lettering was a name familiar to Chloe. Inside, a shop girl came forward to greet her. "Is Madame Blanche in?" Chloe gave the girl her card. Then she waited, fingering the lace collar on a mannequin.

"Chloe, *mon amie!*" Madame Blanche burst from the back room and threw her arms around Chloe. The Frenchwoman looked much the same as she had the first day Chloe had laid eyes on her. Tall, still pencil-thin, still dark-haired, Blanche was dressed in a fuchsia-and-black dress, knee-length in the front and ankle-length in the back. Chloe breathed in the woman's rich Chanel N°5 perfume and luxuriated in a genuine welcome in this foreign land.

"But what has brought you here?" Madame drew her to a chair near a rear fitting room.

"I came to visit my husband's grave."

Madame Blanche made no reply, merely gazed at Chloe as if her words had made no sense.

Chloe voiced the reason for looking up her old friend,

"And I'm looking for a wedding dress. I'm to marry again on the first of November."

Madame stared at her for several moments. "You did not come to Madame Blanche for fashions or to find your husband's grave. You wish to . . ." Madame looked into Chloe's eyes and lifted her own eyebrows.

Madame's words flustered Chloe, as if she were a child caught with her hand in the cookie jar. "But I did. I need a wedding dress."

"*Non.*" But Madame led Chloe to the rear. Through the back door near the fitting room was a sight both familiar and nostalgic to Chloe—the messy designing and sewing room. Madame pointed to a mannequin with a half-finished dress of royal blue. "This will be your second wedding so we do not have to use *le blanc*, white."

Chloe studied the dress. "Too daring. I want something simpler and in a paler color."

Madame led her over to another. This dress, nearly finished, was in a light-rose crepe de chine. "Why are you marrying again? You do not look like a woman in love."

The unexpected, unwelcome question made Chloe fumble, sorting through her thoughts. She avoided an answer. "May I try it on?"

"*Bien.* Of course."

Madame helped Chloe slip off her dress and then took the silk dress off the mannequin. "Careful of the pins," she warned.

Hearing again the familiar words from the past moistened Chloe's eyes. In the rose-pink dress, she walked back out to the three-way mirror in the rear of the shop and looked at herself.

"Exquisite, as always," Madame murmured. "You are still

one of the most beautiful women I've ever been pleased to dress."

Chloe stared at herself in the mirror. She didn't see the beauty. She saw the doubt in her eyes. "I went to the US embassy, but no one seems to know where my husband was buried. If he'd died in a battle, it would be easy. But since he died in Paris of food poisoning—"

"You notice that the skirts are dropping in the back," Madame interrupted as if she hadn't been listening.

"I went to one of the battleground cemeteries. It was awful. All those rows of white crosses—"

"I think this color is excellent for you—"

"Why aren't you listening to me?" Chloe snapped.

Madame met her gaze. "When you say something you really mean, something worth listening to, I will attend."

Chloe floundered as she gazed into Madame's unflinching eyes. At last she said, "I don't . . . I don't seem to be able to get it right."

"What right, *ma chere?*"

"My life." *Everything. What am I doing here in Paris?*

"That is much to fail. I do not believe it. The Chloe Black I knew did much right. She brought her friend Minnie from the unhappy . . . situation to New York City and now Minnie is on the stage, a success."

"That's the only thing I did right. And I didn't do much."

Madame Blanche shook her head. *"Non."*

"I can't put it all into words."

"What of the man you will marry?"

Chloe could hardly keep up with Madame's quick changes. "Drake loves me very much."

"Ah. He loves you, but you do not love him. He must be very rich."

Chloe flushed. "It's not like that. I do care for him and he loves me."

"I do not doubt many men love you. You are *irresistible, oui?*"

"Don't make fun of me." Chloe slumped into one of the nearby velvet chairs, disregarding the pins that pricked her.

"I cannot give you advice." Madame sat in the adjoining chair. "I am a modiste, not a psychiatrist or a priest. But I can tell you that always you mistrust your beauty—you do not revel in it as a woman should. You fear it. You also fear to show any true emotion. Only twice did I see your eyes shine with honesty."

"When?" Did anyone else realize this about her?

"The first showing at my shop on Fifth Avenue. You stared down the ladies who would scorn Minnie as a model. Your eyes blazed with passion."

Chloe remembered. "And the second time?"

"When we marched down the avenue and I sang 'La Marseillaise.'"

"I remember." Kitty had taunted her with this in August, a lifetime ago. *I was real with Jamie, too.*

"I also remember the day your little friend, the cat, brought the news of your husband's death."

Chloe stared down at her lap, unable to speak. That awful day.

"It broke something in you, *mon amie*—not your heart, I think, but something else."

Stung, Chloe looked up. "I loved my husband."

"My dear, *ma chere*, you only knew him for two days. Is love possible in that short time? I think, *non.*"

Tears clogged Chloe's throat. She looked away.

"Love comes in many forms. I think you had passion for your husband, but love takes longer. I will not, cannot give you advice, but I will ask you these questions." Madame paused as though gathering her next words.

Chloe held still as if Madame was about to take a spade to her life, digging deep and finding what?

"Why can you not show the truth of what you feel? Why do you seek your husband's grave? You know that will not bring him back or you back the way you were in 1917. Why do you agree to marry a man you do not love?"

Chloe felt all resistance to Madame shrivel up. "I don't know."

"If you don't know your heart, *ma* Chloe, who does?"

Paris, November 1, 1929

After replying to Jackson's stunning early morning telegram, Chloe walked trancelike out of her small hotel and down the few blocks toward the Seine. She walked along the banks of the sluggish gray river that mirrored her own mood. In spite of the chilling drizzle, she sat down on a park bench. *Today was supposed to be my wedding day.*

A man, probably an American, sat reading a London paper. The headline blazed: "STOCKS STILL FALLING." Jackson's telegram lay crumpled in her pocket. Part of her wanted to take it out and read it again and another part wanted to shred it into little pieces and throw it into the Seine. Restless anxiety forced her up and she began walking again, head down, unwilling to meet any stranger's eye.

It wasn't only Jackson's telegram. She'd saved all of Drake's cables in her drawer at her hotel. The first one she'd received on October tenth had read: "Chloe, may we postpone wedding? Press of business is overwhelming. Love, Drake."

She'd been so preoccupied with her inner struggle that she'd passed this warning off lightly. Too lightly. The ensuing telegrams had become more and more intense and more and more disturbing. The US stock market was rattled and Drake and other businessmen were trying to prop it up.

On October 29 their efforts had failed. Vast "paper" wealth had been lost. Drake had not told her the extent of his losses, but he had admitted that he had lost a fortune that day. How? How could money vanish with something like the wave of a magician's wand?

Now, the sound of chanting penetrated her thoughts. She found herself outside the gray-stone Cathedral of Notre Dame. In spite of the morning's damp chill, the doors had been propped open while the mass was being performed inside. Taking a place just outside the doors, Chloe looked up at the hideous gargoyles that sprang from of the stone exterior. Their ugliness jogged her mind and a memory came to her. She was a little girl, standing outside the parlor at Ivy Manor listening to her parents quarrel over her. Then she'd run away down the path to Granny Raney's cottage. Her heart pounded at the memory. Flashes of endless arguments shouted and sneered over her head from childhood on raced through her mind.

I didn't want my Bette to end up a pawn. I want her to be a person, not a bargaining chip. I left Bette at Ivy Manor so that wouldn't happen over her. But did it make it better for her? I love her, but how will she ever know that? I've run away from the conflict over her just as I ran away with her father. I've run away all my life. Now I've run away to Paris.

"You have to go back tonight," her conscience spoke up. *They don't need me, don't want me.*

"Your father's heart attack freed him from the consequences of his buying too much stock on too slim a margin.
He died in debt. You know how your mother is."

I can't face it.

Her conscience ignored her. "Your daughter will suffer if
you don't go home and take charge. This has nothing to do
with loving and being loved. This is survival."

Breaking into her thoughts, the sound of the priest chanting his singsong benediction in Latin drew Chloe closer. She
stepped just within the open double doors and listened to the
Latin liturgy that she did not understand. She pressed her
quivering lips together. The church service taunted her. The
congregants kneeling inside the church, the priest and
acolytes belonged there, had a place in the solemn sacrament.
Even if she walked inside, she would still be a stranger, still be
unable to take part in the solemn ceremony.

I always stand outside. This thought went through her
like electric current. *All my life, what did I want to run to?*
The reply was easy: until she'd eloped with Theran she'd had
no destination. Had she tried to run to Drake now and then
away from him here? *What did I hope to find in Paris?* Questions—questions like the ones Madame Blanche had posed.
But the last one had been the hardest: "If you don't know, *ma*
Chloe, who does?"

*I have to go back. I have no choice. I have my ticket and
enough funds to get home. That's all. I just don't want to go
back and face everything. Even with Daddy dead, nothing
will be different, not really. My life was a sham.*

How did a person begin to live a real life, not just stand
outside and watch others? How could she let Bette know she
was valued for herself, not as a prize in a war?

The chanting inside the cathedral ended and a bell in the
tower tolled. Chloe watched the priest walk down the aisle,

swinging a censer. The fragrance of strong incense was carried to her on the breeze. The urge to plunge inside the dim cathedral and drop to her knees swept through her like the wild wind that swooped down the tall sides of the cathedral and tugged at her hat. *How do I come inside? How do I live my real life? How do I become a real mother to Bette and show her what a real mother is?*

The answers to these questions eluded her. But she couldn't delay any longer. She had to go back to the hotel and pack her bags. The ship left tonight and she had to be on it. And among this welter, her postponed marriage to Drake still swirled and teased her. Did she have the nerve to go through with it? Would he still want her? A voice in her mind sang something. She couldn't catch it and it was soon gone.

Chapter Sixteen

*C*hloe waited under the center arch at the entrance of the Baltimore Union Station. It was a November evening—darkening, breezy, and chilling. Shadows cast by the overhead lamps stretched down the steps. Against the penetrating wind, she pulled the fashionable wool cape she wore tighter around herself. *I must call Drake right away when I get home.* Her guilt over arriving in and then leaving New York without calling him gnawed at her. Why had calling him been so impossible?

She'd called her mother from New York, giving her the time and number of the train she'd be arriving on and asking her to have the car come for her. Her mother had sounded affronted and miffed, just like she always did. Chloe wished she were going anywhere but home.

For a moment, she let her mind wander, remembering the first time she'd come to these arches, the night she'd eloped with Theran. She had been innocent, hopeful but afraid that night. But that had been 1917, a lifetime ago. Then that tune that kept singing in her mind started up again. If she could only come up with the words, she knew it would probably stop plaguing her. But the lyrics always stayed just beyond her reach.

"Chloe." The voice that hailed her out of her thoughts was the *last one* she'd expected to hear. She turned in disbelief. In a dark, neat suit as though on his way to Wall Street, Roarke stood in front of her. For one long, heavy moment, they stared at each other. Why wasn't he in New York? She took a step forward. "Roarke," she murmured.

And then another voice came, breaking in, "Miss Chloe?" It was Jamie, looking up at her shyly.

And then another, more tentative, "Mother?"

Her daughter had come, too. Bette looked down and then up, hope flaring in her shining eyes.

Awash in sudden joy, Chloe stooped and threw her arms around both children, pulling them close. "Children, dearest children." Her heart soared. Tears moistened her eyes. "Bette. Jamie." She hugged them to her, weeping and laughing. "I've missed you so."

"I've missed you, too, Miss Chloe," Jamie said. "Did you know that Mr. Thomas and Miss Estelle 'dopted me?"

"Yes." Chloe stood up and took a hankie out of her black suede purse to wipe her eyes. Jamie looked happy and well fed. He wore obviously new black-flannel slacks, a white shirt, and a blue-and-black plaid-wool jacket. "Yes, I'm so happy for you, Jamie. They're wonderful people."

"I got my own room and everything," Jamie informed her. "And Mr. Thomas is gonna take me fishing and all."

"Mother, Granddaddy is dead," Bette said, looking up with solemn eyes and then quickly down. Her daughter wore a navy-blue corduroy jumper, white blouse, and gray-wool coat. A navy-blue ribbon tied back her long black hair from her face. Her cheeks were pink from the cold.

"I know, dear." Chloe wished she could pull Bette back for another hug, but wouldn't that be pushing her luck?

"You missed the funeral." Bette stood with her hands clasped in front of her, her head down. Chloe heard the echo of her mother's complaint in her daughter's words.

"I came back as fast as I could, my dear." Chloe bravely kissed the top of her daughter's silken head. This was the first time she'd ever spoken to the child without her mother hovering nearby. "I'm so glad Grandmother let you come to meet me." How had that happened?

"I was over visiting Jamie when Grandmother called to ask Mr. Roarke to drive here to get you from the train," Bette explained. "So Miss Estelle said I should come, too." Bette beamed with pleasure. "I never got to ride all the way to Baltimore before."

"And Mr. Roarke's got the best car," Jamie added with enthusiasm.

Chloe laughed out loud. "Bette, we'll have to see you get around more. You're growing up, honey." Chloe ran her fingers over her daughter's dark, straight hair. And she pinched Jamie's cheek. "And before we know it, you'll be driving." Then she looked up into Roarke's stiff face and her joy ebbed. His face was a rock cliff, a dangerous one.

"Is this all your luggage?" he asked in a gruff voice.

"Yes, I didn't have the heart to do much shopping." *I just bought a wedding dress.* Her heart betrayed her by beating too fast and too hard.

With his good hand, Roarke picked up one of the scuffed brown valises. Jamie hefted up the other with a grunt. "I can get this one, Mr. Roarke."

"I'll get the hat boxes!" Bette squealed and scooped up, one in each hand, the gold straps to two round gold-and-white-striped boxes.

"Then I can get this," Chloe said, lifting up her square brown-leather cosmetics and jewelry case. "And off we go." She looked at Roarke, willing him to smile, say a word of welcome.

"This way," Roarke grunted and turned. As the three of them trotted to keep up with him on the way to the car, she stifled her disappointment. What had she expected from Roarke—a warm welcome, a miracle?

"My, Jamie, you are getting strong," Chloe praised as they waited by the car under a street lamp.

"And I didn't drop the hat boxes," Bette said, evidently unwilling to be overlooked.

"I know, and the wind was just whipping 'round us." Chloe couldn't believe she was actually talking to her daughter. Bette had always been tongue-tied around her. Was it because her grandmother wasn't here or was it the presence of another child? Whatever it was, Chloe could hardly believe it. She hoped she wouldn't say anything that would disrupt this new start. *I must tread very, very carefully.*

Jamie helped Roarke store the luggage in the trunk. Then Roarke held open the door of his sleek black sedan for Chloe and she slipped in, remembering in a flash Roarke picking her up when she'd come home from Buffalo all those years ago. How she wished she had the nerve to mention this. Maybe if the children had not been along, she would have. Like two rambunctious puppies, Jamie and Bette clambered into the backseat with giggles and teasing.

Without a word, Roarke started the car and drove off, heading through the city streets toward the highway. For a while the children chattered and then as the darkened highway rolled past the car windows, the backseat fell silent. Chloe glanced back and saw that the children had curled up on the wide seat and fallen asleep. Now she could speak to Roarke.

But with each mile, the barrier between her and Roarke seemed to expand. The silence roared between them. Finally, she couldn't stand it. "Tell me—" She stopped and swallowed to moisten her mouth. "How are things around home?"

"You mean after the bottom fell out?" Disgust edged his voice.

"Yes, how are your parents?"

"They're worried. How else would they be? Father says the trouble has just begun."

Chloe quailed under his disgruntled tone. "I ... I can't believe it myself. How does money just disappear like that?"

"A lot of people bought way too much stock on margin—on credit, that is—and all it took was some wiser investors taking a good look at the facts and dumping their stocks while they could still make a profit on them. And then insanity took over."

She wanted to ask, "Did you lose money?" But she didn't have the nerve. She gripped the edge of the soft leather seat with both hands.

"Your mother's more upset by your father's death than you might think."

This announcement took her by surprise. "I would think ..." She hesitated to say what she was thinking, but then what didn't Roarke know about her parents? "I thought she'd be gloating. They always competed, argued over everything, and I thought she'd be happy that she outlived him."

The faint light from the dash illumined the contours of Roarke's face. And Chloe realized that she hadn't taken much notice of Roarke's scars this time. The darkness hid them now anyway. She could imagine if she wanted to that they didn't exist, that the past didn't separate them. "Sometimes," he said, "we get what we want and then we realize we don't want it."

And sometimes we don't get what we want and we want it all the more. The unexpected joy of seeing Jamie and Bette made her reckless. *What have I got to lose?* "This reminds me of the night in '18 when you picked me up when I came home from Buffalo." She held her breath. Would he open up and really communicate?

Silence.

She tried again. "Is Kitty here or in New York?"

"Neither." He glanced her way. "Didn't you know she'd moved to California right after Jamie's adoption was final?" Roarke's tone was tart, as though this had angered him.

Chloe was too shocked to respond. *Kitty left without a word to me?*

Another silence.

"How long will you be visiting with your parents?" she asked at last.

"I leave in two days," he said with implacable certainty.

"I . . . I'm sorry to hear that. I was hoping . . ." Words failed her.

"You'll be going back to Washington soon, won't you?" His voice almost taunted her.

The hope of reaching Roarke faded. He'd probably guessed long ago how her father had been using her and despised her for her gullibility. Why did they speak to one another like polite strangers? *I know all about you, Roarke, and you know all about me. Why can't we talk anymore?* She might as well face facts. "How is Miss Talbot?"

"I don't know. She isn't working for me any longer. She finally realized that I wasn't going to marry her and quit me."

Roarke's bluntness surprised Chloe.

"How's Drake Lovelady?" Roarke's voice was more than gruff.

Were they indulging in tit for tat? "Fine. We postponed our wedding until things settle down a little."

Roarke jerked, and Chloe remembered he hadn't known of the engagement. She hadn't meant to be so callous in telling him.

"I see," was all he said.

The news that Chloe and Lovelady were engaged scalded Roarke's frayed emotions. *It's what I expected, isn't it?* Roarke thought of Chloe's father suffering heart failure over the loss of his fortune and of men whom he'd witnessed jumping off rooftops on Wall Street. Could one failure destroy the remainder of a life? That's how it seemed to him, and evidently he wasn't alone.

On the next afternoon after Jackson and the lawyer had departed for Washington, Chloe found her mother sitting in the formal parlor that never changed, staring into the small fire on the hearth. "Mother?"

"Is the lawyer gone?" Her mother surreptitiously dried her eyes.

Was she mourning her husband? "Yes." Chloe sat down on the love seat opposite her mother. Facts and figures still whizzed around in her mind.

"How bad was it?" Lifting an English chintz teapot, Mother added tea to her cup and poured one for Chloe.

"Daddy lost everything and will still owe money after all his property is sold." Chloe accepted the translucent cup and saucer and poured in rich cream and two cubes of sugar. Her father had managed to amass almost one hundred thousand dollars in his life and then had lost it all. What had possessed him to play that deep in the stock market?

"I thought he'd done something like that." Mother sounded harsh but pleased. "I suppose you were glad to hear that *my* father protected this property from your father's sticky fingers. Before we married, Father made Quentin sign away his right to hold title to my family's property. Quentin could call Ivy Manor home, but that was all. The Carlyle land was to and always will remain in the hands of a Carlyle heir."

This news had been as surprising to Chloe as her father's losses. Chloe stirred her tea, making sure her teaspoon never touched her cup—another undeniable mark of a lady. "Was that the reason you deeded the property to me when I turned twenty-one?" *Why didn't you ever tell me?*

"Yes, I always thought your father would gamble everything away in the end, just like his father and grandfather had, and I was right." Her mother sounded grimly satisfied.

Chloe couldn't believe she was gloating in light of their losses. Didn't she realize that her late husband's money was what they lived on? *We can't eat land, Mother.* "But he . . . we don't have anything left but Ivy Manor."

"My family has kept this land for over two hundred years, Chloe." Mother straightened her shoulders as if her ancestors were crowded around them, watching. "We have held it through a revolution, financial panic, and war. I protected it from your father by deeding it to you. Anything in my name could have been seized to pay his debts, but nothing in your name can be touched. When you marry Drake, he will bring money with him and he will help you oversee the land that the croppers work. That will give us income."

Chloe didn't respond. She sipped the warm, sweet tea and drew what comfort from it she could. Her mother was confident Drake would be interested in handling the family business and that he still had money to bankroll their farming. Did he?

"I will insist that Drake sign the same prenuptial agreement that your father signed." Her mother punctuated this with a decided nod. "Ivy Manor must remain solely in the hands of a Carlyle. That way Bette will retain it just as you have."

As if on cue, Bette, still wearing her black school dress and black cotton stockings, walked in. "Grandmother, I finished my homework. Can I go outside now?"

"Your diction, please," Chloe's mother scolded primly.

"May I go outside, please?" Bette amended, not even acknowledging Chloe with a glance.

"I don't know why you want to go out on a dreary day like this. And you probably want to run off to see that boy the McCaslins have taken in."

"Yes, ma'am, I want to go there, please."

Chloe smiled at Bette, but the child didn't respond, just stood stick straight by her grandmother. Did Bette fear permission would be withheld?

"I don't know what the McCaslins were thinking of, taking in somebody's brat like that. But that Kitty has been a disappointment, not marrying and living way up in New York City. That's what they get for letting her go off to college."

"They couldn't have kept Kitty home, Mother," Chloe murmured, wondering why her mother could never say anything nice about anyone. "You know that."

"I've always faulted Kitty McCaslin for introducing you to that Theran Black. Thank heavens you came to your senses and came home to have your daughter." Her mother added more tea to her cup. "You've run wild living in Washington with your father, but you left your daughter here to be brought up like a Carlyle at Ivy Manor. That much you did right and I give you credit for it." She bestowed one of her rare smiles on Chloe.

Her mother hated Theran, but he was Bette's father. Chloe wanted to run out of the room, screaming.

"Now, Bette," Mother's tirade continued, "dress warm and tell Jerusha where you'll be playing. And come home on time for supper."

Bette turned away from her grandmother and glanced shyly at her mother, but said nothing. Did the child know not to speak to her in front of her grandmother?

Chloe stopped her as she started from the room. "Honey, I haven't given you what I brought you from France." She drew a fan from her dress pocket. "Here."

Bette took it and moved the little hook so she could open the black paper fan. The fan had *"Gay Paree"* written on it in gold lettering and had a picture of the Eiffel Tower sketched in white behind the words. Bette's eyes widened. "Thank you, Mother. I love it."

"Let me see it," Chloe's mother commanded in her queenly way.

Bette displayed it proudly.

"A cheap paper fan," her grandmother snapped. "Why didn't you bring her something that would last—a porcelain doll or a miniature china tea set?"

Chloe flushed. Her mother's words hit their mark. Chloe should have gotten her daughter something better, but the days in Paris had been filled with worry and sorrow. Chloe had bought the fan in one of the tourist shops on the quay right before departing. "I'm sorry, Bette."

"I like it, Mother," Bette murmured and fluttered the fan.

Chloe's mother sniffed. "Just like your father," she muttered loud enough for Chloe to overhear.

Bette left the parlor and Chloe heard her feet pelting down the hallway to the rear of the house.

Chloe stared at her mother, but made no effort at remonstrance. What good would it do? She set her cup and saucer on the sterling-silver tea tray without making the slightest sound. *And that proves I am a lady indeed. How much more of this can I stand?* "I have an errand to run. I'll be back for the evening meal."

In the front hall, Chloe put on a warm hat, cape, and gloves and stepped outside into the cold November afternoon. Roarke should still be at the McCaslins. *I am a fool. He'll just insult me again.* She saw Bette already on the lane and ran to catch up with her. "Wait for me, honey!"

Bette halted and Chloe raced up the lane to her. Would she be able to recapture that tenuous connection with her daughter again? "I have a souvenir for Jamie, too." Then Chloe hoped she hadn't said the wrong thing. Would Bette be jealous?

"What did you get him? Or is it a secret?"

Chloe was relieved at Bette's tone. Her daughter merely sounded interested. "I got him a book of picture postcards. Do you think he'll like them?" *Maybe boys didn't like such things.*

"He'll be able to show them in class. I bet nobody else will have stuff all the way from Paris, France. I'm going to show Teacher my fan tomorrow." Bette patted her coat pocket.

Soon the two of them knocked on the McCaslin door. Comfortable Maisie opened it and drew them inside the warm house. "Our boy, Jamie, he waitin' for you, Miss Bette."

"We got a present for him," Bette announced.

"You do? Then come right in the dinin' room. He's sittin' there finishin' up his homework."

"I'm done with mine," Bette bragged. She hurried ahead. "Jamie. Hey, Jamie."

"I'm glad you come, Miss Chloe," Maisie said in an undertone. "Mr. Roarke gone back to New York City a day early and his mama is that unhappy. Why did Miss Kitty have to go off to California? And what is Mr. Roarke doin' in New York when he lost his job anyway?"

This news hit Chloe in her heart. She hadn't guessed that Roarke had lost his job. She'd been too deep into her own troubles. But he'd been a broker. How many still had jobs?

For some reason this made Chloe recall that she still hadn't let Drake know she was back in the States. *What am I waiting for?*

"Chloe, dear." Miss Estelle—still slender and reminding Chloe of Kitty—came down the stairs. "I thought I heard your voice. Thank you for coming. Do you have time for tea?"

"Certainly." Chloe didn't like the way Miss Estelle looked. She'd lost some of her spark, that lively quality that she'd passed on to Kitty, and looked much thinner. For the first time, Chloe wondered if the McCaslins had also invested too heavily in the stock market. Surely not.

"You have our sympathy on the loss of your father," Miss Estelle said, reaching the bottom step.

"Thank you." A sudden completely unexpected rush of tears poured down her face. *Daddy's gone. And everything's turned out wrong.*

Miss Estelle tucked her arm into Chloe's and walked her to the dining room. "Losing a parent, even one...who caused pain, still hurts, honey. You'll grieve. Yes, you'll grieve."

*　　*　　*

On the way home in the deepening twilight, Chloe wondered why her daughter was behaving so naturally around her. Was it just because Chloe's mother wasn't nearby or was it something else? Whatever it was she was grateful but cautious. "You like Jamie a lot, don't you?" she asked.

"Yes, I never had a friend before."

"No friends?"

"No, Grandmother said there wasn't anyone suitable for me to play with 'round here."

Chloe was suddenly grateful that her mother had spent so much time away at spas during her own childhood.

Bette started to run. "It's cold." Chloe had to agree with her and began running, too. "Let's cut through here," Bette urged.

Chloe found herself running down a path she'd nearly forgotten. Ahead through the evergreens and oaks, she glimpsed an old cottage. Even if she hadn't been running, her heart would have pounded at the sight. Memories flooded Chloe. "Do you know who used to live here?" she called to her daughter as they ran.

"No."

"My grandmother, Granny Raney. My daddy's mama."

Bette nodded and ran faster as the sharp, cold wind whipped at the skirts of their coats. Chloe kept glancing over her shoulder back at the cottage, deserted and forlorn in the early winter's night. The melody that had haunted her since her last day in Paris came again. This time she dredged up a few words, "Just as I am . . ." She didn't know the rest, but it was Granny singing. That much she recognized.

That evening, Chloe sat at her vanity writing a letter to Drake. Crumpled pink, rose-scented paper littered the vanity top.

What did she want to say to the man she'd agreed to marry? Everything had been turned upside down and not just for her. Drake must be struggling, too. She was afraid simultaneously that he might not want to marry her now—and that he might still want to marry her. She glanced at the clock. Nearly midnight. She began again.

> *Dear Drake,*
> *I came directly home to Ivy Manor after returning from Paris. Will you come and see me? We need to talk about many things.*

Chloe halted and twisted the pen between her fingers. Did he still want to marry her? The thought that the stock market might have changed Drake, changed his feelings toward her, was a bitter one. *I gave you my promise, Drake, and I won't break it. But maybe you don't want me anymore.*

> *Please come.*
> *With love,*
> *Chloe*

Chapter Seventeen

New York City, January 1930

On Saturday morning, Roarke hurried down the thread-
bare carpet of the stairs of his rooming house. The smell
of last night's fish soup still lingered. The plump, glum landlady stood at the bottom, holding out the receiver to him.
"You won't hold up the line too long?" she recited the usual
question.

"No, ma'am." Roarke took the receiver from her.
"Hello."

"Roarke," his father's brisk voice came over the line, "I
need you to come home."

"We've had this discussion before," Roarke muttered,
aware that the other unemployed men and his landlady, all sitting just through the arch into the overly neat parlor, were
hanging on his every word.

"Your mother is dying of cancer."

His father's stark words hit Roarke squarely in the head
like a claw-hammer. His throat constricted. "It's for sure?"

"Yes. She didn't want me to tell you over Christmas. But

the diagnosis is accurate. A tumor in her uterus has spread its malignancy throughout her body."

Weak-kneed, Roarke leaned back against the polished staircase. "How long?"

"The doctor can't tell me. She could die tomorrow."

"Does Kitty know?"

"Yes, I just finished calling her but . . ."

On Saturday morning, Chloe stood in the midst of the kitchen of her Granny Raney's three-room cottage. The January wind rattled the old windows, but Jerusha's husband had come over this morning and cleaned out the pipe on the old wood stove and started a snug fire for her. Still, she wore a thick green sweater and knit gloves against the chill. She looked around at the dusty interior and lifted the broom to sweep away the draping cobwebs. Nearly twenty years of neglect. Was she crazy for planning to move here?

A timid knock came at the back door.

Chloe glanced over her shoulder and glimpsed her daughter's wind-rosy face looking in. A thrill of pleasure zipped through Chloe. "It's open, Bette. Come on in."

The little girl in her dark wool coat hurried inside and shut the door firmly behind her. "Brrr." She shivered.

The temptation to hug the child to her and kiss her over and over rocked Chloe, but she resisted. *Easy does it.* "Come warm up by the stove, honey. I did."

Bette obeyed the beckoning wave of Chloe's hand. "Grandmother says you're crazy to clean up this place, that a servant should do it."

Bette's unsurprising words triggered a vivid memory. Chloe gazed at the center of the kitchen, seeing herself at Bette's age with her granny and mother facing each other.

Chloe was standing at the ironing board with the heavy, well-heated flat iron in hand, poised over a white pillowcase she'd embroidered with butterflies for her granny. "My daughter doesn't need to learn how to iron," her mother had snapped.

"There be some things every woman should know how to do," her granny had countered, standing slightly bent.

Her mother had sniffed. "My daughter will always have servants to do for her. She is a Carlyle."

Her granny had put her arthritis-twisted hands on her narrow hips. "We're all the same to God. He loves us just as we are—Carlyle or Kimball, master or servant."

Chloe pulled her mind back to the present. "Grandmother mentioned that to me." *And a lot more.*

"Why do you want to move out here?" Bette asked, still holding her arms around her, trying to get warm.

Chloe heard the uncertainty, the worry in her daughter's voice. She heard Bette's real question: "Why are you leaving me again, Mother?"

"I love you, Bette, and I'm not going to leave you behind anymore."

Her daughter worried her lower lip.

I know you don't believe me, honey. Her mother's resentful voice replayed in Chloe's mind: "You hold me responsible for the fact that you've spent Bette's whole childhood in Washington, D.C., suiting yourself. The truth is that you could have taken her from me any time you really wanted to."

What Chloe had hated most of all was that her mother merely spoke the truth.

Moving into Granny Raney's cottage had been triggered by the desire to put some distance between her and her mother's waspish tongue. Each time she'd walked past the cottage it had beckoned her, just like her granny had in life, invited her to come inside and lay down all her burdens on a sympathetic lap. But her granny was long dead.

Bette had come closer to Chloe, who stroked the child's soft hair. *I've got to stand on my two feet or I won't be able to teach Bette how.*

Another knock at the door. Chloe turned and froze. Drake stood outside . . .

"Is Kitty coming home?" Roarke asked his father, desperate for an excuse to refuse.

"No."

Just no? Roarke clutched the phone. "What's happening with Kitty?"

"I don't know." His father suddenly sounded two hundred years old. "Son, I need you. The county's in trouble. The bank's on the edge. I don't know how I'm going to be able to extend credit for seed this spring. Your mother's dying. I need you."

Roarke struggled with himself. Could he go home to stay?

"Roarke, I've never hounded you to tell me what happened to you in France. But whatever it was, it's history. A scarred face and a stiff arm haven't kept you from home. I need you now. Will you come home?"

Roarke stared ahead, but saw northern France, a battleground. The image still had the power to—

"Son, will you come home? I need to know . . ."

Chloe opened the door and Drake walked in, handsome in a gray pin-striped suit and looking very much out of place. Surprise held her speechless.

"The butler told me where you were," he said.

She stared at him. Then she felt Bette burrowing under her arm. "Drake," Chloe said, "this is my daughter, Bette."

"Hello." Drake smiled down and took her daughter's hand. "It's a pleasure to meet you, Bette."

Bette pressed against Chloe, tongue tied. Chloe patted her arm. "Why don't you go keep warm by the stove?" Bette fled to the kitchen. "She's shy," Chloe murmured.

"I've surprised you." Drake stated the obvious, rubbing his chilled hands together. "But I finally was able to get away for a few days, so I drove down. I . . . we have to talk."

Chloe nodded. His grandmother's engagement ring tingled where it still encircled her finger under her glove. "You didn't answer my letters."

He drew her toward the front windows, which rattled in the persistent wind. "Some things can't be said in ink or over a phone line."

Chloe felt her stomach sliding toward her toes. She wanted to say, "I know." But she couldn't find her voice.

"I told you that my family has suffered major losses in the crash."

"Yes, Daddy lost everything." She pulled up the collar of her sweater against the chill. But was it just the wind or the distance she perceived that stood between her and Drake?

"I'm sorry I couldn't be here for his funeral." He shoved his hands in his pockets like a boy. "But I was trying to help my father shore up what remained of our corporation. My father didn't speculate wildly, but others did with our stock."

"I'm sorry." She wrapped her arms around herself.

"Me, too. As the dust has settled, we've managed to keep the corporation and our oil refineries going, but our stock price is dreadfully low—less than half of what it was. And everything around us seems to be slowing or shutting down. The market for our petroleum shrinks daily."

For the very first time she saw worry crease Drake's forehead. She reached over and rested her hand on his arm. "This must be very difficult for your parents."

"Very." He put a hand over hers. "But you and I must discuss our future . . ."

"Roarke," his father prompted, breaking the silence on the line.

"I'll be home within a week," Roarke said the necessary words, the only ones he could say. "I have a few loose ends to tie up and then I'll come down on the train."

"What about your car?" Father didn't sound surprised.

"I sold it." *To buy food and pay rent for one room.*

"Then send me a telegram and I'll meet you at the station."

"I will." Roarke hung up and felt as though he'd just hung up his last hope. *I can't support myself and my mother is dying and my sister won't come home.* Every eye in the parlor was turned to him. He cleared his throat and felt his back against an invisible wall. "I'll be leaving in a few days, ma'am."

His landlady said something polite, but his thoughts were already home. *I can't run away anymore . . .*

Before the words came out of Drake's mouth, Chloe knew what he was going to say. She closed her eyes and waited.

"I still want to marry you, Chloe."

She opened her eyes. That wasn't what she'd expected.

He took her wrists in his hands and pulled her closer.

"That hasn't changed. But I'm not the wealthy man I was. I'm not destitute, but—"

"I wasn't marrying you—" Chloe paused and softened her harsh voice; Drake hadn't meant to insult her. ". . . for your money, Mr. Lovelady."

Drake folded her deeply into his arms with familiar ease. "I still love you. I still want to marry you."

But standing there, Chloe suddenly knew what she had to say. Her mind was as clear as polished glass. "I'm going to give you back your grandmother's ring."

"No, I'd rather—"

"No, it's a family heirloom and I want you to keep it in your care." She tugged off her glove and then the ring, put it into his hand, and closed his fingers over it.

"You don't intend to marry me, then?" Drake sounded defeated, hurt.

"No. I've not taken back my promise. I told you I wouldn't. All I know is that right now I belong here. My daughter, my mother, the county need me. I've an obligation just like yours to family and to business."

"Business?" His eyes met hers.

"Yes, I'm one of the largest landowners in the county. Times are hard. People are worried."

Drake slipped the ring onto his little finger between the first and second knuckles. "We thought the party would never end," he said wistfully, wryly.

"We were wrong."

"I still intend to marry you. I'll be back." With a last smile, Drake kissed her wrists above her glove cuffs and left her. Chloe shut the door behind him and rested her back against it. Where would it all end? What was she doing moving into this cottage? All she knew was she could think clearer here.

Bette ran from the kitchen and wrapped her arms around Chloe's waist. "Don't leave us again."

Chloe felt her heart swell with both joy and sadness. Her daughter couldn't talk to her in the big house. Away from her grandmother, though, they had a chance. "Don't worry. I'm not going anywhere you can't come with me."

But Chloe looked around her at the musty dust and cobwebs. Her father's lawyer had given her a quick education in her responsibilities. Property taxes on the Carlyle acres loomed ahead. After years of prosperity, where had this deflation or recession or depression come from? Where would it all end?

February 1930

*H*er nerves jittering, Chloe walked into the McCaslin bank with its polished maple, brass fittings, and deep green carpet. Over the winter, she'd taught herself how to drive and had come alone. She needed advice and plenty of it. After smiling at the teller and his one customer, she walked through the gate into the bank office area and halted. The door was open; Roarke McCaslin in sober gray sat at his father's desk. Awareness pulsed through her.

She cleared her throat. "Welcome back, Roarke." Jamie had talked of nothing else but Roarke's return a week ago. But she hadn't seen Roarke since last November. After all their years apart, how did he still have the power to make her react to him?

With an impersonal expression, Roarke rose and motioned for her to come in and sit. She followed his invitation and perched on the chair in front of his desk, afraid of letting him know how the sight of his stony face unnerved her.

"What may I do for you, Chloe?" His voice gave nothing away.

They might have been strangers! All the polite words she'd practiced became molten lead. Chloe leaped up and snapped the door to the office shut and whirled to face the stubborn man once and for all. "I'm tired of us acting like we're strangers until we decide to rip up at each other."

The truth of her words slicing through him, Roarke stared at her. She still wore mourning for her father. The black made her look paler, more vulnerable.

"Kitty won't answer my letters." Chloe plumped back down into the chair. "Your parents won't talk about her. And no one knows or will tell me what's wrong with your mother." Chloe leaned forward. "Roarke, you have to be my friend again, or else."

He wouldn't be cornered. "I'm supposed to make everything right for you?"

She repressed the urge to throttle him. "I don't have the patience for this. What's wrong with your mother?"

Her quick change of topics ripped the scab off this particular wound. "Cancer. She doesn't want Jamie to know so she is keeping it as quiet as possible."

Chloe blanched. "Dear God, no."

"Don't faint on me." *I hate sitting here saying this to Chloe. God, are you listening? Are you there?*

Shock registering, Chloe pressed three black-gloved fingers to her unrouged lips. "I can't say how sorry I am, Roarke. How long?"

"No one knows." He picked up his pen and gouged his blotter with it.

"That's why you came home." The hope that he'd come for any other reason died another nasty death.

"Yes." *That and insolvency.*

Looking up, she studied the ivory crown molding and calmed her jangled nerves. "If you need me for anything, I won't fail you."

"Thank you." For the first time, his tone was honest. Suddenly he wanted to tear off the mask he'd worn since the raid at Seicheprey. He wanted to be honest with Chloe, with someone.

"It will hit Jamie hard," Chloe murmured. "And Bette. She's become very attached to your mother."

He couldn't risk letting down his guard yet. "What do you need from me, Chloe?" His tone sharpened.

She longed to give him a personal reply. But no, she'd given her promise to Drake and wouldn't renege for any reason. No more lies or half truths in her life. "Advice," she replied briskly. "I'm worried about our croppers. They're going to need seed next month and I don't have the money to buy it and loan it to them against the crop."

She was here on business then. He glanced up and saw only her lips, remembered how soft they'd felt against his so long ago. He gripped his pen tighter. "What is the balance in your savings account here?"

"Don't you know?" She looked up, wide eyed.

His mouth curved into a reluctant smile. "I don't memorize the balances in all our accounts."

She sat back, suddenly feeling lighter. But why, she didn't know. Her savings account wasn't heartening. "We have a few hundred dollars and the first installment of property taxes comes due in June."

"That I knew." *I was already thinking of how to help you.*

Old habits die hard, I guess. But he'd come up with exactly nothing.

"All Daddy's property and money were swallowed up by his debts to banks in Baltimore and Washington. I have some jewels I can sell, but friends have written me, saying that they've tried to sell items and have been offered ridiculously low sums."

Roarke tried to see from her gloved hands if she still wore Drake's engagement ring. He couldn't. He knitted his fingers in front of his vest. "Supply and demand. Many are selling. Few are buying."

She clutched a black handbag in her lap. "I need help or my croppers will have nothing to plant this spring."

"Maybe they shouldn't plant anything," he said in sudden disgust. Couldn't anything go right? "Commodity prices have dropped through the floor. Neither tobacco nor cotton will bring much this year—again supply and demand. People without money don't buy cigarettes. If people aren't buying clothes, factories won't buy cotton to spin into cloth—on and on. Tariffs have killed trade internationally."

"I hadn't thought of that." She released her purse and it slid to the floor. "Good heavens, Roarke. What should I do?" For weeks now, singly and in groups, both black and white croppers who worked Carlyle land had stopped at the back door of Chloe's cottage, voicing worries about the coming crop. Underlying all these had been, "You're the Carlyle. What are you going to do to keep us going?"

"Everyone's depending on you," Roarke said grimly, hunching over his desk.

Chloe looked up surprised. "How did you know?"

"People stop in, just to chat. But everyone knows your daddy supplied the money that kept everyone working their acres. People are worried about that and whether this bank can keep going. Banks are closing all over."

"What should I, can I, do?" She leaned forward, resting one hand on his desk.

"Let's keep talking," Roarke said without much hope. "Maybe something will come to us." Her face only inches away tempted him.

Moving to the edge of her chair, Chloe had never felt less capable of answers. Without thinking, she repeated something her Granny Raney used to say, something she'd been thinking of these past few weeks: "'People got to eat.'"

At that, Roarke's eyes suddenly sharpened. He nodded thoughtfully, then grinned. "Chloe, I think you've got the germ of an idea."

On the next sunny but cold Sunday, still in mourning, Chloe donned one of her plainer black dresses and hats. Then, without powder or rouge, she set out on foot for church and to launch the plan she and Roarke were counting on. Also dressed soberly for church, Bette met her at the end of the lane.

"Honey, I'm not going to our regular church today. Where's your grandmother?"

"She has a bad headache," Bette replied. "Where are you going?"

"To the Baptist Church over on the river."

"Why?"

Many reasons. "Because that's where Granny Raney went to church."

"You mean you live in her house so you gotta go to her church?"

That was as good a reason as Chloe could come up with

now for her daughter. She smiled and offered Bette her hand. In the weeks since Chloe had moved into the cottage, her daughter had become her friend. Not yet her daughter, but Chloe accepted what she was offered gratefully. "Coming?"

Bette took her hand and they walked to the church, only a mile down a rutted field road and across the churchyard. Inside the white-clapboard church, they sat in the rear. Many heads swiveled back to gawk at them. No doubt people were tallying up all that Quentin Kimball's wild daughter had to repent of. Chloe ignored them and Bette concentrated on swinging her feet back and forth as she sat on the high pew.

Preacher Manning had been young when he had officiated at Granny Raney's funeral. Now he was in his middle years, still wiry and black-haired. He looked her straight in the eye and she felt his welcome. Then the preacher's text made her tingle with unexpected joy. "'Give and it shall be given to you; good measure, pressed down, and shaken together, and running over, shall men give into your bosom. For the measure that ye mete withal it shall be measured to you again.'" He preached on giving rather than receiving. It gave Chloe new heart, confidence that her plan was right before God.

The congregation shuffled to its feet to sing the closing hymn. Sudden recognition made Chloe's breath catch in her throat. The Baptists sang out loud and robust, "'Just as I am without one plea, But that thy blood was shed for me . . .'" Granny's tremulous voice sang along in Chloe's memory, the song she'd been humming in her mind all across the Atlantic.

"'Waitin' not to rid my soul of one dark blot . . .'" Chloe started singing. "'Just as I am though tossed about with many a conflict, many a doubt . . .'"

Bette stared up at her and joined in, keeping up with her

mother. "'Just as I am Thou wilt receive, pardon, cleanse, re-
lieve . . . Because thy promise I believe . . .'"

Chloe suppressed laughter as many heads turned to her,
obviously waiting for her, the woman who painted her lips
and danced the Charleston, to walk forward at this invitation
to sinners. Well, after all, why not? She stepped into the aisle.
She had much to repent of and something important to say.

"I don't understand what you were thinking," her mother
scolded Chloe roundly later that afternoon. They sat together
in the indigo-and-white parlor at Ivy Manor. "What do you
mean, *giving* our croppers seed? You'll bankrupt us and we'll
lose the land."

Chloe listened for the brass knocker on the front door.
Roarke had promised to visit this afternoon to back her up,
but her mother had jumped the gun. "Mother, the country is
in a depression."

"I know that," her mother snapped. "What has that got
to do with you giving sharecroppers free seed! Who's going to
give *us* free seed?"

The knocker sounded and a well-dressed, confident-
looking Roarke walked into the parlor.

Her mother glared up at him. "Roarke McCaslin, you
must talk some sense into this daughter of mine. She's giving
away seed!"

Chloe drew strength from Roarke's presence.

"I know, ma'am." He bowed and then, at Chloe's nod of
invitation, sat down on the blue wingchair by the cozy fire.
"Chloe and I discussed the situation at length a few days ago."

"You approve of this insanity?"

"Ma'am, please let me explain." Roarke unbuttoned the
last button on his suit jacket.

Chloe's mother humphed.

Chloe realized that Bette and Haines stood, eavesdropping in the hallway. "Mother, I've explained it to you."

Her mother glared at her with a haughty lift of her chin.

"Times are hard, Mrs. Kimball," Roarke began. "And both my father and I agree that this is just the beginning. There isn't going to be much of a market for cash crops, tobacco, or cotton. And this county has never boasted large crops of those anyway."

"But the cash crops are what bring in money," she objected, red creeping into her wrinkled cheeks.

"They won't bring in much this year," Roarke countered. "Commodity prices have all dropped through the floor."

Motioning for Roarke to stay seated, Chloe stood up and walked over to stand beside him.

Her mother gaped at Roarke. "But President Hoover says our economy will revive again—come spring."

"He must say that," Roarke said. "He can't tell the truth. The country's already in a panic."

"But giving away seed." She held out both hands. "It doesn't make any sense."

"Doing what's right does," Chloe said, resting her hand on the top of Roarke's chair, near his shoulder. She wished he would reach up and take her hand. This still felt risky. "People need to eat. If we buy seed for truck farming, at least, we'll eat."

"But that won't pay the taxes," her mother snapped.

"We're hoping that our croppers will share their produce and profits from what they sell in Baltimore and Washington with us," Chloe said, leaning against the chair and Roarke. Her promise to Drake still held in her mind whether she wore his ring or not. But she'd freed him to let him decide if his circumstances had altered his feelings toward her. Nevertheless, Roarke had the power to draw her. *But I gave my word.*

"I announced," Chloe went on, "this at the River Baptist Church this morning and plan to visit the A.M.E. Church tonight to tell them also. Most of our croppers attend one of the two. I said if we all work together, I won't have to throw anybody off their land."

"It's our land, Carlyle land. If the croppers that are on it can't make a go of it, they should be thrown off. Besides"—her mother looked disdainful—"do you think they'll just hand over the money they make to you?"

"They will," Roarke asserted. "They understand that taxes must be paid and that if Chloe loses the land because she can't pay the taxes or has to sell because she can't keep her family fed, the next owner might not be so generous."

Chloe couldn't have said it better herself. Confident that they were going to prevail, she rested her hand on his shoulder. Still, she kept her pleasure under wraps, unwilling to give her mother something to use against her sometime in the future. No wonder she was afraid of showing real emotion. And Bette had caught the habit, too. *Dear Father, you've got to help me with my girl.*

The phone rang and Haines answered it. He stepped into the parlor. "Mr. Roarke, your father, sir."

Roarke immediately rose and went to the phone. "Dad?"

"Come home quick, Roarke, and pick up the doctor on the way. Your mother is having trouble breathing. She says bring Chloe and Bette, too."

CHAPTER EIGHTEEN

*J*ust after sundown, Chloe soundlessly paced the floral-carpeted landing outside Mrs. McCaslin's closed bedroom door. Jamie and Bette sat huddled on the top step at the other end of the landing. Their drawn expressions wrung Chloe's heart.

The door opened. Dr. Benning walked out. "Chloe, Mrs. McCaslin would like to speak to you."

Chloe stepped close to him. "How is she?" she whispered.

"I've had her under an oxygen mask for about an hour and her breathing is better. She can talk for a while."

"She's better then?"

He leaned close to her ear. "She has maybe a day or two at most. The tumors are crushing the breath from her."

Chloe closed her eyes, drawing up her strength to face this. She walked into the ivory-and-beige room, lit only by two small bedside Tiffany lamps, and Roarke closed the door behind her. She halted, startled—awed—by the terrible and beautiful scene before her. Mr. McCaslin stood by the bed, treasuring his wife's hand in both of his. Their love radiated in the shadowy room, almost palpable in its force. Each face searched the other; a tender smile lifted both. Their private communion separated them, set them apart from Roarke and her. Mr. McCaslin was losing the love of his life.

Chloe pressed the back of her hand to her trembling lips. *Why aren't you here, Kitty?*

Pale and thin, Miss Estelle looked over at Chloe and lifted her other hand. "I need to talk to you, my dear, while I can still make sense." Resistance to pain flickered across the woman's face. "The doctor is giving me more morphine and pretty soon I'll just come and go in dreams, I guess."

"Roarke and I'll leave you, then." Mr. McCaslin started away.

"No, dearest, my heart, stay," she pleaded. "The time for secrets is over. Please sit down near me." Her husband nodded and sat on a vanity chair close by the bed.

On the other side, Chloe approached and accepted Miss Estelle's frail, outstretched hand. She couldn't believe how quickly the woman had lost ground since Christmas.

"Chloe, I'm glad you finally came home." Miss Estelle gazed up with eyes now too big for her face. "Bette and your mother need you and you need them."

Chloe only nodded, not trusting her voice. Roarke's presence so near and yet untouchable brought fresh desolation to this parting.

"You lost your nerve when Theran died," the woman said with searing accuracy, "but I think you're getting it back. Your father's mother was a wonderful person. It was fortunate that she and Jerusha's mother had the raising of you." Another twinge of pain etched itself on her pallid face. "Bad times are here, but you'll find your feet." The woman tried to squeeze Chloe's hand.

The meager effort brought tears to Chloe's eyes. "Don't exhaust yourself talking to me." *I'm not worth it.*

"Why did Kitty leave us?" Deep, hopeless sadness infused each of Miss Estelle's words.

"I don't know. She left me, too." *Just like Roarke.* The double loss dragged at Chloe's heart.

Miss Estelle closed her eyes. "I can't believe we lost her. Something happened in New York and not that bad alcohol—something else. When she brought Jamie to us, I thought we might get another chance, a chance to start over. But as soon as we'd adopted him, she left." A single tear dripped from the lady's eye. "I guess she just didn't want to leave us—Thomas and me—all alone."

Chloe could think of nothing to say to this, so she tightened her hold on Miss Estelle's hand.

The lady opened her eyes. "Roarke, come stand beside Chloe."

Roarke obeyed his mother. His face was a dangerous rock cliff again. His brooding anger at this new sorrow vibrated in the air around him. Chloe longed to turn to him, hold him against the loss he now faced. But no.

"Son, I don't have any time left for sensitivity or discretion. I don't know what you did or was done to you in France, but it's time to put it behind you."

Chloe clung to the lady, reckless hope glimmering—hope that his mother could break through at last.

Roarke's face softened. "Mother, I—"

She shook her head. "No, I don't have the strength to hear it even if you're ready to tell me now. I've prayed and prayed that shadow would pass from you, but it hasn't. You've nearly lost Chloe. And your father and I have nearly lost you, too, along with Kitty." Sweat beaded on the lady's forehead. "We must have been sadly poor parents to lose both our children this way."

"That's not true," Roarke accentuated each word. "You

and father were, are wonderful. Kitty and I failed you. You didn't let us down."

"Then, don't disappoint us now. Tell your secret to Chloe and clean it out of your soul and your life. Thomas and Jamie are going to need you when I'm gone. Your father's heart is frail. You must shoulder the load and keep the bank afloat." Miss Estelle looked transparently pale, as though she were vanishing before their eyes. "I think it will take all your strength and intelligence. But the county needs the—" She faltered.

"I'm getting the doctor again, Estelle." Her husband left.

"Call in the children," Miss Estelle murmured, writhing silently in pain.

Chloe moved away from the bed, taking refuge in the shadows. Roarke stepped to the doorway. "Children, Miss Estelle wants to see you."

Jamie and Bette tiptoed into the room as though afraid of waking someone. Miss Estelle patted the bed on both sides of her. "Come. Lay down one on each side of me. I'm lonely."

The children obeyed hesitantly. Jamie lay down and gazed into his mother's eyes. On the other side, Bette tenderly patted Miss Estelle's shoulder and whispered, "I love you." Chloe pressed the back of her hand to her quivering lips.

Dr. Benning walked in and replaced the celluloid oxygen mask over his patient's mouth and nose. He turned on the valve on the green oxygen tank standing beside the bed as Miss Estelle closed her eyes. Her husband sat back down in the chair while the doctor checked his wife's pulse.

Roarke and Chloe walked out of the room as in a dream. Roarke led her down the hall without one word. Chloe found herself in his bedroom, a room she hadn't entered since childhood. She looked around at the masculine room done in navy and white, at the gold cuff links tossed on the highboy and the brown silk tie hanging over the closet door knob. Awareness of Roarke brought gooseflesh up on her arms.

"I didn't want to take you downstairs. Maisie and the cook are there," Roarke explained, feeling hoarse as if he'd been screaming. "We won't be overheard here."

Chloe stared at him, unwilling to chance believing he would finally open up. "You're really going to tell me?"

His expression was harsh yet rueful. "I know you were never close to either of your parents," he voiced the first thought that came to mind. "I've watched you quietly mourn your father. It does you credit." The woman he loved stood so close and when she had heard the truth she'd leave him once and for all.

"I think I've mourned for what might have been between us. Are you going to tell me then?" Her audacity shocked her. They were alone at last. Roarke was close enough to touch. She shuddered with the nearness of him.

He nodded. "Sit down." He motioned toward a blue-plaid armchair near the hearth where a low fire burned. "These old houses. We should have put in a modern furnace but now we won't be able to afford to."

"Don't talk to me of furnaces." She let herself down into the soft chair and thought of Roarke sitting here each night reading, all alone.

Roarke eased down on the edge of his high antique bed, covered by a thick quilt in blues and white. He pressed both hands down on either side of him. The haunting image of the battlefield crinkled in his mind like a photograph about to catch fire. "The funny thing is that I think I can tell it now. Knowing I'm about to lose Mother makes it easier somehow. I don't know why."

Chloe waited, tense, hardly daring to hope yet at the same time fearful of what he might reveal. The intimate setting was lowering her resistance and she was remembering the times Roarke had held her in his arms. Dangerous memories.

Roarke gazed at Chloe, drinking in the way she glowed in this room, the beauty she brought wherever she was. Then the image of the battlefield, shells exploding all around, men screaming, cursing; dust spurting up as bullets bit the earth. "I was a coward, Chloe."

She looked at him, her lips parting. "No."

He closed his eyes, seeing it all over again. "I ran and hid under enemy fire."

Chloe couldn't believe her ears. He'd put them through all these years of agony because he ran? "There's more to it than that," she said flatly.

"I was the lieutenant." He pushed back his hair with his good hand. "I was to lead my squads as we repelled a German raid and . . . I didn't. I hid behind dead bodies and cowered while my men led themselves into the fray."

The words, spoken so matter-of-factly, seemed almost unreal to Chloe. This man wouldn't do that. "Roarke, you're not a coward. You're not."

"Chloe, how can I say it any plainer?" Acidic irritation spurted through him. "I did not stand and fight. I turned and ran. Theran wouldn't have turned tail. I did."

Of course, Roarke would demand the most of himself. Struggling for words, she looked down. While she searched for what to say, she spread her white hands out on the lap of her black dress. Her hands and nails were no longer those of a lady. Scrubbing floors, washing her own dishes, rubbing clothes on a washboard had taken their toll. After years of running away, she'd come home. She'd finally turned to face the fight. Her calluses and broken nails were her badges of honor. "You're not a coward—not anymore. You came back."

He stood up in one angry, fluid move. "I don't know what you mean." Why couldn't she get it?

"I was a coward, too." She clenched her hands, two fists in her lap. "But I've come back to face . . . everything. My mother, Bette, our people. And so have you."

"That's not the same. You're not a man. You don't understand." He'd waited all these years and now she had no idea what his cowardice had cost him.

She looked into Roarke's dark, anguished eyes. "There are all kinds of courage. I don't think you were ever meant to be a soldier. And you never got a second chance to face the enemy, did you? I mean, you were wounded in your first battle?"

"It wasn't even a real battle, just skirmishes at Seicheprey in Lorraine, just German raids. I deserved worse than this." He glanced down at his stiff arm. But he'd often wondered if he would have been able to conquer his cowardice if he'd had another chance.

"Roarke, I've known you all my life. You are a good person. Does one day, one action, define a man? I'm sorry you didn't do what you feel you ought to have." She stood on shifting sand. One false step and she would take them both down to disaster. "The Great War's been over for a decade. Isn't ten years of banishment enough?"

He paced, unable to stay still. "Every time someone thanked me for serving my country, I wanted to blurt out the truth." Even as he fought her, hope forced itself into his heart. "But I couldn't."

"Don't you think people ever asked about my daughter?" she asked him. "I was a coward, too. I deserted my post as mother. Don't you think that guilt's as real and as harsh as yours? What could I have done that was worse than leaving my child with my mother?"

Halting, he stared at her. "It's not the same." But he recognized the torment in her eyes and the suffering in her tone. It touched a deep chord in his own guilt.

"Every day I want to run away again," Chloe said, daring him to belittle her woman's cowardice. "I look at Bette and the guilt nearly strangles me. Then I ask myself—what's best for her now? I wasn't here for the first ten years of her life, but I can be here for the rest of her life."

Strength deserted him. He sat back down, his head in his hand." I can't . . . there isn't any way I can make up for what . . ."

Chloe rose and went to him, the thick carpeting cushioning her steps. She knelt before him and rested her head in his lap. "Let it go, Roarke. It's history. You can't change it. You should ask yourself, what's best for your father. He's such a good man. And what about Jamie and Kitty? *And me?* Be rid of it now."

"How can I?" His voice came out muffled, agonized.

Chloe combed her mind. It was now or never. "Didn't you hear your mother? The county needs the bank and your father can't do it alone. You're here now to fight the battle of this depression."

"And you think that will redeem me?" he jeered. Her words were persuading him, but it couldn't be this easy.

The song that had finally come clear this morning at church sang in her mind, compelling, irresistible. "God takes us just as we are." Over the past decade, she'd forgotten the most important thing Granny Raney had ever taught her. Truth flooded her, emboldened her. "Ask Him for forgiveness and let it go. Don't make yourself and the rest of us suffer on and on."

"It's not that easy." But the photograph, frozen in his mind, was crinkling more. Chloe's presence was realer than a faded memory of the Western Front.

"It's not easy for me to stand up for Bette against my mother and do it with respect." Chloe took his good wrist in her hand. The contact after so many years apart shivered through her. *This is Roarke, my dearest . . . friend.* "I have to do it for my daughter. Drake told me, 'We thought the party would never end.' But the party's over. We've got to face this new decade together or we'll let . . . *make* others suffer. That's not right."

He was fighting a losing battle. Chloe knelt on the floor in front of him, holding him, and it was as though a storm were flooding his soul. He ached with emotions long held in check, and he moved to push them away. But in the act of removing her hand, he looked down, and he finally noticed something he'd overlooked. In a heartbeat, his long-denied need for this woman stirred. "You took off his engagement ring," he whispered. He gripped the last shred of his resistance to her.

Chloe looked up at Roarke, her large blue eyes filled with a longing even he could read. "I can't marry Drake. If the crash hadn't come, I would have and it would have been a mistake. One in a long list of mistakes I've made." She took a deep breath. "I want to marry you."

He stared down at her, so beautiful, so earnest. Where had she gotten the courage to say that? Could he do less? With a sigh he gave up the fight. "Good. Because I want to marry you."

He stood then, dragging her up with him. All the longing of wasted years surged through him. *She's right.* A frenzy to claim her overwhelmed him. He kissed her deeply, searchingly. His heart pounded and, one-armed, he wrapped her tightly to him and felt her heart beating against him. "Forgive me for all the years I've wasted."

"Forgive me—"

He stopped her lips with another kiss. He sucked her breath into his lungs. Pressing his good hand to the back of her head, holding her in place, he devoured her mouth. Then he broke away from her lips, gasping for air. "Chloe, my Chloe," he murmured.

Chloe felt his passion for her and yielded to him, not pulling away. "I'll take you, Roarke, just as you are. Will you take me just as I am?" She pressed her face against him, reveling in the roughness of his wool suit jacket and the latent strength of his broad shoulders, shoulders that could carry heavy burdens. *That's your courage, Roarke.*

"Yes." He tightened his hold on her, reveling in her softness. "I'll take you just as you are."

"That's all I've ever wanted," Chloe whispered. She lifted her face, asking for another kiss. Roarke obliged and left her shimmering with the need for him. The long, lonely, fearful time of separation was over. They would find their way together.

She and Roarke had come home. Just as they were. Just in time.

HISTORICAL NOTE

"Wars are the locomotives of history" is a truth that can't be denied. Wars force humans to make advancements in weaponry and medical technology. And they put the fighting-age generation through a fiery furnace that forever changes them and, hence, their society. To me, the twentieth century started with WWI and not the arbitrary date of 1900. A living example, Chloe led a completely different life before WWI than she did after it.

Also, two new amendments to the Constitution at the beginning of the twenties—women's suffrage and prohibition—ushered in vast societal changes. Women started voting—a good thing. But the prohibition amendment actually had the opposite effect on society than it was supposed to—it closed the male domain of the old-time saloon, but the nightclub took its place and made cocktails popular for women as well as men. The generation that had been told they were fighting in the "War to End All Wars" returned from that first brutal modern conflict—with air battles, mustard gas, machine guns, and tanks—disillusioned and ready to drown their sorrows in bathtub gin. So criminals organized and reaped huge profits from speakeasies while the FBI grew stronger, trying to stop the illicit trade.

The "Lost Generation" of the twenties took nothing seriously if it could help it and flaunted its new freedom with bobbed hair, rouged lips, short skirts, and automobiles. For the first time, the name of Freud and the word *sex* worked its way into modern conversation. Couples stopped courting and started dating—shocking their elders by kissing people they had no intention of marrying. They danced the wild Charleston and the Black Bottom to honky-tonk jazz. Chloe, Roarke, Kitty, and Drake all portrayed the different ways Americans coped with this new age.

Finally, WWI was the first war in which American black men were drafted in larger numbers as citizen soldiers. Both the South and North were rocked by racial unrest when black men donned uniforms and shed a servile manner. Of course, Minnie portrayed the hope of the disenfranchised black population. She was born into poverty and Jim Crow, but Minnie had dreams and the will to make them come true. Go, Minnie! In the new century, Chloe and Minnie found a way to break through the barriers that had separated their families for generations and Chloe found her greatest joy in seeing her friend's success.

In the subsequent stories in The Women of Ivy Manor series, these many themes—tyranny, injustice, freedom, equality—will repeat, since they were the great struggles of the twentieth century and continue today. Just check the evening news.

If you are hungry to know more about the fascinating time in history portrayed in *Chloe, Only Yesterday* by Frederick Lewis Allen is the classic guide to the twenties. Great nonfiction that reads like fiction.

READING GROUP GUIDE

1. What historical facts in the story surprised you? What hadn't you known that took place in this colorful period?

2. How did Chloe's life differ before the war versus after the war? Was she the better for having gone through it? Why?

3. Which character did you find most interesting? Why? Would he or she be someone you'd befriend in your own life?

4. Which character did you think was the most pivotal to the storyline? Why?

5. Chloe's Granny Raney was very important in her life. Was there anyone in your past who influenced you for good? For evil? Is there anyone you are trying to influence for the better here and now?

6. Chloe found comfort and direction for her life in an old hymn. Do you have any songs or verses that are special in your life? Which ones and why?

7. There were four men in Chloe's life—her father, Theran, Roarke, and Drake. How would you characterize each? How are they different? The same?

8. Which man appealed to you most? Why? Which did you dislike the most? Why?

9. Kitty was Chloe's best friend, but in the end, Kitty left, stealing Jamie from Chloe. What clues point to why Kitty did this? What do you think compelled her to wound Chloe like this?

10. Chloe's moment of decision came in Paris in 1929. Have you experienced a similar moment in your life? Did it change things for the better or the worse?

ABOUT THE AUTHOR

Lyn Cote (pronounced "co-tee") is the award-winning author of a number of historical novels including *Echoes of Mercy* and *Lost in His Love*. She was born in Texas, grew up in Illinois on the shores of Lake Michigan, and raised two children in Iowa. A full-time writer, she now lives in northern Wisconsin with her husband and two cats.

If you would like to contact the author with more questions, please e-mail her at l.cote@juno.com or write to P. O. Box 864, Woodruff, WI, 54568. Also you might want to visit her Web site at www.BooksbyLynCote.com for more information about the other titles in The Women of Ivy Manor series.

Tidewater Maryland, April 1936

*B*ette screamed herself awake. She jerked up in her bed. A feeble glow outside her window pierced the predawn gray. Her heart pounded hard and fast. She fought for air. What? What had happened?

A second blast exploded outside.

Gretel's scream joined another of hers. Her friend lay in the trundle bed beside her. *"Was ist los?"*

Bette heard the sound of bare feet pelting down the hardwood hallway and then down the steps. Her mother's voice called out, "Roarke, wait! Get your gun first!"

Bette tossed back the covers and nearly landed on Gretel. "Come on!" She grabbed her friend's hand and dragged her from their bedroom. Mother was before them, racing down the stairs to the foyer. "Mother!" Bette screeched, afraid her mother might run outside into danger.

"Wait!" Mother held up both hands to stop them. Bette and Gretel halted near the middle of the staircase, both winded and panting.

Her stepfather hurried from the rear of the house, his rifle in his good hand. "All of you stay in here till I see what's out there." He threw open the door. Cold damp air rushed in and they all saw it at once.

A cross burned on their wide and long front lawn.

Bette gasped so sharply that her tongue slammed against the back of her mouth, nearly making her gag.

"*Was ist los?*" Gretel repeated in a hollow voice.

Shock and fear shimmered through Bette. She tightened her grip on Gretel's hand. "It's the Klan," she whispered.

At this, Gretel pressed herself close to Bette as if seeking refuge.

Her stepfather stalked outside.

"No, Roarke, they might—" Mother's voice was overcome by a blast from stepfather's rifle.

"Come out, you lousy cowards!" he roared. "Show yourselves and face me like men!"

Silent night was the only response.

"Cowards!" he shouted. He stalked to the cross and, using the butt of his rifle, he beat it to the ground. It sizzled in the early morning dew. Bette knew she'd never forget the sound—a hissing like a poisonous snake. A snake poised to strike them.